OLD BONES

a mystery

Ron Chudley

VICTORIA · VANCOUVER · CALGARY

TouchWood Editions
#108 – 17665 66A Avenue
Surrey, BC V3S 2A7
www.touchwoodeditions.com

Library and Archives Canada Cataloguing in Publication
Chudley, Ron, 1937–
     Old bones: a mystery / Ron Chudley.

ISBN 1-894898-33-8

     I. Title.

PS8555.H83O64 2005   C813'.54   C2005-905605-3

Edited by Marlyn Horsdal
Book design by R-House Design
Cover design by Erin Woodward
Front cover photo by Colin Stitt/iStockphoto

Printed in Canada

TouchWood Editions acknowledges the financial support for its publishing program from the Government of Canada through the Book Publishing Industry Development Program (BPIDP), Canada Council for the Arts, and the British Columbia Arts Council.

The Canada Council | Le Conseil des Arts
for the Arts | du Canada

BRITISH COLUMBIA
ARTS COUNCIL
Supported by the Province of British Columbia

for my wife, Karen,
who makes it all worthwhile

PROLOGUE

Rudy Magee's buddies had both been grounded, so he was all by himself on the day of the big discovery.

That summer had been suck city. Two weeks after the end of school the bloom was off the rose. By that time he and Pete and Napster had done all the cool stuff they could think of: ridden their dirt bikes up to the dam and thundered back down at bum-numbing speed; fixed the ancient sailing dinghy that Pete's dad had given them and nearly sunk the thing out by Snake Head Point; persuaded some girls—who had mysteriously become more interesting since Grade Eight—to go on a night swim and been roundly heckled when someone suggested skinny-dipping; hung about the Beer & Wine Store until they finally got Pinch Murphy—who was old enough to be *able* and stupid enough to actually *do it*—to buy them a double-sixer of Molson's.

It was this final escapade, in fact, that had caused the above-mentioned grounding. They'd quite masterfully sneaked the hooch, along with a pack of Marlboros, into the old fort at the bottom of Rudy's garden. But hardly had they got lit up and taken a couple of good swigs on the man-juice when Rudy's swinish sister spotted them and blew the whistle. The outcome of all this was that both Pete and Napster were grounded for a month. Rudy's punishment was more painful but shorter; his father took the beer and cigarettes for himself, gave Rudy a most un-PC whaling, and sent him on his way.

Which, indirectly, is what led to the big discovery.

Without his buds to hang out with, Rudy had been at loose ends. The tiny hamlet of Melton, on the south shore of Christina Lake in central British Columbia, was not exactly awash in available entertainment. So on that day, the desperation of terminal boredom made Rudy do something quite foreign to his extroverted nature: he went alone on a hike.

Five minutes walking on Highway 3 and he was out of what passed for town. Apart from the odd isolated dwelling it was now just greenery; dense, second-growth pine on the left of the highway, smaller trees and scrubby bush on the uneven hillside descending to the partially visible lake. Rudy kept on for a few kilometres, oblivious to the passing procession of cars and holiday campers. Then, when he was beginning to grow bored and seriously thinking of trying to hitch a ride anywhere, he saw something unexpected: a half-interesting-looking path leading off in the direction of the lake.

Investigating, he found that it wasn't really a path at all, just an elongated open space where stuff didn't seem to grow so thickly. At this point the highway took a long swing left and headed uphill away from the water. The open space that wasn't really a path swung in the opposite direction, and Rudy realized that at some time this might also have been a road.

To his surprise and dawning delight, he found himself intrigued. A small mystery. He'd never noticed the old road. Now, with a distinct lift of the heart, he decided to explore.

Twenty metres or so in it became rough going. What was definitely a flat ribbon of evenly graded ground curved away and down in the direction of the lake, but it was choked with dense undergrowth through which it became increasingly difficult to force a passage. Rudy was wearing only runners, shorts and a light tee, little protection from the prickly tangle. Then, about to turn back, he found himself abruptly in the clear.

The reason for this was simple enough: what had once been a roadbed now ran along the edge of a small precipice that had recently crumbled away, taking the road with it. A 20-foot gap, filled with earth and torn scrub and rubble, separated Rudy from where the road continued. But it was not hard to scramble across, and when he reached the other side he found progress much easier.

From here on the bed had been carved out of rock, which was both solid and inhospitable to growth. Moss, parched and sun-brown now, was all that clung, and in the bald spaces between, Rudy could actually spy traces of ancient asphalt.

So where did this old road go? And why had it been abandoned? Feeling a sense of real mystery, Rudy hurried on eagerly. Suddenly, as he came around a sharp curve, there was the lake. It was right below. A 30-foot sheer drop. Then he was standing on the edge, the toes of his runners peeking out over nothing, feeling a delicious surge of vertigo.

"Holy Christ!" Rudy whispered, staring down in wonder. "Wait'll I tell the guys about this!"

The road continued on for about 50 metres—then vanished. All trace of it was gone, snatched from existence by an act of vast devastation that had swept a huge slice of it into the lake.

Thoroughly awed, Rudy drifted along what remained of the road. The landslide that had destroyed it was obviously no new occurrence: the spreading rocky scree was weathered and covered with lichen. Brush and even some quite large trees grew out of it, all the way down to where it spewed into the lake. Larger chunks of rock that had rolled farther out, partially or completely submerged, were stained and water-weathered by time exactly the same as everything else at the lake's edge.

With one exception.

Rudy paused, paying attention to something new. An anomaly. What he was looking at was one of the rocks. It was separated from the main slide area but quite close to the shore. The water wasn't very deep and the thing was clearly visible and—it wasn't a rock at all. Rudy's 14-year-old vision was excellent. He had no doubt of what he was looking at. The lines had a uniformity that nature never made; dead straight on two sides, rounded on one end, flat on the other. Near the middle was a square area that was almost at the surface. A cab. The thing was a pickup truck.

Without any conscious decision, he was scanning the cliff face, looking for a way down. Then, taking great care, Rudy picked his way through the rubble to lake level.

But now what? The cliff face, above where the truck lay, plunged sheer into the water. In fact, though the vehicle itself was now quite close, he could scarcely see it. Refracted light on the water surface made it nearly invisible. Had he not happened to spot it from above, he realized that he would never have noticed anything at all.

With his whole gut he longed to be out there, taking a real look at this mysterious object which, he understood, must be as ancient as the road itself. There seemed only one way. Peeling off his runners and his shirt, he examined the water briefly and plunged in.

Keeping a lookout for submerged rocks, he swam in the direction of the drowned truck. It took less than a minute to get there. Looking from above, he expected to be able to touch the roof with his feet. He was not disappointed. The truck was farther down than it looked, but he could still stand easily on the cab with the water well below his neck.

Rudy stood there a moment, feeling an exhilarating sense of

accomplishment and power. So—what was he going to do now? From here, he discovered, he could see even less of the truck than from the shore, just a wavery outline that might or might not have been filled in with faded red. If he was going to learn anything, get any more information to embellish the adventure tale he meant to take back to his buds, he had to get down for a closer look.

Jackknifing his body, he flipped up his legs and dived into the deep.

Getting down to the level of the top of the cab was easy. Staying there was another matter. Before he had a chance to find out anything, natural buoyancy pulled his body back to the surface. Again he dived and again the same thing happened. But on the third try he was more successful. Feeling below the roof, at the top of the driver's side door, he discovered there was no glass. It was easy to get his fingers inside the hole, grasp the door top, and draw himself down.

But his air was gone. So he came up, gasped big breaths to oxygen-load, and swam down again. This time he went right to the truck, got a good hold, and thrust his head into the driver's side window.

What he saw was at first very little. Water, decay and time had turned everything into a scum-encrusted blur. The steering wheel was clear enough, as was the sweep of the dashboard and the crouched shape of the seats. Pulling his head clear, Rudy swung his gaze sideways to examine the bed of the truck. Except for a thin coating of grime it was completely empty.

Running out of air, Rudy fought the urge to surface and, with the desperation of a reporter losing a big story, he stuck his head back inside again.

His eyes had adjusted and he could see more clearly. On the floor of the cab was a formless shape, difficult to differentiate from the lake debris, just sort of a big knobby hump. That seemed to be all ...

But it wasn't.

Resting on what was left of the driver's seat was something else; lighter in tone than the background, round, about the size of a cabbage. There were two large holes close together, a smaller pair below, and a double row of wedge-shaped objects: a pattern that suddenly coalesced in atavistic and chilling familiarity.

Rudy gasped, almost ingesting a mouthful of lake, and shot to the surface. Treading water, not wishing even to *toe-touch* what was below, the shocked young adventurer took in the enormity of his find.

He had a tale to tell to his buds, all right: that is, if he could make it to shore without choking on his own breakfast.

ONE

His father was huge and splendid and strong as a steam shovel. His father was the king of creation. His father hoisted him with tough, brown hands, powerful, iron-muscled arms, and swung him around with the exciting, terrifying force of a tornado. Before his child-eyes, the world went by in a sweet, multi-hued blur. And he laughed, oh how he laughed: at the speed, the colours, the beauty, and the mind-numbing, gut-tingling, soul-surging thrill of it all.

His great father laughed with him.

As well as feeling electrified he also felt splendidly safe. His father not only possessed god-like power, he also loved him, his only son, beyond all things. That was the truth that sang at the very core of his child-being, all other matters paling in its great shadow.

His father loved him and would never let him go.

For what seemed an eternity the magic, whirling dance continued. Then somewhere in the midst of it all a single, coherent sliver of shining truth pierced his consciousness.

He had never been so happy.

That knowledge, when it first flowered, was ecstasy. His heart throbbed with the joy of it. This is what he had been missing always, this wonderful sensation of peace and security and—belonging.

This was the element that had never been there. But then came an extra understanding.

He would never be so happy again.

As that final truth took hold, all joy leaked away. What was left was something dreadful that sucked at the very core of being. The whirling in his father's arms began to take on the temper of punishment. He screamed for it to stop—but only in his mind. The silent cries were not heard by the laughing giant who was mercilessly spinning him faster and faster.

By an immense effort of will, he managed to fight the centrifugal force, wrenching his gaze from the careening universe to the one whose gift of wonder had turned so swiftly to pain. Only then was the full truth revealed.

His father had no face.

An explosion of astonishment and revulsion, of terror and unspeakable disappointment wracked him. His whole being shattered into a million tiny pinpoints of stars that faded into black.

And *he* was in the black—sitting in the black—which wasn't black at all but grey—depressing grey—and he was himself—Jack himself—sitting in the bed of Jack—in his own mundane bed—with heart-thump and sweat-stink—staring bug-eyed at nothing more fearful than the cold light of dawn.

"Fucking hell!"

Jack lay in the bed for several fitful minutes, wondering if he should try to doze again, remembered the dream and thought, *why bother.*

He got out of bed, clad only in his old sleeping boxers, and slouched to the kitchen. Despite his morning stumble, and the 42 years that nibbled at the edges of his sturdy frame, Jack was in good shape. Even barefooted, he was tall enough to be dangerously intimate with the tops of doorways, a fact that had given him some bruises but was of compensating advantage in his job as a cop.

Right now, as he filled the coffee maker, this particular police-man felt like one of his scruffier felons. Moments later, glancing in the bathroom mirror as he peed, Jack saw that he looked pretty much the part of a villain too. God, he thought, if they asked me to go undercover on Main Street, Vancouver, I'd fit right in.

Not that he'd ever served in Vancouver, or any large city, come to that. Twenty-one years in the RCMP had seen Constable Jack Marsden with a half-dozen postings across the country, the largest in Dartmouth, Nova Scotia, the smallest right here in Melton, on Christina Lake, B.C.

He flushed the toilet, brushed his teeth, then—feeling a bit cheerier—caused the villain in the mirror to grin. The guy's teeth were in good shape. Beard stubble disguised a strong jaw and healthy skin. The eyes, though sleep-squinted, were steady, clearing even as they watched themselves.

But—abruptly—the sight of the mirror-face reminded Jack of something disturbing. Then it came. Of course, *the dream*. It was stupid, but the echo was still powerful enough to cause a hollow feeling at the bottom of his gut.

He tried to brush it off, but found himself going over the night-mare sequence in his mind. Unsurprisingly, the more he examined it in the cool light of morning the more absurd it seemed. So, what else was new? Dreams were almost always ridiculous. That business of being whirled around, for instance, was just Alice-in-Wonder-land bullshit. Meaningless, as far as he could see. And the giant twirling-guy being his father—*a dad without a face*—that was just terrific. As good a Freudian cliché as any pop-analyst could come up with—especially since Jack had never seen his real father.

"Jesus, give me a break," he muttered and went back to the kitchen. He poured coffee, drank a whole cup down, as hot as he could bear. Then he slung on runners and a sweatshirt and tumbled out the door to try to jog himself into some semblance of sense.

His route took him along the back of town and past his girlfriend's house. Margie must be giving an early class, he realized, because though it was before 6:00 her lights were already on. They were due to meet for lunch so he had decided to run right by, but something—an emptiness that he would have been loath to admit was an echo from his dream—made him want to see her right now, and he turned back.

He went up on the side porch and tried the door. It was unlocked and he went in, calling. "Margs! *Me!*"

The house was small, a bungalow with two bedrooms; one for Margie, the other for her son, Doug, who was 12 and at summer camp. That last fact meant that Jack could have spent whole nights here, but actually he never did. Somehow, after making love, even after falling dead asleep, he woke with the need to get back to his own place. Of course, there were always good reasons: he had to get up early for a shift, he didn't have the stuff he needed for the morning, he didn't want to start gossip—she being a respectable lady and he a cop: all of which was bullshit, of course, which they both knew. This would have to be talked about sooner or later, and he wasn't looking forward to it.

Now, as he entered the kitchen, he could hear the shower running. He stuck his head into the bathroom, seeing her tiny but exceedingly well-made figure through the glass of the shower stall.

"Okay, lady," he yelled over the water racket. "This is a bust!"

"Hey!" Margie called delightedly. "I didn't know you were coming by, copper."

"I was just passing."

She slid the door back, sticking out her head. "Oooh, you look all hot and sticky. What're you waiting for, Constable? Get that sweaty bod in here."

He did as she suggested, pronto. There was scarcely room for the two of them, which was altogether the opposite of unpleasant. They soaped and rinsed each other happily, she all of five foot three, barely coming up to his chest, slim and curvaceous but also well muscled, befitting her job as a fitness instructor. At one point, when she looked up at him, with the water dripping off her nose and lashes, Jack was moved to reflect that Margie looked scarcely half her 36 years. Following that, as it sometimes did, the other sly-little-bastard notion slipped in: what in hell could this lovely creature see in him? But he was used to that, buried the thought before it could take real form, instead putting full attention on the wet, wonderful comfort of her soapy womanliness. At one point, however, he did take a moment to note that the hollow-gut that had pursued him since waking was quite gone.

As they were having breakfast a while later Margie said, "Hey— what about that truck in the lake, eh?"

WHEN JACK CAME on shift the first thing the sergeant asked him was if he'd heard about the truck in the lake.

Not mentioning he'd got the news from his girlfriend, who'd had it from the sarge's own wife, Jack said that he'd heard something but not much. Once the officer had filled him in, he said, "Seem like any foul play?"

"God knows," Ridgely said. "Whatever happened, it was one hell of a long time ago. I had Jim Oakton from the *Cleaner* on the horn this morning."

"That bugger got wind of it already?"

"Nah! It was news to him too—for once. Anyway, I asked him to look up when they changed the route of Highway 3 and he came up with 1952. So—whatever happened—that thing's been down there at least half a century."

"Jesus! Why do you think no one spotted it before?"

"Well, to start, it's in the middle of freakin' nowhere. Also—you haven't been here long enough to know—but the lake level's gone down a fair tad in the last few years. So, if and until I get more evidence, how it seems to me is this: at the time that truck took its last dive, nobody knew it had happened. And you couldn't see anything afterwards. Apparently, that part of 3 around the lake was always a bitch, so they gave up on it and took the route over the south ridge. The remains of the old highway grew over and by the time the water level finally went down, no one was around to notice."

"Until this kid."

"Yeah—Bill Magee's oldest. He found it by some kind of accident. Jim Oakton thinks the national papers will pick it up. Bizarre human-interest piece. He could be right, I guess. Depends on who we've got down there, and what happened to him. Anyway, Creston says they can get a mobile crane over here by this afternoon, and we can get it out there on that old roadbed. You supervise that, okay?"

"Sure."

"You've only got the rest of this week till your vacation, right?"

Jack felt a little twinge of surprise. For some reason, he kept forgetting about his coming time off. "Oh—yeah. That's right."

"Well, that should be plenty of time to get this sorted out. Whatever we discover in that wreck, I don't expect it'll be much. We'll be lucky if we even find who was the registered owner. Of course, that may be the bone pile in the cab. We'll just have to see."

The bone pile in the cab.

Despite Jack's 21 years on the force he found the sarge's description oddly disquieting. But he didn't mention it, and went to his desk, attacking a stack of paperwork and looking forward to the afternoon. Though a mite on the ghoulish side, this promised to be an interesting break in routine.

IN FACT, THE crane had to come down from Kamloops and didn't arrive till the next morning.

By that time, word had got around and half the town was waiting on the bluff overlooking the lake when the crane arrived. Jack got a couple of the locals to take charge of crowd control, his only real concern being that no idiot topple off the cliff edge in the excitement.

Just as the big crane began setting up for the job, Jim Oakton from the *Gleaner* arrived, carrying his heavy old camera and panting because of his jog in from the highway. Jack liked Jim well enough. When the tubby little guy came wheezing up he gave him a grin.

"Hi, Jim—here for the big scoop?"

"I wish!" Oakton puffed. "What's happening?"

"Not much so far." Jack pointed to where wetsuited figures were swimming and plunging out by the wreck. "Just getting the cables under her, by the looks of it."

One of the swimmers lifted an arm and signalled. From the long arm of the crane, a hook descended to water level. The swimmers began connecting cable loops to the hook, an operation that took several minutes. Finally everything was ready. The cable inched upwards until everything tightened, all taut and secure. One of the wetsuits made a take-it-away gesture to the crane driver and they both swam clear.

There was a pause. Dead silence from the watching crowd. Then came a number of clanks and grinds as the crane operator fiddled with gears and levers, preparing to raise his heavy load. The engine hummed and, carefully, the half-century-delayed rescue began.

The truck rose like some ancient leviathan from the deep. First appeared the cab, dark and slime encrusted, but still with a ghostly underglow of its original red. The windshield and back window, though filthy, seemed miraculously intact. But the driver's-side glass was gone, the gaping hole like the eye of some primordial beast.

The rest of the wreck followed and, as it emerged and hung, gently rotating, spewing its cargo of water and mud, the watchers gave an audible sigh. Then, soft and almost reverent in its intensity, there followed a round of applause.

Now the crane arm began to retract, starting the retrieved vehicle on its last journey home. As it swung into profile, Jack could see that the bodywork seemed undamaged. It was an old International, not large but squat and built like a tank—which was probably why it had survived so long. It looked intact, no indication of an accident. Probably the driver had simply lost it, trying to take a curve too fast or maybe falling asleep, and plunged off the cliff into the water.

The truck was now swinging around toward the land. Jim Oakton's camera began to flash and people started to surge forward for a better look. Waving them back, Jack kept things clear so that the wreck could be lowered onto a waiting flatbed. Jim wanted to get up there to take a picture inside the cab but Jack held him back.

"Leave it, Jim. We don't know what we've got yet."

Jim laughed. "What you've got is some bones and 50-year-old sludge. Surely you're not going to call this a crime scene?"

"Probably not. But we'll just have to take a look. Come by the station later. Whatever we find out, I promise you'll be the first to know."

Oakton nodded, grudgingly satisfied, but sauntered to the back of the flatbed. The old International crouched, still leaking water, flattened tire-remnants splayed from its wheel rims. The rear bumper must have been made of 20-gauge steel, because even now it looked as if it could crush a regular auto into junk. Attached to one end was a small oblong of metal, within reach of the reporter who stretched up and briskly wiped it with his hand. Layers of mud came away, revealing the distinct markings of raised letters.

WT45874
BC 1951

Jim Oakton's camera flashed, then the reporter backed off. "That'll do just fine for now. I've got a story to write." He waved. "See you later, Jack."

PAT SMOLENSKI, THE local doctor who worked with the police on the occasions—rare in this part of the world—when his services were needed, was on hand when the cab was finally opened. They had brought the truck to the workshop in back of Fraz Orloff's Petrocan station, which was large enough to accommodate the thing and also had the equipment that might be needed to breach it. After half a century, locks and hinges were fused solid, so it took Fraz a few minutes with a torch to remove one of the doors.

Since Jack was in charge, he also got to do the dirty work. But the operation wasn't all that stomach-turning. What they found was pretty much as Jim Oakton had predicted: mud and bones.

The doctor first investigated the skull and after a brief examination shook his head. "Nothing to tell us much here."

Jack peered at the object, so stained with age and water that it looked more like stone than bone. This object that had—presumably until some time in 1951—held all the intricate thoughts and persona of a human being, now looked like a relic from an archeo logical dig. "What might we have expected?"

Smolenski slowly revolved the skull. "With the degree of age and decomposition, there's no way to tell what happened to the guy, other than that the poor bastard probably drowned. If there was a bullet hole, now that'd tell us something. But—as you can see—it isn't the case. So, pending a look at the rest, which won't take long, I reckon the story here is going to be death by misadventure."

Which was the way it turned out. The cab contained just one set of bones: male, maybe six feet tall, and probably between 25 and 40 years old. Apart from the bones, there was nothing identifiable save two flattish lumps that might once have been boot soles and one bottle: a pint container—or mickey—for liquor. Seeing it, the doctor nodded wryly. "There you go. If you're looking for a smoking gun, Jack, I'd say little mickey here is it. The guy was probably drinking."

Jack sighed. "What else is new?"

The whole thing was over in less than an hour. Conclusion: there was no point in any more formal examination of the remains. Smolenski said he'd drop his findings off at the station and Jack was left to clean up and get the bones ready for the undertaker. It wasn't too bad. Vastly preferable, he reflected, to working the scene of a bad road accident, something which, even in this quiet neck of the woods, happened all too often and was the only thing he really disliked about his job.

He moved the flatbed outside to the back of the lot, then hosed down the inside, mostly to make sure he hadn't missed anything that should be cremated, but it seemed they'd got everything. About to finish up, he noticed something on the floor, near the atrophied ruin of what had been the gas pedal. It was not much more than a lump, like a squarish pebble, which was what he at first took it for. After a couple of taps with the hose nozzle it came away. He picked the thing up, finding it lighter than expected. It was reddish brown, like a hunk of rock containing a lot of iron, but not heavy enough for that. Peering closer, he saw that although it had at first seemed to be entirely natural, there was actually a faint echo of man-made shape. He shook it and was rewarded with a sluggish rattle. He tried wiping it, but only flakes came away, still leaving no clue as to what it was. He started to toss it aside, then changed his mind and stuffed it into his pocket, meaning to take a last look at it later. Finally he washed up and called the undertaker from the Petrocan phone. Old Fraz would want those bones out of there ASAP.

He arrived back at the station just as Jim Oakton drew up in his ancient Toyota. "Hey, Jack, watcha find?"

"Not much. About what you said: mud and bones."

"No indication of funny business?"

"Not unless you count the presence of an old rye bottle."

"So you say the guy was driving drunk?"

"I'm saying no such thing. The bottle in the cab may mean everything or nothing. It's just an accident. An old, sad, pathetic story. Don't try to make anything more out of it, Jim, for Christ's sake."

He stopped, embarrassed at the heat in his own voice. But Oakton didn't seem to notice. "Just kidding," he said mildly. "Anyway, my story has already gone to press. I've got something for *you*."

"Oh?"

The reporter shrugged. "It's stuff you'll find out anyway. But since my sources are quicker—and it's in my story—I figured I might save you guys some trouble."

What Oakton had tracked down, from the number on the ancient plate, was the registered owner of the International. Information as far back as 1951 was not in the electronic database, but a contact had found it in Motor Vehicles Branch records in Victoria. He'd come up with one Herbert Johan Reddeki, living in the town of Duncan on Vancouver Island; 1951, not surprisingly, was the last year for that particular vehicle. Jim's final information, obtained on the Internet through some process he would not divulge, was that no one of that name had filed any kind of tax return in Canada within the last half century.

"I know that doesn't prove that the driver was old Bert," Jim shrugged. "I mean, he could have left the country, skipped taxes, or even changed his name. But all of that I sincerely doubt. There may be no way to prove it—but my bet is Bert's our boy."

Jack had to agree. The sarge did also. On the police report, the owner of the vehicle was listed as one Herbert Johan Reddski: the victim of the ancient mishap "in all likelihood" the same person. Since there was no evidence of foul play and no known family, and the tragedy was really ancient history, the brief account went into the files and the case—if it even merited such a name—was closed.

JACK WENT HOME, threw off the old clothes he'd used for the cleanup, and got into the shower. The hot water and soap smell was a relief, and made him realize that working on that rotting wreck—even though the scent of real death had long departed—must have affected him more than he knew. As he emerged from the shower the phone rang.

"Hi, hon," Margie said. "I just got home. You?"

"Yeah—just out of the shower."

"I'm about to go in."

She laughed. "Hurry on over, buster. Get here while I'm still naked and we can play!"

Margie hung up. Jack, with a smile of pleasure and some embarrassment, glanced downward, seeing the clear evidence of her suggestion upon his own anatomy. Margie was such a wonderfully frank and free spirit. Though she was only a bit younger, he sometimes felt she came from an entirely different generation: folk who were comfortable with their sexuality in a way not possible for him. Oh, he enjoyed making love all right, and being with Margie was better than anything he'd ever known. But she also had the capacity to stir confusion in him. Her openness, her unquestioning acceptance of the basic, animal nature of the body, that he found amazing—and on some level disquieting too.

One thing he did understand: if there was a problem, it was his alone. But maybe the trouble wasn't really about sex. What if his disquiet at Margie's frank sexuality had its root not in prudishness but in simple panic: fear of closeness? What if? *What if?* For a sensible guy with a great lady and a fine job, he was definitely too introspective.

A little later at Margie's place, introspection was given the swift boot. When he arrived, as promised, she wasn't wearing much of anything save perfume and fresh talc, and they had a wonderful time. As well as being uninhibited, she brought the strength and agility of her job to the business of lovemaking.

Afterwards, as they lay, damp bodies sandwiched like one creature, aglow and stupefyingly spent, Jack had to admit that his mind felt as relaxed as his body. For a time, delicious if all too short, he did feel genuinely at peace.

LATER, THEY WENT out to eat. On their way into Billy's Kitchen, the tolerable local diner, Margie swooped a copy of the *South Kootenay Gleaner* from the outside box.

"Wow, hot off the press," she cried. And a moment later, "Hey, copper, looks like you're a star."

Jack grabbed the paper and perused it as they threaded their way to their usual booth at the back. Under the headline "Ancient Accident Victim" was a picture of the wrecked pickup being lowered onto the flatbed, with Jack and the watching crowd in the background. The story that followed was brief but clear. They ordered burgers and, while they were waiting, read it together. Then Margie gave a sudden little intake of breath.

"Hey," she said. "I know that name—Reddski!"

"You've heard it?"

"Yes—I think so."

"But the truck was registered on Vancouver Island."

"Yeah, but what I'm saying is I've heard the name *here*."

"So?"

"So—maybe the guy had family here. Did you think about that?"

He grinned. "Gee, lady, actually we did. Next of kin is kinda one of the first things we tend to think about. If there were ever any Reddskis around here, they're long gone."

Margie grinned. "Sorry. I didn't mean to sound patronizing, but, Jack, I have heard the name. I don't know where or when—but I'll think of it."

AND SHE DID. But it took until the end of the evening. In fact, they were just pulling up in front of her place when Margie thumped her hand on the wheel of her zippy little SUV and cried, "Got it!"

"What?"

"Where I heard the name Reddski."

"Great! Where?"

"Well—it's a bit of a story. Want to hear?" Margie was quite a one for her stories. They tended to be long but were always interesting.

"Fire away!"

"Okay. When I was young there wasn't much to do around here. But one summer, when I was about 13, there was this magic-mushroom craze. And one kid had this older brother who was kind of latter-day hippie. From him we found out all about crazy magic mushrooms. Wow! And that the hills round here were supposed to be just *swarming* with them. So one day a bunch of us went on a magic-mushroom hunt. You know the old road that leads up to the dam? Well, we went up there. We searched the woods and high meadows for hours, but couldn't find anything. Then way up toward Jimsons Ridge.

"We found this farm. Just a few small fields and a big old log house. But there were magic mushrooms. We'd just started in picking when suddenly there was this gunshot."

"Gunshot?"

"Scared the poop out of us, I can tell you. We looked up and there was this guy on the stoop of the house. He was old, looked like a hillbilly. Had this shotgun still smoking in his hand, and behind him was a much younger woman. His wife or maybe his daughter.

"Anyway, the old guy says, 'What are you doing, girl?' His voice was soft with a bit of a foreign accent. And he was looking more anxious than angry. So I said, 'Just picking mushrooms, sir.' I didn't want to tell him about the psychedelic thing. I said we were just passing and saw the shrooms and decided to get some and that was all. So he calls for me to come to him, then surprises me all over again. He says, 'You would like drink of water?' I guess I nodded. The woman went inside and came back with a cup of water."

Margie had a bemused expression on her face. "Jack, it's so weird. This is like a dream I'd forgotten. But the more I talk the clearer it comes back. So—I drank the water, and he finally said, 'You look like nice girl, so I do you big favour. Tell you secret. Those are bad mushroom. Poison! That is why I fire gun—to stop you before you eat poison. All mushroom on Reddski farm poison. So—no good to come here for mushroom. You tell friends—never come again to Reddski farm. Okay?' "

"And I bet you didn't?"

"Damn right. I don't know if we believed it about the poison. Probably not. But I know we thought anyone weird enough to make up stuff like that could be real trouble."

"But are you sure his name was actually Reddski?"

"Absolutely. We made silly jokes about it: imagined this old hillbilly going round on red skis. Old Farmer Red Skis we called him. Kids do shit like that to death. I guess that's what made it stick. Anyway—that's my weird Reddski story. What do you think?"

"Well, like you say, it's weird. It definitely could explain why Herbert Reddski was in the area. But we've checked it out. There's definitely no one of that name around here now."

JACK DIDN'T STAY long that night at Margie's.

She wanted him to stop over and, since Doug was due back from camp in a couple of days, this time she was more insistent. Not sure exactly why, he nevertheless resisted—and was greeted with stony silence. This, in Margie, was dangerous. It meant that she was more than just mad at him. He had the distinct feeling she was teetering on the brink of a sad—and possibly irreversible—process: the idea of actually giving up on them.

He tried to figure out what was wrong with him: why he seemed to be running from the best thing that had happened to him in years. But then something else started bugging him. Whether he was avoiding thinking about what needed to be thought, or whether he just couldn't stop being a cop, he didn't know, but his mind was working on the business of Bert Reddski.

Old Farmer Red Skis.

Apparently there once had been Reddskis in the area. Okay, then so what? Now the rest of the family were dead or long gone. No one left to say if Bert was a relative. No one to remember. No one to care. No claimant for the lost pile of bones.

And—for God's sake—what was so unusual about that? Even in this peaceful land, unidentified bodies turned up all the time. Police files were filled with records of unknown remains. Bert Reddski had only been identified by the wreck in which he was found, but at least his file had a name. Surely that was something.

Something: but, in some irritatingly persistent corner of Jack's mind, evidently not enough.

The next day was Friday, the last before Jack's vacation. In midafternoon a call came in to the station: some folks had just returned from vacation to find their house burgled. Jack was sent to investigate.

The place in question was on a road behind town with several expensive and newish homes. The householders, Irene and Gil McCann, both in their 70s, had come back from a visit with family in Vancouver to find a back window broken and the house ransacked. A mess had been made and a lot of small stuff stolen, but a computer, a flat-screen TV and couple of VCRs were untouched. The thieves had probably been kids, on foot, disturbed before they could get comfy. Jack took notes, gave his usual spiel about locks and holiday precautions, promised to inform them if any of their goods should turn up and headed out.

About to get into the cruiser, he paused. Something had begun flitting around at the edge of his mind. Then he realized what it was and returned to the house. The McCanns hadn't heard about the truck in the lake so he told them the story, ending with the question that was the real reason for his return.

"I know you've lived around here a long time. Over the years you probably met just about everyone. I wondered if either of you had ever heard of a family called Reddski."

Gil looked blank, but Irene nodded vigorously. "I know that name. I used to go to school with a girl called Reddski. Norma? Nora—that was it. Nora Reddski."

Scarcely able to credit the intuition that had made him come back, Jack said quietly, "Do you know if she had a brother?"

Irene shook her head. "No idea. She wasn't in my grade. I didn't know her all that well. And she was kind of odd, too, with a weird accent. Oh, not like some Doukhobor kids had back then. Foreign. Her folks had a farm. Way up in the boonies, I think. But a brother? If she did he wasn't in school with me."

"Well, thanks," Jack said. Then, almost as an afterthought, "Any idea what happened to Nora?"

"None at all." Irene said, then frowned. "Just a minute—I lie—I did hear she got married. But I've no idea to who."

And that was that. Jack thanked them for their help and headed back to town. Why he seemed impelled to keep on with this Reddski thing he didn't know. He did still have the slim excuse of seeking next of kin, but there was no way he could justify spending much more police time on this sad little saga.

Back at the station he filed his report on the McCann crime spree. As he was signing off for the night, the sarge said, "You and Margie planning on going somewhere on your vacation?"

"I hadn't really thought about it."

"You don't sound very enthusiastic."

Jack shrugged. Seeming casual about such a thing as a vacation must appear a bit eccentric. But, whatever the reasons—the current ambivalence of his feelings for Margie, the annoying obsession with the Reddski business, or the strange disquiet that of late seemed to be lurking at the edge of his head—he just couldn't get in the mood.

"Oh, Margie can't get off. And her kid's been away. But we may work something out. Go to the coast or something."

"Well, have a good one."

After he left, he didn't exactly hurry, still feeling vaguely as if there was unfinished business. Margie was running a late exercise class, which was a relief. After last night's cool departure he wasn't too sure of his reception when they next met.

At home he changed and threw his soiled uniform into the hamper, noticing at the bottom the old things he'd used for the truck cleanup. Well, plenty of time to do a wash later: like three full weeks, for God's sake. He shut the hamper and automatically started to tidy his apartment. The place was a mother-in-law suite, just one big basement room with kitchen and adjoining bath, so that took all of five minutes. He was just thinking of maybe turning on the TV when the phone rang.

"Hello?"

"Constable Marsden?" It was the voice of Irene McCann.

"Hi again, Mrs. McCann."

"I hope you don't mind me phoning so late. I called the station and they said you'd gone home."

"That's okay. How can I help you?"

"Actually—it's the other way round. Remember we were talking about Nora Reddski? Well, I just remembered the name of the man she married, if you're still interested."

"I certainly am."

"It was Abel Welsh."

JACK BIT THE bullet and drove over to Margie's place. By now, he figured, she would have returned from her class. Resisting the urge to sit and think about it, he got out of his car and went in.

Margie was in the kitchen with her work-sweats still on. Trying to keep the momentum, Jack took hold of her hand. "Listen," he said quickly. "I'm sorry I didn't stay over last night. I want to be with you. This—us—is more important to me than anything. I just haven't quite worked out how to deal with it yet."

Margie's gaze was stern. "I love you, you know that, copper?"

"Yes. And I love you."

"So what's to deal with?"

"I don't know. But something I'm going to work on it, I promise. I just need to know that you won't—give up on me."

"Oh, honey!" In a single, agile movement, she plastered herself onto him. "You big goof. I thought you were giving up on me!"

For some time they just stayed like that, hugging hard, squished together like a single, crazed creature.

That night Jack did stay over.

NEXT MORNING, AS they were getting up, Jack said, "You remember that story you told me, about the magic mushrooms and the Reddski farm? You talked of a young woman there?"

"Yes."

"Well, it was his daughter, I think—name of Nora. She was married to a guy named Welsh. Did you catch sight of him?"

"No. Wow, you've been busy. How did you find all this out?"

"Oh—lucky break. The point is, though there aren't Reddskis around anymore, there may be Welshes. In fact, Nora Reddski-Welsh may still be right on that farm where you last saw her."

"Golly."

"Yeah, it's a thought, isn't it? Anyway, I figured today I might just take a little trip up there and check. I mean, if it is her, and the guy we found is her brother, then she has a right to know."

Margie looked puzzled. "I guess so. But—since you're starting vacation, why are you bothering with this?"

Jack looked puzzled. "To tell the truth, I've been wondering the same thing."

She studied him shrewdly. "Could it be that, somehow, you feel personally responsible?"

"If I did—does that make me seem like a jerk?"

"A jerk?" She laughed and hugged him hard. "No, copper dear, like someone who maybe cares. Look—I'm not working and Doug won't be back till tonight. So why don't we get in my car and I'll show you where the place is."

THE JOURNEY DIDN'T take very long. They started out just after two and were soon on a winding road past the reservoir, heading for what Margie had called Jimsons Ridge. On the other side the country opened out, trees giving way to high meadows and, lower down, some fields where a few cattle grazed. At last, they came around a steep bend and found what they were looking for. A narrow dirt road, little used. But Margie was in no doubt that this was the place. Farther on were the fields of the magic-mushroom story and, in the distance, an old log house. It looked even more down at heel than Margie had described.

But it was inhabited. Smoke curled from the chimney. Chickens scratched in the yard. Out front a Datsun pickup was hunkered down like an old tired dog.

They stopped the car and Jack walked up onto the stoop. The front of the house was overwhelmed by a massive spume of ivy, covering the windows and almost blocking the door. Pushing aside the tendrils, Jack knocked. The sound was muffled, flat, as if the place was so ancient and stale that it could not even echo. After a short wait he knocked again.

A muffled voice said, "Door stuck. Go round back."

Jack and Margie did as they'd been bid. The path to the rear was through a garden, both vegetables and flowers, in sturdy rows and healthy profusion. However, many had gone to seed and there was a major encroachment of weeds. Work here had been recently but severely curtailed.

The back door, like the front, was half-hidden by hanging vines. But this was open and a voice called from inside, "Come in! Whoever is there—come!"

Jack and Margie entered and stopped short, blinking. Because the house was made of logs, the windows were small. All were shrouded with outside growth, so it felt like a world beneath the sea and it took a moment before they could properly see that world's sole inhabitant.

Even before Jack focussed on the woman herself, it was clear that she was alone. Single cup by the sink; single plate with half-eaten meal on the table; single clear kitchen chair (all others piled with papers and junk); single rocker by the fireplace. Also, the place had an atmosphere: a distilled essence of loneliness.

The solitary one herself was very thin and very brown and very tall. Dressed in overalls, a checkered shirt, sagging cardigan and ancient boots, she stood in the kitchen, regarding them solemnly. Her gaunt face was rigid with will, her eyes dark pools mirroring the bleak ambience of the house, She moved toward them, upright and straight—but also very slow. Only then did Jack notice that her gnarled right hand held a walking stick.

"Who are you people?" The woman's voice was as strong as the lines on her face. It had a faint but unmistakable accent. "Why do you come to my house?"

"Are you Mrs. Welsh?" Jack asked. "Mrs. Nora Welsh?"

"Yes." Without ceremony. "Who are you?"

"I'm Jack Marsden, from the RCMP in town. And this is my friend, Margie Peroff. We came up here to—uh—talk to you."

The old woman regarded them, not hostile but considering. "What does RCMP want with me?"

"Just a little information, Mrs. Welsh. Is this a bad time?"

The woman began to move across the kitchen. Her steps were slow, her right side obviously causing much pain. "A month ago I fall down," she muttered, as if they had asked for an explanation. "Now everything go to hell. You have tea?"

Jack opened his mouth to decline, but Margie cut in, "If it's not too much trouble."

"Tea is tea," Nora said, as if this were a major philosophical statement. Making it, she was remarkably dexterous. Putting aside her stick, she supported herself against the counter and set to work. Soon three steaming mugs were produced. "No milk," Nora said abruptly. "Can't milk, so cow go dry. Garden gone to hell too."

They all settled at the kitchen table. The tea was scalding but good. Finally Nora said, "All right, Mr. RCMP—what you want?"

Jack glanced at Margie, took a breath and plunged in. "Tell me, Mrs. Welsh, was your maiden name Reddski?"

The woman looked at him without surprise. "Of course. This was the Reddski farm. My pa's farm. I was Nora Reddski." She gave a rustling chuckle, though her face didn't smile. "Might as well be Reddski still. Wish it was Reddski, if you want to know."

"Why is that?"

Nora shook her head. "Well, what was good of him?"

"Ah—who would that be?"

"Abel Welsh! Stupid man. Stupid, *stupid* man."

"What did he do?"

The old woman looked at Jack as if he was stupid himself. Then her expression softened. "Of course, how would you know? Abel was my pa's hired hand. Not much of man, but only one around. My pa didn't think he was good enough for me. But I am getting on, almost too old for babies. Pa doesn't care. He only want grandkids from his precious Johnny anyway. But by then even he has to admit that Johnny isn't ever going to take over farm. So he give his permission and we get married." She shook her head bitterly. "Abel Welsh! If that man wasn't so stupid I wouldn't be like this now."

"What did he do?" This time it was Margie.

Nora's expression was pure outrage. "Goes and kills his stupid self! Rolls the tractor and squashes himself flatter than a bug. Three months after we wed—and me not even yet with baby."

"Wow!" Margie said.

"I'm sorry," Jack said.

"Three month wife, and 40 year widow. Pretty good, eh? Nothing to show but a broke-down old farm and a broke-down old woman. And no one to look after either of us." She broke off. "But why we talk about this? Sad tales from foolish old women are nothing to police. Mr. RCMP, what you want from me?"

This was it. Jack took a breath. "All right, Mrs. Welsh. Did you ever have a brother?"

Her glance was like a knife. "Brother?"

"Yes. You see, why I … "

"Stupid!" she burst out. "Do you not listen? Of course I have a brother. That's all Pa ever think about. That's what I am telling you."

"Johnny!" Margie cried suddenly. "The one who wouldn't take over the farm. Your brother's Johnny?"

Jack's eyes rolled up. "Short for Johan?"

"Yes."

"Herbert Johan Reddski?"

"How you know?" Nora stopped, an entirely new expression filtering, muscle by reluctant muscle, across her features. At last she said, "You have come to tell about Johnny?"

"Yes," Jack said quietly. "I'm afraid I have."

AFTER THE STORY was told there was a long period of quiet. Finally the old woman's stunned look eased into neutral. Then she began to smile. The expression grew increasingly complex: amazement, relief, pain, understanding, grief, irony and joy, somehow all coexisting on the bleak landscape of her face.

Watching, Jack and Margie remained silent. Minutes passed. When the old woman finally spoke, her voice was quiet, but very clear. "That night was terrible."

Silence. No interaction indicated. This was not conversation but an opening statement. The rest would follow in its own time.

"Johnny had only come home day before," Nora continued at last. "That time he was away a year. Working as logger on Vancouver Island. Me and Ma were real happy. Pa is thinking Johnny come home for good.

"I never see my parents so happy. Pa—like he's in heaven. And I am thinking, nothing I ever do make them happy like that. We have special homecoming feast. Pa finds bottle of slivovitz he is saving from Old Country. Makes toasts to the family and the farm and Canada. I never see him so happy. Then Johnny tell us about the girl."

The shadows in the house seemed to have lengthened and thickened. The old woman's eyes glowed with memory, staring 50 years back through the dark conduit of time.

"She is nurse, he says, in some hospital on Vancouver Island. One day in the bush Johnny get this gut pain. Appendicitis. They drag him out to hospital where he nearly dies. But he gets better, meets this nurse girl. Falls in love, he says. And that is that.

"This girl loves him too. Her name is Doris Day. This I remember because that was also name of big film star back then. She is very beautiful, he says, but sweet and not proud. She is not Catholic, but from good family, and her and Johnny plan to get married and have family too. Well, then Pa full of joy. Lots of room at the farm, he says, for Johnny and new wife, and for all the kids they want.

"So now Johnny gets all quiet. At last he tells truth. He's not going to live on farm. Not ever. He's not back to stay. Only to tell about his marriage and get our blessing.

"I never hear such a sound like Pa make then. It is a kind of scream, like wild animal in pain. 'Blessing!' he yells in Polish. 'You tell me you throw away everything I work my whole life to give. You tell me you marry slut and have bastards and go away forever—and you want blessing? What I give is curse! *Curse!* Now, get out! Never come back. Go—and never come back again!'

"The two of them stand, glaring. Hating! I think there will be murder. Then Johnny say, 'Okay, old fool, if that's what you want. I go and never come back! And you can all go straight to hell.' He spits on floor at Pa's feet and runs out. I can still see his red truck, kicking up stones as he drives off like crazy man. And that is last time any of us ever sees him."

Nora gave a long sigh, like air escaping from a corpse. "Next day, after everything calms down, Pa is sorry. Says he is wrong. Says Johnny will know he was wrong too. He'll come back and say sorry and all is forgiven. Pa is believing this until day he dies."

The old woman's shoulders gave a heave. "So strange now to think Pa was right," she whispered. "Johnny would have come—except he couldn't. All that time we wait. All those years. And not just us. His poor nurse girl, she waits too. She must think he doesn't love her no more. And we think he don't care about us. The grief kills Pa inside. Kills Ma even quicker. For years I am here alone. And all the time Johnny is there"—she gestured sadly in the direction of the lake—"down there, waiting for some little kid to find."

Margie said quietly, "But now at least you know Johnny didn't mean to leave everyone. Isn't that something?"

Nora considered this, finally nodded. "Yes, you're right. My poor brother Johnny was not a bad man. Just unlucky. This is terrible thing that happens—but I am glad I know. I only wish Pa and Ma could know too. But that poor nurse girl—I think she needs to know most. How her heart must have broken, how she must have waited." Nora smiled mournfully. "If she is anything like Pa—maybe she waits still."

THE SHADOWS HAD lengthened to late afternoon by the time they left. On the way back Margie drove silently and very fast. Both were deeply affected by the events of the afternoon, Jack perhaps more than he cared to admit.

Margie was fetching Doug from town, where the bus was due at 6:00. On the way, Jack had her drop him at her place, where he retrieved his own car. It had been decided they would all go out for supper later. Jack made a swing around to the store, where he picked up the Saturday *Globe and Mail*, then headed home.

He walked inside and was halfway across his living room when he stopped, looking about with a frown. Nothing had changed. Certainly no one had been in there. Yet everything seemed subtly different—as if he were looking at it for the first time.

Which could only mean that the change was in himself. What exactly it was, he had no idea. The events of the last days had certainly had an impact, revealing hidden drama in the everyday world. But the change in him was more than simply a response to them. What had been intensified was a process that had started long ago. Jack had no idea what the result would be but he had the uncomfortable feeling that it was somehow inevitable.

To distract himself from these thoughts, Jack began leafing through the paper he'd bought earlier. He read the sports section first, then turned to the news. Flipping pages, on his way to the international section, he paused at the column called "Across Canada." Catching his eye was a paragraph two from the top:

Ancient Accident Victim

The remains of an ancient accident were found near Grand Forks, B.C., earlier this week. A pickup truck with 1951 plates was discovered by a youth while swimming in Christina Lake. It was totally submerged and contained the bones of one 25-to-40-year-old male, yet to be positively identified. The truck apparently plunged into the lake some time in 1951. Highway 3 was later diverted to a safer route away from the water. Officials believe this is why the mishap has remained so long undiscovered. CP

Jack smiled. So old Jim Oakton had got his story picked up by the wire service after all. Pretty slim coverage though. A big sensation in a small town was small potatoes to the outside world.

A knock came on the door that separated his apartment from the house above. Amy Beakins, his landlady, descended a couple of steps. She was a short, round woman, sweet-natured, wearing a print dress and kitchen apron. She was carrying a laundry basket now, and was on what Jack had come to think of as a "mothering run."

"Hello, Jack, I'm just doing a bit of laundry. Anything you want to put in, dear?"

"Well—if it's not too much trouble."

"Of course not. We must keep our policemen spic and span, mustn't we? How's your friend Margie?"

"Fine. Her kid just got home from camp."

"That's nice. Margie's a nice girl. The two of you are so nice together." Amy's expression grew impish. "Perhaps it won't be long before I'll have to start looking for another tenant, eh?"

This was not the first of Amy's forays into such territory; she was an unashamed matchmaker. Jack grinned. "I'm not going anywhere right now, Amy. But, if anything changes, you'll be the first to know."

"Of course, dear, of course." Suddenly embarrassed, the plump lady retreated upwards, leaving the laundry basket. "Just leave your stuff in there, dear. I'll get it later."

She departed. Smiling still, Jack loaded the basket with soiled laundry. He put in all his regular stuff, then came to the clothes he'd used when gathering the remains of Herbert "Johnny" Reddski. A phrase drifted into his head: *dust to dust.*

Jack lifted the grubby shirt and pants to throw them into the basket. Something fell with a solid clunk upon the floor. A small reddish rock. He picked it up, and it was a moment before he recalled what it was: the object he'd found on the floor of the drowned truck. He'd put it in his pocket and then entirely forgotten it.

He moved to a better light. The thing was dry now. Rusted metal, because layered shards were peeling off. He shook it, producing a dull rattle. Intrigued, he looked closer, realizing that what he held was a small metal box. He carried it to the table and took out a heavy knife. He poised the knife vertically, point touching the surface of the rusted metal, and struck the handle a sharp blow with his other hand.

The knife went through the rotted top as if it were paper. It split neatly in half. What had been inside spilled out, dropped, skittered under the table. Jack had to get on his knees to peer around. At first he couldn't see anything. Then he spied it, way in a corner. He fished it out and took it under the lamp.

A plain gold wedding band.

Feeling a strange sense of inevitability—of something akin to déjà vu—Jack found a rag and rubbed the ring clean. Watery entombment had not affected the precious metal. Soon it gleamed, as fresh as the day—half a century ago—some snooty jewellery store clerk had put it into the hand of a young logger.

A hand never destined to put it on the finger of another.

On the inside of the ring was an inscription, quite clear because it was only four solidly engraved letters:

J. R. D. D.

Without any surprise, nor even a sense of having made a decision, Jack knew what he had to do.

TWO

Emily sat in the doctor's office reading *Saturday Night* magazine, deeply absorbed in an article on the Queen Charlotte Islands. She was very upright and very still. Her reading glasses were half lenses, small and neat, and sat on a nose that was fine-chiselled and also neat. The surrounding face was olive brown, tanned from a lifetime of tending gardens, but remarkably unlined. Her hair had a moderate amount of uninhibited grey. Her eyes were blue-grey. Her lips were full, not exactly forbidding, but held in lines more than passing stern. The hands that held the magazine were square and competent; when she turned pages her movements were as decisive as those of a policeman directing traffic.

Emily was 66. In fact, today was her birthday. It was just a year since she'd retired from her post in the English department at the University of Victoria, but that year, free from classrooms and lectures and the stifling round of university politics, had been the nearest thing she could imagine to heaven. No longer to inhabit the world of academe, to live in sweet solitude, reading, looking at her paintings and working in her demi-paradise of a garden; it was almost too good to bear. Consciousness of the miracle was with her always, simmering in the substrata of her thoughts, the nearest thing possible in her agnostic heart to prayer.

Emily put down her magazine and looked at her watch. It said 1:51 and her appointment had been for 1:00. Dr. Quayle was running almost an hour late.

Emily felt a niggle of irritation, which she swiftly squelched. The poor man was overworked to distraction, but he always called her in for a quick chat after her annual checkup, to go over diet or cholesterol counts or something equally minor. She was just lucky that old Quayle was so conscientious. She smiled to herself; "Old Quayle," as she'd thought of him, was at least 20 years her junior.

"Emily Muller?"

Emily was jolted from her thoughts by a voice from the reception desk.

"The doctor will see you now."

Dr. Quayle was writing notes when Emily entered. He indicated a chair with a nod, pursed his lips in—she thought—a slightly theatrical display of concentration, and went on scribbling.

She sat and calmly waited, watching him. Dr. Peter Quayle was a big man, thoroughly scrubbed, with small hands and carefully manicured nails. He wore heavy-framed glasses, which he removed as he finished writing.

"Hi, Emily," he said quietly. "How are you?"

"Not too bad, thanks, Doctor."

Not for the first time, she was amused to note the unspoken hierarchy in their forms of address; a fortyish man calling a sixty-ish woman by her first name while she called him "Doctor." On a couple of occasions she'd tried using his Christian name. He didn't seem to notice, while she'd actually been embarrassed. Which meant perhaps that the need for hierarchy was actually seated in her own psyche. Her generation, she knew, was more likely to fall into the doctor-as-priest fallacy. Though she tried not to worship at the flawed shrine of science, some probably cowardly essence made her more comfortable within older established patterns.

The doctor was consulting her file. He looked up,with what for him was an unusual expression: he actually looked uncomfortable.

Thinking back later, Emily realized that that was when she should have started to be alarmed.

"I see today is your 66th birthday," the doctor said. "How have you been enjoying your retirement?"

"Very much, thank you."

"Good," he said. "Very good, yes. And how have you been feeling since your last checkup?"

"Not too bad. But that tiredness I mentioned before—that arrived after the flu—that seems to be still hanging about a bit."

"Ah!"

The doctor tried to smile, but came up again with that unusual, uncomfortable expression.

Alarm bells began to go off in Emily's head. She experienced an aching, hollow feeling that she only belatedly recognized as fear. She attempted a smile—which was no more successful than Dr. Quayle's had been. "How's my cholesterol, doctor?"

"Very good. In fact, most of your tests, as usual, were just fine."

"*Most?* Does that mean not all?"

"Ah—that's right. Not quite all, I'm afraid."

Emily stared. A sensation more painful than the previous hollowness clutched at her gut. Finally, she began to comprehend the situation; what she saw, slinking its way through the controlled professionalism of her doctor's face, was awful compassion.

"What is it, doctor?" Emily said, her voice sounding to herself like the rustle from a tomb. "What's wrong with me?"

EMILY DROVE HER Subaru Forester—the one big indulgence

she'd allowed herself upon retirement—out of Victoria, heading home to Cobble Hill.

The traffic hadn't yet started to build on the Island Highway, so the flow was fast and unimpeded. The road had been recently improved and was now a virtual expressway almost to the start of the Malahat Mountain Range, 10 kilometres north of the city. From there the route was both lovely and majestic. Goldstream, where the mountains began, was an emerald chasm of coast maples and towering cedars, through which the road wound discreetly, as if given reluctant dispensation. It slipped through a narrow gap, then—released—soared steadily away. To the west reared a wall of granite, encrusted with moss, ferns and occasional nets to guard against rock falls. To the east the land collapsed into Finlayson Arm, a watery gulf all but severing the southeast corner of Vancouver Island. In that direction, as the road climbed, an alternating pattern of land and water could be seen, misty islands stretching to the United States mainland, and the volcanic silhouette of Mount Baker.

This view and this drive were major reasons why Emily had moved north to the village of Cobble Hill. She never tired of its charms when travelling to the city. On the way down today her reaction had been in the usual range: wonder, satisfaction, a comfortable feeling of rightness in the whole world.

Coming home, she might as well have been in another universe.

Emily drove like an automaton, oblivious to everything except the deepening realization in her head. It was like a ravenous insect consuming her future. Everything she held dear, all the years and seasons she had unquestioningly anticipated—the entire sum of the books to be read, friends to be enjoyed, art to be loved and gardens to be planted—all had been crushed, negated, rendered null and void, by a simple procedure that had taken place in some faceless medical lab.

A blood test.

At the annual checkup, because of that flu and subsequent tiredness, Dr. Quayle had added one more test to the routine stuff. What it turned up was far from routine.

She had a fatal disease.

Of course, the doctor hadn't been that blunt. In fact, he'd been ludicrously reassuring, waffling on about treatments and remissions, percentages and average survival times. But when all the medical bullshit was done, what remained was a stark fact: she had a condition that was going to kill her. Acute Lymphoblastic Leukemia: ALL to those in the business. It struck at random, cause generally unknown.

Randomly, it had struck at her.

ALL—initials from hell.

Chemotherapy was the treatment to kill the cancerous—the only time Quayle actually used the C-word—blood cells. What else would be killed at the same time, Emily shuddered to think. As if this weren't enough, there were other tests down the line: needles to be thrust into her bones, her spine, perhaps even her brain. Not to cure. Simply to measure the disease's progress, to see just how far the rot had got.

To see if her wondrous retirement might now run to perhaps a few more months or, if she was very lucky, one pathetic year.

THE VILLAGE OF Cobble Hill drowsed beside the Esquimalt and Nanaimo Railway track, 40 kilometres north of Victoria. Once a thriving community, it had at first faded when the main highway was relocated, then quietly renewed itself as the surrounding community grew. Nestled under Cobble Hill Mountain, the village centre was still little more than a pub, a post office, a grocery and a couple of antique stores. The houses, some a century old, were modest but most had carefully tended gardens, tall hedges allowing glimpses of lawns and flower beds, arbours and rockeries, tasteful and discreet. Inevitably, discovery had meant that brash subdivisions had begun to gather around the lady's venerable skirts. But the feeling—particularly in summer—was still not unlike that of a corner of rural England.

Emily's house was on a rise, half a kilometre from the post office. It was one of the oldest in the area, dating from the beginning of the 20th century. The property was large, surrounded by cedar hedges on three sides. The front had a tall wooden fence, broken only by the driveway entrance. This ran up beside the house, divided from the front garden by bushes, gated arches and clipped greenery. Thus the whole of the interior was a magically private domain.

Emily's Subaru arrived in the driveway just before 5:00. The engine stopped, but the door did not open. In silence the vehicle just sat, immobile as a photograph, while the sun swung slowly west, shifting all the shadows of the world in its slow march toward night.

A very long time later, when car and occupant were in deep gloom, another figure appeared from a driveway on the far side of the road: a woman, 40, fair, heavy-set, broad hips and ample bosom, wearing sandals, shorts and a flowing orange shirt. In a habitual gesture, the woman pushed a clump of hair out of her eyes, folded her arms across her breasts and began to slip-slop her way up the street.

Reaching Emily's drive, and moving alongside the Subaru, she stopped, seeming to sense the presence inside. She leaned down, peering, then gave an exclamation and tapped on the window.

"Emmy!" The woman called. Then, with alarm, "Emmy!"

The figure in the car jerked into life. The other woman opened the car door and stared in. "Emmy, dear—what's the matter?"

Emily shook her head, snagged her bag and fussed her way out of the car. "Nothing, Joan, I was just going to go in."

"But I saw your car go by hours ago. And I phoned several times. I thought you must be in the garden. Is everything all right?"

Emily was heading briskly for the front door, key already poised.

"Of course," she replied, voice gathering strength. "When I got home I felt a little tired—I didn't sleep well last night—so I just sat for a bit in the car, and I must have dozed off. That's all."

Emily opened the front door open and Joan followed, but she was not entirely placated. "It's not like you to do that."

Emily hurried into the living room. It had tall ceilings and waist-high wainscoting, old-fashioned windows with yellow and purple stained-glass insets, and many original paintings on the walls. The furniture was Arts and Crafts, dark oak and paisley; an ambience that was comfortable, scholarly and artistic in near equal proportions. Everywhere there were plants, succulents and ferns, creepers and flowering tropicana, standing, hanging and draping in profusion, as if the outside garden had crept in to take over that domain as well.

Emily went to where a spindle-beaked watering can sat on a stand. Automatically she began to water a Boston fern. "I'm just fine, Joan," she said quietly. "Have you had supper?"

Emily had known Joan Scully ever since she moved into her house in Cobble Hill, 15 years previously. Joan was an art teacher, on the staff of Brentwood College in nearby Mill Bay. She was a fine watercolourist, with a local reputation. Her husband, Fred, was a music teacher and a quiet drunk. They had no children.

Over the years Joan and Emily's friendship had grown, from casual to the realm of indispensable.

Joan had eaten, but she poured them both wine and sat while Emily microwaved leftover stew and fixed herself a salad. Joan had not been fooled by her friend's earlier assurances. It wasn't just the oddity of finding Emily asleep in the car. Much stronger was the thing she *felt*. All assurances to the contrary, she knew that something hugely important had occurred. Though she couldn't put a finger on exactly how, this was an entirely new Emily she was seeing. And the change didn't feel good.

But Joan said nothing of what was in her mind. She sipped her wine and watched Emily and waited.

After Emily had eaten, they retired to the living room and put on a CD: a *Concerto Grosso* by Arcangelo Corelli. The music was stately and sweet, violins, harpsichord and cello in harmonious and orderly array, soothing all discord with its baroque measures of light and reason. They sat for a long while, drinking wine and listening to the music. Emily gazed steadily at the night-filled garden beyond the windows. Joan gazed at Emily—and still waited.

Finally, not looking at her friend, Emily said, "Joan—I think I have to tell you something that no one else knows."

"I see."

"It's about—my mother."

Was this what she had been waiting for? Joan had no idea. But this was apparently the moment's necessity. So she nodded and sat back, waiting for the revelation to begin.

Emily leaned forward abruptly, as if finally making up her mind. She rose and went to the kitchen, returning with more wine. She filled their glasses, then with agitation stared out of the window. Finally she briskly clapped her hands together. "Hell!" she said, with a grimace. "The only way to do this, I think, is to tell it to you in the same way that I found out."

"You don't look much like you want to."

Emily laughed weakly. "Actually I don't! But I think I must. So listen. You knew my mother died when I was young? I did tell you that? But what I haven't said is that it was actually when I was born."

"Giving birth to you?"

"Yes. For years my father let me think she died much later. But that wasn't so."

Joan frowned. "But why would he lie to you?"

"That's what I'm going to tell you. When I finally work up the nerve. Anyway—after my mother died we moved from Alberta to Ontario, where I grew up. My dad never married again—and we never talked about my mother."

"So how did you find out about her?"

"Be patient with me, dear. I'm getting there. One day, when I got home from school, there was a reporter from the old *Toronto Telegram*, which was still around in those days. He told me it'd taken him ages to track me down, but he was doing a follow-up on a big story from a long time ago. 'What story?' says I.

"'Why,' says he, 'Your mother's, of course!'"

"YOU SEE, IT turned out that at the time of my birth my mother created a sensation. She and I were—how can I put this—a national phenomenon."

Joan stared. "What on earth do you mean?"

Emily took a gulp of her wine, then continued determinedly. "Prepartum metabolic imbalance! That's the term for it now, but it was hardly understood in those days. My mother had it very badly. It literally made her crazy. That sometimes happens, though now they have drugs for it. But not then. My mother developed what amounted to schizophrenia. She saw shadows, imaginary monsters, everywhere. She became obsessed that these horrors were plotting to steal her unborn child. Early on she confided this to my father, but he didn't take it seriously. And later she became very cunning. She never told anyone of her plans for what finally happened."

There was a silence, which Joan did not dare break. Then her friend continued.

"On that last day, when my dad was at work, my mother slipped away from the woman who was supposed to be watching her. She was eight months pregnant. The town water tower was only a few blocks from where we lived. The gate was supposed to be locked, but she managed to get in—climb up. My dad got there just in time to see her reaching the top.

"I don't know exactly how tall that tower was. But the platform where my mother stood—arms spread, looking like she was trying to fly—was at least a hundred feet up. My dad called out, but she didn't seem to hear. But he could hear her—chattering away to her to unborn child. To me! 'Don't worry, darling. No one is going to take you. No one will hurt you. I love you. I love you.' And then—she jumped."

Joan's horrified gasp was followed by a silence: the quiet of the grave. Finally, in soft tones, Emily concluded, "She must have fallen like a stone. Of course she was killed. But the bizarre thing, the extraordinary thing, the thing that got us in the news, was the other thing, that makes it possible for me to tell you this now. Because you see, when my mother—hit—it was in such a way that I was completely shielded. Not only wasn't I injured but—well—people could actually see I was okay."

"See?"

"My mother's body, while protecting me, had split open on impact. So when my father rushed up, there were the two of us; in a ruin of blood, side by side. My mother was dead. But her head was twisted around so that she seemed to be looking at me. And me—well, I was just lying there—still attached by the cord. But right then, my father said, as he knelt down beside us—I cried."

VAST, ALL-FORGIVING dark had slipped like slumber into the garden beyond the windows. Inside, the silence was an almost physical presence, a screen upon which ancient, sorrowing images flickered like phantoms in a silent movie.

Joan moved first. Unselfconsciously wiping her damp eyes, she went to a cupboard on the far side of the room. She hauled out a gin bottle, poured a slug and drank half of it at a gulp. "That poor woman," she whispered. "That poor goddamn woman ..." Then, "So—until that newspaper guy tracked you down, you knew nothing?"

"Not a thing. That's why we left that town. My dad hoped I'd never find out. How could a father possibly let his child know she'd been born in such an utterly ghastly manner? But still, I was furious at him for keeping it from me. And, running away as we did, it seemed like a betrayal."

"Of whom, for God's sake?"

"Of my mother. It's not logical, I know. It's a feeling I could never shake, but there's no doubt my poor mother was crazy."

"But Em, if you were angry at your dad for keeping it a secret, just think what he must have felt at not being able to stop it."

Emily sighed. "I know. I know! But at the time I was a teenager. Self-righteous and so judgmental. It makes me ashamed to think of it now, but—largely to punish my father—and myself, for surviving when my mother didn't—I quit school and ran off to Toronto."

"What did you do there?"

"Became a sort of vagrant."

Of all the revelations of the evening, this seemed to astonish Joan the most. "You a vagrant?"

"I even had a baby."

That did it. Joan literally gaped. "But—Em—I mean—you!"

"Surprised, eh? Your goody two-shoes, spinster buddy getting herself knocked-up."

Joan gave an explosive little giggle, then her face clouded. "But after—your mother—weren't you scared the same thing might happen to you?"

"The schizophrenia thing? Dear, I was terrified. But I was fine. Absolutely normal pregnancy. A boy, actually."

"What happened to him?"

Emily shrugged. "No idea. I'd agreed to give him up for adoption, so he was taken away and I never saw him again."

"Oh, I'm sorry."

"Don't be," Emily said briskly. "I didn't want to be a mother—then, or since."

"But don't you ever wonder where he is? What he'd be like? Somewhere in the country there's this man walking around who's your flesh and blood. Don't you ever wonder what became of him?"

After a moment Emily said with quiet conviction, "No, not really."

They sat for a long time after that, gazing out into the dark, each woman lost in her own thoughts. Then Joan rose resignedly. "Well, dear, thank you."

"What for?"

"For telling me all this. For trusting me with your secret."

Emily smiled. "Silly cow—who else would I trust but my best friend? It's I who should thank you."

"For heaven's sake, why?"

"For listening, dear. For caring. But mostly—for being you!"

AFTER JOAN LEFT, Emily sat, unmoving. What on earth had she been thinking of? Not to have told her best friend the one thing that absolutely needed telling—but instead the one that absolutely didn't.

But then, maybe that wasn't true. The longer she thought, the more she admitted that the story about her poor mother, and her own exotic entrance into the world, *had* needed sharing. For decades the secret had been held inside, brooding, festering, swelling from simple—if astonishing—tragedy into something almost evil in its encrustation of embarrassment and shame. Now, at last, the secret was out.

All irony aside, one thing at least was understandable: that it had taken something as shocking as the news of her own imminent demise to shake the horror loose from hiding.

So now she was free.
Free to do what?
To die in peace.
Within the year.

IT WAS A strange night. For hours Emily wandered the house, neither exhilarated nor sleepy, just incredibly calm. Unburdened at last from the one big secret that had haunted her existence, it seemed that everything else—even death—was unimportant.

Yet she knew this was an illusion. She was probably in shock. Shock enabling her to reveal the secret of her birth. Shock cushioning against the full impact of impending death. Not that her body felt anything of its inner decline. Perversely, she actually seemed to be feeling better than she had in months.

Quietly, woodenly, Emily drifted through her little realm—the sum total of all that had been her life. At one point she found herself rooting through her desk, examining letters, files and photos, the evidence of an existence that now seemed like the ancient detritus of a stranger.

Later she explored other parts of her house, examining the pictures displayed there. For years she'd collected fine art and the collection, including an Emily Carr, a Jack Shadbolt, plus three small sketches by the Group of Seven her father had purchased eons ago, was quite valuable. It was, Emily admitted, an old-fashioned array. But it was very beautiful and had given her much joy. Now all she could see were meaningless patterns of form and hue, accumulated over years, which themselves seemed utterly pointless and empty.

When the full realization of this hit home, Emily hovered in front of the last painting—a lovely pastel of a wooded clearing—feeling the faint, dry whisper of despair.

HOWEVER, AFTER SHE'D made tea and stood in the living room, watching the silver dawn rise beyond the high hedge at the end of her garden, her heart felt strangely lighter.

After a while she took the long-spouted watering can and began doing the rounds of the indoor plants. The normalcy of this routine was sweetly soothing, dispersing the sense of unreality that had prevailed since her fateful visit to the doctor. After that she opened the doors and walked outside.

In the back garden, metamorphosis was at work. Dawn had slipped into pale morning, transforming darkness to shadow, shadow to ghostly light. Feeling like a shadow herself, Emily glided down the steps and into her other domain.

Ahead was a sloping lawn, bordered on the left by a curving arbour, festooned with wisteria and climbing rose. To the right reared a rockery which, with a group of flowering shrubs, separated this intimate area from the mysteries beyond. A path led through the arbour, beside an ornamental pond. Emily drifted along in the gloaming, scarcely looking, her feet long familiar with every pebble and stone.

On the far side of the pond was a small fountain. Facing it, a sun umbrella and garden chairs. Emily sat. For the first time since yesterday she felt true relaxation seep in. She listened to the fountain and watched the light grow in the sky. Ever so slowly, white became pale yellow, yellow merged into pink, pink evolved into blue. In a time measured only by the peaceful beating of her heart, true morning arrived at last.

Over the far corner of Emily's high hedge the sun thrust its rim, sending slanting rays to bathe her in morning gold. As warmth seeped in, relaxation gradually evolved into drowsiness, a delicious sense of well-being. Without intention, or awareness of transition, Emily slept.

CONSCIOUSNESS RETURNED, ALONG with a feeling of being hot. Slowly she arched her back, stretching her arms and shoulders, before cautiously blinking open her eyes.

A voice said, "Good morning."

Not surprised, Emily looked up. Joan was sitting in the chair opposite, smoking a cigarette. A tray with teapot and cups was on the table between them.

"Good nap?" Joan said.

"Yes, I think so."

Joan nodded matter-of-factly. "Good. You needed it. I made us tea. Ready for some?"

"Yes, please."

Joan poured tea, handed it over.

"Thanks," Emily said, and then quietly, "Joan—I'm going to die."

"What?"

"I went to the doctor yesterday."

"I know that, woman. What did you just say to me?"

"That flu I thought I had—well, dear, I'm afraid it's leukemia."

Joan, frozen in the act of pouring, just stared. "Leukemia?"

"Yes."

"You're sure?"

"Yes. I'm sorry I couldn't tell you last night."

Joan looked off into the distance, blinking hard. Composing herself, she finally looked back at her friend, studying her a long time. Finally she said softly, "Well, I suppose you'd better tell me now."

A LONG TIME later, after the full story had been told, and the pot of tea had been finished, and Joan had cried and Emily had comforted her, and Joan had wondered why Emily seemed so calm, and Emily had stopped being calm and cried too, and Joan had cried again, and they had comforted each other, Joan said quietly, "So—how long?"

"If I'm lucky—six months."

"And nothing can be done?"

"Well, there is chemotherapy. That might buy a little more time, but it'd also definitely make me a lot sicker. And then there are all the tests: needles in my back, and in my brain. Just to check on something that can't be stopped anyway. I'm not going to do any of it. And I'm damned if I'll ruin what little good time I've got left just to get a bit of extra bad time later on. Can you understand that?"

Joan nodded, the gesture small but unequivocal. "Yes."

"Good. Of all people, I thought you would."

"So—what are you going to do now?"

"In the time left? Well, I've been thinking. And all I can figure so far is what I don't want."

"Which is?"

"Well—I don't want any of the usual things. To read more books or hear more music or to do special things or see more of my friends—except you, of course. And—most important—I don't want to travel."

"Really? There's no place in the whole world that you wouldn't like to see before … "

"Before I die. You can say it."

"I know, hon. Just give me time. So?"

Emily thought for a while. "Let me put it this way. There's not a place in the world important enough that I'd be willing to miss one single day in my garden."

"Yes," Joan nodded slowly. "Okay, I do understand that." She gave a little start and a giggle and reached behind her chair. "And speaking of gardens—here!" She drew out a package, long and thin, with a red ribbon tied around one end. "Happy birthday," she said.

Emily was about to protest, then realized that that was just a reflex, a meaningless pose from another life. Yesterday, as it turned out, had been her final birthday. So any celebration of it, especially by the one she cared for most, was not only right but as important as anything could ever be.

"I know it was yesterday," Joan said, "but last night I believe we sort of got sidetracked."

Emily took the package. "Thank you, Joan," she said softly. "Thank you very much."

"Okay—open it up."

Smiling, feeling ridiculously moved, Emily did so. Inside was something utilitarian and mundane, yet so right that she laughed with pleasure.

"I knew you'd been looking for an undersized garden spade. Fred found it. In Canadian Tire."

Emily had wanted this because the "flu" had left her feeling a bit weak. Now understanding why, Joan's choice seemed almost prescient. "It's great. It'll be very useful. Thank you."

The two sat quietly, contemplating the garden. Beyond the pond was a large bed of tree peonies and roses with, farther back, a criss-cross of brick paths separating beds of marigolds, in varying shades of yellow and gold, and impatiens in every tone of red graduating almost to black. Pale cornflowers and dark-blue century plants, chicory and bachelor buttons contrasted with the deep green of the hedge beyond. After a while Emily said, "Joan—this business of dying—I intend to think about it very little."

"Can you do that?"

"Yes, I think so. For a while anyway. Later I'll be probably be contemplating my mortality a lot. But now I want to be—like a plant in this garden. Only a short life ahead, perhaps, but rich and real, caring only for the moment. All my life I've been haunted by the past. By history. And I only just realized it."

"Oh?"

"It was only when I knew that I didn't have a future that I could finally cope with the past. Last night I could tell you about the thing that's always haunted me because finally it didn't matter anymore. Getting that into the open was actually more important that what was happening to me. Do you understand?"

"I do," Joan said. "And even if I didn't, what the hell. We're here! Together! I don't care about anything else."

Emily reached out and, though Joan was unreachably far, clenched her fingers as if squeezing her hand. "I know," she said quietly. "I know! Our friendship is like this garden, more important than any past or future. And if that sounds inexcusably mushy— well—too bloody bad."

LATER, EMILY WENT inside, showered, changed and made herself lunch. Ironically, having just found that her days were numbered, she was actually feeling better. How long would this situation last? She didn't know and didn't care.

After lunch she went back into the garden, making a slow tour as was her usual routine, picking off deadheads while she decided what she was going to do. This generally didn't require much conscious decision; she just found herself immersed in whatever needed to be done, without ever having the sensation of beginning. Sometimes—quite often, actually—having other chores in mind, she would go into the garden meaning to stay just a few minutes, only to discover hours later that she was still there, happily oblivious, with her original plans forgotten.

So it was without surprise that, a couple of hours later, Emily emerged from a bucolic semi-stupor to find herself contentedly weeding away. She was in the southeast corner of the property, in a less developed part of the garden, an isolated place backed by the thick hedge that ran around the property and screened from the rest by a thick row of rhododendrons. For a moment she wondered idly how she had come to be in this particular place. Then a line of pulled weeds, leading back out into the open, told their tale: she'd simply been led in here, as her hands had moved from weed to weed, following the work.

In fact, she was in a place that her conscience had been pricking her to tidy for some time, deep under the rhododendrons. Because the area wasn't visible, it was easily forgotten, which, as every gardener knows, is the poorest excuse for neglect.

Well, she was doing it now, but what had brought her up short was a practical problem. Long overlooked, the weeds here were monsters, with long roots resistant to pulling. She was without tools.

Emily remembered her birthday gift, the little spade from Joan. It would be perfect for the job. It was still by the pool. Picking it up, she whimsically wrapped the ribbon around the handle. Then, smiling, she took the freshly adorned tool back to her weed culling.

It worked like a charm. The new instrument had a nice sharp edge and bit sweetly into the earth, blade sliding easily under the most unyielding roots. In a short time she was nearly finished.

Just one weed remained: a stubborn old dock with a root going all the way to China. Emily plunged deep and twisted the blade sideways in time-honoured fashion. The dock came up all right but at the last moment the tap root broke in the middle, leaving a thick and very viable end far below. Emily had the irritated urge to ignore it. Hell, if she did, the result wouldn't even be visible till next spring, when she and all her concerns would only be a footnote in someone else's memory.

But that last thought did the opposite of the expected. Suddenly, getting that root became a matter of stubborn principle. To give up on this task, simply because she wouldn't be around later to be embarrassed, was such a sad comment on the futility of all endeavour that it just couldn't be tolerated. She was damned if she was going to be bested by one pesky weed.

With a determined grimace, Emily thrust her spade into the soil one more time. The blade hit something hard and unyielding, making a clunk and bringing her up short. Damn. There weren't many rocks in her garden, but they could be quite big. Glacial debris from the last ice age. They could give the spade a jolt and be hard to remove. However, the stones themselves tended to be colourful, and made interesting additions to her rockery.

So, after her first small annoyance, Emily began philosophically to dig. It took just a few minutes to get the job done, to scoop out the earth, capture the reluctant root, then get right underneath and pry out the stone.

She gave the thing a sharp rap to remove some of the dirt, then bent to examine it more closely. It was round and about the size of a cabbage. With growing interest she turned it over. On the other side were two large holes close together, a smaller pair below and a lower row of wedge-shaped objects.

Teeth.

Finally, Emily understood what she had discovered. In the shock that followed, one thought was immediately clear: this was definitely not something she'd be putting in her rockery.

THREE

Joseph shaved meticulously as always, relathering and inserting a new blade for the final taming run over the growth which each day sought to bury his finely chiselled features beneath a dark jungle.

When he finished he showered, washed his hair, then applied some of the new special Swedish conditioner that Roy had presented him with the evening before. This product was supposed to provide twice the body of regular conditioners, which wasn't a bad idea, since his thinning upper growth—unlike the forest below—needed all the help it could get. Joseph wasn't too concerned about that situation: it was Roy who worried, always trying to make him look glamorous, younger than his 52 years.

Joseph might have been forgiven for wondering whether this was for his benefit or because Roy was concerned by the evidence of his partner's advancing age. Were it the latter he'd have understood, seeing how Roy might be embarrassed at being tied to an aging old frump like himself. But strangely—wonderfully—he knew this wasn't the case. Roy, sweet, free spirit that he was, didn't care a whit about what other people thought. Genuinely, he wanted Joseph to look good just for himself.

What wasn't there to love about Roy?

Joseph dried off and combed his hair, applied a subtle aftershave and even more unobtrusive deodorant, then carefully donned a pale blue shirt, dark socks and tie, ending with a conservative navy suit: what Roy called his banker's motley.

After he'd breakfasted, he walked into Roy's bedroom. His partner was asleep, sprawled sideways across his big yellow bed. He was on his back, arms splayed sideways, palms up and fingers wide. Although he'd just had his 35th birthday, he looked no more than 20. To compound this impression, he was sleeping with the intense dedication of a teenager. Joseph found himself smiling, feeling, as he sometimes did—though he'd never have admitted it to a soul— more like parent than lover.

Roy's auburn hair fell in waves across the pale skin of his forehead. Looking down, Joseph had an unexpected vision of how that brow had once looked: bruised and battered. A long time ago, that had been. In another life. Why the memory had chosen to surface right now was a mystery, for Roy looked as if he'd never known a moment's care. Determinedly dismissing the intrusion, Joseph reached down and ever so lightly touched Roy's hair. As he often did at such tender moments, he thought, I must have done something right.

"Roy. Roy!?"

"Whaaaaa ... ?"

"Sweetie, it's 8:30. I'm just off."

"Oh—okay ... " Without opening his eyes, Roy lifted a hand, stretched it in Joseph's direction. "See you at lunch?"

Joseph, squeezed the hand. "Sure, Melanie's. Usual time. Don't forget you need to be at the gallery early for the hanging. Okay?"

"Okay, thanks for the reminder. Have a good morning."

"You too. Bye." Still smiling, Joseph headed out of the house. On the stoop was the morning Times Colonist. He leaned down, snagged it, did a quick swing back and deposited it on the kitchen table; Roy always liked to glance through the arts section—such as it was—over his breakfast coffee.

They'd been together 14 years: among their immediate friends, almost a record.

JOSEPH GILLESPIE'S HOUSE was on Dallas Road, a winding, scenic route that traversed the cliffs on the tip of Vancouver Island and formed the southeastern edge of the small compact city of Victoria. James Bay was a 30-square-block area, bounded by the harbour and the ocean, and filled with hotels and many immaculately restored heritage homes. The oldest part of town, it had once been in decline, but now it was rediscovered, restored, moving from penury to fashion with scarcely a real-estate hiccup.

Joseph's house was a squat, stucco bungalow built in the 1930s, not as grand or venerable as many of its neighbours. But, with only a narrow road between itself and the cliffs, the house commanded a breathtaking view of the vast, light-filled, sky-filled, weather-filled Juan de Fuca Strait.

Joseph had bought the house 20 years previously, from an elderly widow. It had been neglected, so it took imagination to see its real prospects. Now, with interior refurbished and small garden beautifully landscaped, the house was what in the trade is known as an architectural gem.

As was his habit, Joseph took one last proprietary glance at his home and headed out. He was on foot, wearing stout runners that he would change when he got to the office. It was a 20-minute walk into town, much of it through Beacon Hill Park, with its flower beds, ponds and twisty Garry oaks. As Joseph came out of the park, passing the old Anglican church and heading up into the city, he found himself waxing happily philosophic: thinking of the sun, the morning, the walk, his wonderful home and dear Roy, sitting in the kitchen, reading the paper and drinking his first cup of coffee. Conscious of all these things as he pumped along, Joseph couldn't help feeling that he was the most fortunate being on the planet.

He came down a bit when he got to the bank. That was only fitting: as senior loans officer, he couldn't waft about grinning like a fool. His office was at the far end of a row of cubicles that housed loan officers and the investment managers. But it was the only one that had a window, a fitting tribute to his rank.

Consulting his computer, he saw he was fully booked with appointments right through to lunch. He had paperwork to do and phone calls to make and had barely made a serious dent in those chores when, promptly at 10:00, his first customer was announced. It was evidently going to be one of those days.

The window of Joseph's office looked out on a small courtyard behind the bank; it linked two busy streets and was a popular thoroughfare. It was also sheltered, and had a small café, complete with tables and umbrellas. In occasional quiet moments, Joseph found it pleasant to sit unobserved at his desk, watching the passing parade.

He had no time for such activities this morning, however. So it was by the merest chance that, during the small hiatus between the departure of his 10:30 client and the arrival of his 11:00, he happened to glance out of the window.

And saw Roy.

His partner was entering the courtyard from the alley at the left. There was no doubt that it was he. But Roy was not looking in the direction he knew Joseph's office to be.

He seemed utterly preoccupied.

Joseph was astonished. By this time, he knew, Roy should be deep into the hanging.

The Balshine Gallery, where his partner worked, had been angling for years to get an exhibition by the fashionable eastern printmaker Adrienne Kilgaron. The main reason they'd snagged it ahead of Vancouver—and even San Francisco, yet—was the hard work of Roy. The exhibition was a triumph for him, raising considerably his status at the gallery, and he'd been looking forward desperately to organizing the hanging.

So what the hell was going on?

After Joseph's first surprise, his immediate thought was that the hanging must have been postponed. But Roy's face told him it had to be more than that. The young man's expression was tense, almost anguished, and his movements put Joseph in mind of a sleepwalker.

Joseph jumped up and leaned toward the window, frantically waving to get Roy's attention—but to no avail. The young man was in such a daze that he charged right on, crossed the courtyard and disappeared out the other side.

Joseph stood wide-eyed, aware that he was breathing so hard he was almost panting. Then the intercom buzzed, announcing his 11:00 a.m. appointment.

For the rest of the morning, Joseph conducted business with his usual pleasant efficiency, not one of his clients guessing that his mind was miles away, horribly concerned about what was happening with Roy. It was well after 1:00 before he could leave the bank.

Melanie's was full but their usual table sat empty. No Roy. Joseph took his seat and John, the head waiter, was there at once. "Gee, Mr. Gillespie, I thought you guys weren't coming. What happened? Is Roy sick?"

What indeed had happened? By this time Joseph was consumed with curiosity, but he had to eat his lunch in ignorance, because Roy never showed up.

At five minutes before 2:00 he should have headed back to the office, but he couldn't ignore what was happening. Roy's strange behaviour earlier and his absence now made it seem that something awful must have happened. Joseph was suddenly reminded of the memory-vision he'd had that morning: of Roy's face, battered as it had been so long ago. This could have no connection with whatever was going on now. Nonetheless, it added its own dark weight to his growing fretfulness.

Abruptly he made the decision. On his cellphone he called his secretary, telling her he'd taken unexpectedly ill and was going home. Then he turned his steps toward the one place where it might be possible to still the turmoil in his heart.

The Balshine was one of a number of galleries in a small street near the Bay Centre. Befitting its exclusive nature, it had a quiet but opulent exterior: plain marble facade, simple metalwork around plate-glass widows, elegant gold lettering on the door. Also on the door was a "closed" sign, in preparation for the Kilgaron opening tomorrow.

Joseph entered quietly. The place was long and low, with pearl grey carpet, black roof and plain, off-white walls. The ceiling spots were unlit, waiting to be positioned when the new pictures were hung—a process that was going on right now.

Conducted by Roy.

In fact, his partner had just hung a picture and was standing back to see the effect. The first thing that Joseph noticed was that the young man seemed utterly normal, completely absorbed.

As if absolutely nothing in the world was the matter.

Standing nearby was the gallery owner. Monty Balshine was a man in his mid-60s, with a white beard trimmed like an old Spanish don's and a mane of silver hair to match. By contrast, his face was a mottled and unhealthy scarlet, due to a dermatological condition that was the bane of his mild existence.

"Oh, hi, Joseph," Monty said.

"Afternoon, Monty," Joseph said. "How's it going?"

But his real attention was on Roy: Roy, who was still staring at the picture in apparent concentration, as if nothing else in the entire world was on his mind.

Joseph wanted to scream: *Roy, what are you playing at? What in shit is going on? I'm here and you know I'm here. Can this stupid charade and talk to me!* But he said, "Hello, Roy. What happened to lunch?"

Roy gave what appeared to be a genuine start of surprise, then turned with a brilliant smile.

"Lunch?" Roy said. "Oh, God, sweetie—I'm sorry. I completely forgot."

AND HIS PARTNER looked—totally unconcerned.

Yet three hours ago Roy had seemed at his wit's end; like someone to whom something terrible had happened.

Astonishment was followed by a wave of relief so massive that Joseph felt physically ill. But then came huge anger. Jesus Christ, he'd been crazy with anxiety, and here was Roy, the cause of it all, acting as if nothing the fuck had happened.

"God, sweetie!" Roy was saying. "You look awful."

"I feel awful," Joseph managed to reply. "I've been sick."

"You look it. You should go home. Sit down and I'll phone for a cab."

"Not that kind of sick, Roy. Sick with worry."

Roy looked nonplussed. "Because I didn't show for lunch?"

"No, it's ... "

"Well, I'm sorry, really. But I just forgot. I got here at 10:00 and it's been so exciting I haven't sat down for a single minute." He actually looked genuinely hurt. "Sweetie, I'm sorry I stood you up, but ... " He gestured around the gallery. "You understand?"

Joseph didn't understand. Not one thing. Especially he didn't understand Roy claiming to have been at the gallery since 10:00 when Joseph had seen him behind his office an hour later than that.

He opened his mouth to say something to that effect, then shut it. Whatever was going on, they couldn't talk here.

Right now only one thing was totally clear: he must shut his mouth and leave. So he gulped and said, "Yes, of course I understand. Everything's okay. Sorry to make a fuss. I'll see you later—at home. Bye." He gestured around the gallery as he backed off toward the door. "These look wonderful. It's going to be a great show. Bye, Monty. See you later, Roy."

And then he was stumbling off down the street like the fool he felt. He just kept walking, drifting as if in a dream, amidst the shoppers, late-lunchers, tourists and panhandlers who thronged the early summer streets of his neat little city.

Some time later, he found himself standing on the stone causeway in the Inner Harbour. Behind him were the ivy-laced towers of the venerable Empress Hotel, to his left the stone eruption of the provincial legislature. In the harbour, yachts, including an impeccable three-masted schooner, rocked gently on a sparkling sea. Beyond shimmered an azure panorama, with a backdrop of purple-green hills. A postcard picture of demi-paradise.

Gazing at his sweet city right then, Joseph felt as though he'd been transported to some small corner of hell. He sat on a bench, the sun hot on his immaculate suit, and at last started to think about the question he'd been trying to avoid ever since leaving the gallery.

Was Roy being unfaithful?

That was ridiculous. Insane. The idea of his loving partner having a liaison with another person—another man—was the most impossible thing that Joseph could imagine. The idea that he, Joseph, could be entertaining such a notion was utterly fantastic.

And yet.

The man in the courtyard had been Roy, who had claimed categorically to have been at the gallery.

So … deception!

Which could only have one explanation.

Joseph rose and began to walk again, instinctively heading south toward his own neighbourhood. He moved more briskly than before and after a while the familiar exercise began to soothe him. At last, he began thinking more rationally.

Granting the deception, that didn't have to mean anything as extreme as a liaison. Surely there could be a dozen other reasons for Roy's actions, perfectly innocent reasons, but private enough not to be blurted out at the gallery in front of Monty. Okay. Possible. But even in his cooler state, Joseph couldn't imagine what one of them might be.

Added to that was the recurring memory of Roy's face: the extremity, the real desperation of his expression, as Joseph had clearly witnessed it from his office.

Something *had* happened. Something was going on. If not ordinary, yet not underhanded—then what?

JOSEPH WAS NO nearer any ideas, let alone conclusions, when he realized that his walk had taken him home. He opened the gate and approached the house, feeling in his orderly soul more than a trifle odd to be returning at this time in the afternoon.

He let himself in and walked into the kitchen. It looked untidy, as if Roy had left in a hurry. On the table was an unfinished breakfast: half-eaten toast, half-drunk coffee. An open *Times Colonist*.

It wasn't until he went into the living room that he found the devastation. Well, "devastation" was the word that first leaped to mind, but after his initial surprise, Joseph realized that it was just a bad and thoroughly uncharacteristic mess. The bureau in the far corner was hanging open, letters and papers scattered in disarray. The bookshelves nearby had been similarly disrupted, books half out or piled oddly, others carelessly tossed on the floor. The junk drawer from the kitchen had been literally upended upon the coffee table, its contents crouching in an indescribable heap on the polished oak.

Roy's room revealed a similar scene of semi-chaos. Every one of his drawers had been emptied, clothes and underwear dumped on the floor. All the hanging things had been pulled from the closet, along with suitcases, and a heap of boxes from the top shelf, all of which had been thrown upon the bed.

The house must have been broken into.

Nervously, Joseph crept down the hall toward his own room. In queasy apprehension he looked in—finding the place as pristine as when he'd left.

Dazed, Joseph drifted back to the living room and stood helplessly, shaking his head. Finally he began to take note of what had not occurred. First and most obvious, nothing seemed to be missing: paintings, ornaments, TV, all manner of electronic stuff, everything was safely in its place. Nothing had actually been harmed or broken. Finally, there was no hint of other damage, no scrawled graffiti or similar marks of vandalism.

Meaning?

This was not the work of an intruder at all.

Conclusion?

This chaos could only have been created by Roy. Roy, whom Joseph had seen in a state of agitation behind his office, at a time when the young man was supposed to be hanging pictures. Roy, who had later denied the whole thing.

IT TOOK JOSEPH an hour of painstaking effort to get the house back into order. Everything but Roy's room: he closed the door and left that can of worms strictly alone.

By then it was after 5:00. Had this been a normal day, Joseph would have just been arriving home from work: setting up before-dinner drinks, talking to Roy about his day.

Sweet, straightforward Roy—who today had turned into a Roy of strangeness and secrets.

Also, at any moment, Roy would probably be arriving home. What on earth would he have to say? God, what possible explanation could Roy produce for his odd and disturbing actions? Thinking about that, Joseph went back to the newly restored living room, poured himself a stiff vodka and tonic and at last sat down.

At that moment, with almost theatrical timing, his partner came home.

The back door slammed and familiar footsteps clicked across the kitchen. Roy marched—almost skipped—into the living room, a huge, impudent grin on his face. Seeing Joseph, he stopped dramatically. "Well, *hello*, cute mouse," he said with an exaggerated lisp. "What's my sweetie doing sitting all alone in the dark?"

Of all things, this bizarre act was the last thing Joseph had expected. Sickened and now even more afraid, he whispered, "Waiting for you to tell me what the hell's going on!"

"Going on?" Roy stared at him, with astonishment that was camp and hysterical. And quite bogus.

At which point there seemed no alternative but to cut directly to the chase. "You can quit the bullshit. Roy. This morning—I saw you."

Roy was now very still. His eyes narrowed. "Saw me?"

"Crossing the courtyard behind my office. At 11:00 o'clock, when you said you were at the gallery. Don't try to deny it."

Roy sucked in a breath, half shook his head, then stopped. His body grew limp.

"I saw you as plain as I see you now. You looked terrible. I thought something absolutely ghastly had happened. I was just about out of

my mind with worry. Then at the gallery when you lied about it ...
and then—when I found what you'd done to our home. Christ, Roy,
if you care about me at all, tell me what's going on!"

Roy just stared. His wide eyes were moist now, his brow
contorted with lines of tension. His bottom lip began to quiver.
He looked simultaneously like a beautiful, tragic figure—and a
naughty kid.

At last Roy whispered, "Oh, Joe!"

Somehow those two words, uttered so simply, without art or
campiness, but coming from some awful well of despair—those
words went right to Joseph's heart, thrusting aside everything but
love. And then he was on his feet, arms extended, beckoning, and
Roy gave a little animal yelp and ran into them.

"Never mind, Roy," Joseph whispered. "Never mind. Whatever
it is, we'll handle it together."

There was a long silence during which they clung. But then Roy
pulled away. "I don't see how we can handle this."

"Why not?" Joseph pulled Roy back again, looking deep into
his eyes. "We've faced everything else, haven't we? That's why it's all
worked so well. Right?"

Roy nodded wordlessly.

"So—whatever's happened—why not this too?"

Roy didn't move. He just hung, suspended in Joseph's grip. His
expression was calm but contained something else—something that
caused Joseph to feel a sudden quiet chill.

"Because," Roy said quietly, "'this' is about murder."

THE BOY STOOD in the big garden, gazing at the posh dwelling,
scarcely able to believe his eyes—or his luck.

At last!

Not two hours before, he'd been on the streets of Victoria, alone, homeless, with not the slightest idea of where his next mouldy crust was coming from, let alone a proper meal, let alone a fucking *bed*.

He'd hated being a street person. He'd discovered he was very bad at it and had never intended for things to turn out that way.

When, a few years earlier, he'd realized that he was beautiful, that men were attracted to him, and that he liked being lusted after, it had all seemed very simple: he'd use his body as a one-way ticket to paradise.

Being 16 then, living in the small town of Brantford, Ontario, he'd thought paradise was any city with a gay community large and rich enough to sustain a young courtesan in the style to which he hoped to become accustomed. Precipitating him into this life was an incident in his last year of high school. He'd been having an affair with a boy who, though stupid and smelly, was the only game on offer. One night they were caught lustily banging away in the boys' shower. Both were expelled, and his father had expressed his own outrage by beating him up and throwing him out of the house.

Late the next night he crept back home, collected some things, stole a pile of cash—and spent a quiet half-hour ripping up every stitch of his father's clothing. Then he hit the road for the west coast. On the way his first act was to ditch his old name, adopting the one he'd always fancied.

He became Roy.

Vancouver was good to Roy. His fine auburn hair and pale beauty made him a natural for the high-class sex trade; youth and education meant he could be moderately choosy. Early on, he received golden advice from a flaming old queen, who was a survivor and kinder than most. "Sugar, you're young and pretty. If you want to stay alive—never take it without a condom. Don't matter how much moolah the old gals offer, or how sweetly the bitches beg for skin—if you don't want to end up on a memory quilt like 20 friends of mine, you'll take it with rubber or with mouth or not at all. Now, gorgeous, you promise me that."

Roy did promise, if only to stop the old fart yapping. But the advice stuck. Within a short time he had his own little place in the West End and began to build a nice list of prosperous clients. He had money, freedom, a sexy wardrobe. For a year or so he was actually almost happy.

Then he found mother.

"Mother" was what one client, a rich stockbroker named Walter, called cocaine. Walter liked coke a lot and could afford it and pretty soon he had Roy liking it too.

Not long after his first encounter with mother, Roy was hooked. The feeling of well-being, of power, of marvellous *rightness in the world*, enveloped him like a long-lost love. In fact, young Roy, so well versed in sex, had never known real love. And deep down he knew that, no matter how skilled he was in instigating lust, he could never be someone that anyone actually cared about.

Mother changed all that.

On a coke high, Roy felt not only pretty but lovable, someone worthwhile. Someone who actually belonged on the Earth. And mother miraculously expanded sex. At last he understood the true meaning of the term "making love." Gay young-man-of-the-world, he was yet a stranger in the strange land of the heart.

With mother—a stranger no longer.

Which was all very fine when he had her. When he didn't, the flip side of the sweet coin was all too clear: the loneliness and tawdriness of his life, once easily ignored, came painfully into focus. The only remedy was another date with mother. Before long these liaisons were all that Roy could think about.

After a while, instead of buying clothes and jewellery, instead of keeping his person in the state his dainty old fags appreciated, he was spending all his money on coke. Gradually his clients stopped coming around. One day he spent the rent money on one last mother-blast and, soon afterward, he found out not only what life was like without his beloved cocaine—he was homeless as well.

He went up to the Lions Gate Bridge, but couldn't bring himself to jump. Desperate, finally starving, he was forced into selling himself on the street. Here his youth and fading beauty were of little help amongst the competition. Without pimp or protector, he was often cheated or robbed, and sometimes even beaten. His looks and health were rapidly deteriorating. Out of brutal necessity, his old condom rule became a hatefully comic relic—the consequences, a terrifying reality he faced daily.

Then, amidst the sordid flurry of his day-to-day struggle for survival, he heard about Victoria. Life in Victoria—tucked away on Vancouver Island—was much easier, according to a kid who'd worked the game there. The market was smaller and less dangerous, and a lot of the old gays were retired with piles of cash. If Roy would help him get there, he'd show Roy the ropes and together they'd have an easier life. Did Roy believe this? God knows. But, somehow, he managed to get the money for two bus tickets to Victoria. On arrival, the kid vanished, never to be seen again.

Alone, penniless, in a strange town, starving and growing ill, Roy had been living on the street for three months—when he found deliverance.

"WHAT DO YOU think of my little place, Roy?"

His questioner came out from the house into the secluded garden, where Roy was standing. He was a tall man, in his 50s, with fine features, delicate hands and a thin, spare frame. His hair was thick and silver. His mouth was full and, in contrast to the rest of his skin, very red. His eyes were ice-blue.

His name was Trevor.

When they had arrived, Trevor had parked close to the house, carefully checked that the street was empty, then hurried him indoors. Now, as the man approached, pausing to survey him, Roy felt himself actually blushing. "I think your place is wonderful, Trevor," he said. "But I must look awful."

Trevor grinned, showing perfect teeth. "You do, dear. And the smell is even worse. But we'll take care of that. Hungry?"

Roy realized he was starving. "Yes."

"Okay—take off your clothes."

"Now? You mean, before I even get to eat you want to ... "

"Screw you?" Trevor gave a cold laugh. "Are you *kidding*? Sweetie, the state you're in, I wouldn't bring my pretty cock within 10 feet of you. I don't know, yet, if I ever will."

Roy's jaw dropped. "Then why am I here?"

Trevor continued to dissect the young man with his gaze. "An experiment."

"What do you want to do to me?"

Trevor laughed again. "Not that kind of experiment. For a while now I've been on the lookout for—a special companion. And when I saw you downtown, despite your wretched condition, I got a sort of feeling."

"Oh—but I'm just ... "

"A shadow of your sweet self? No doubt. But right now you're filthy. That's why I won't let you loose till we've stripped and scrubbed the street out of you."

Which was exactly what happened. Roy was not only bathed and fed, he was put to bed on clean sheets in a little private room. For many weeks, Trevor didn't lay so much as a finger on him.

DURING THAT TIME Roy rediscovered what it was to live like a human being. He got his health back and his pale, fragile-seeming good looks. Instead of hustling him into bed, as expected, Trevor spent endless hours in conversation.

He wanted to know everything. How long he'd been in Vancouver, where he'd grown up, when he'd "come out," and all his interests beyond the narrow confines of sexuality. Trevor was particularly concerned with his young protégé's education. Roy had been a bright student, showing a real flair for history, literature and the arts. Had he not run off, he might have gone on to higher education. His intelligence was high, his general knowledge fair and his esthetic taste developed beyond his years. All of the latter seemed to give Trevor particular satisfaction now.

"From the moment I laid eyes on you, Roy, I had the feeling you were different. Ass—even real sweet ass like yours, dear—is cheap. But quality ass, intelligent ass, ass that a civilized person can live with—that's different. And I'm definitely coming to believe that yours could be what I've been looking for. So, I'm very pleased with my intuition about you. Delighted that I found you in Victoria."

As to the reason why Roy had ended up there, however, Trevor's reaction was chillingly different. "Drugs are shit, Roy," he said, cold blue eyes boring into the young man. "And—most important, as far as I'm concerned—drugs are illegal." He put his hand on Roy's knee, but not to caress: the grip was cruelly hard, like the teeth of a dangerous dog giving warning. "Do you know what I do for a living?"

"You've got some kind of job with the government."

"Not just some kind of job, you silly little queer. I'm a deputy minister, a senior honcho in the administration of this fucking province. So not a hint of scandal must ever touch my life. Your being here depends on a complete understanding of that fact. Am I clear?"

Roy nodded, excited but also a bit afraid.

"Right now, no one even knows you're here. And no one will:

not till you've learned to play straight, and been given a new public identity as my nephew."

This was intriguing. Roy grinned, but quickly stopped when the pressure increased on his leg. Trevor leaned in close. "But if I ever—ever—find that you've taken drugs, or brought drugs into this house—and by drugs I mean anything that isn't legal, or legally prescribed for you, personally—I'll make sure you're sent to prison, where they'll certainly spoil that pretty ass for good. Am I understood, sweetie? Are we on the same page here?"

Roy did understand, said so fervently. He was on the same page all right, Trevor could depend on it. What he suddenly wasn't entirely sure of, however, was if he wanted to be in the same book.

BUT, NEEDLESS TO say, he stayed.

Roy's life with Trevor lasted two years. During that time existence was sweeter than it had ever been. As the man's official "nephew" with the brand-new name of David—a charade meticulously constructed and adhered to—he was outfitted with two complete wardrobes: a dull, preppy array of suits and sweaters for public display, a full range of lounging pyjamas and other exotica for the privacy of the house. There—quite apart from the lovemaking, and fine food and wine they shared—Roy, for the first time in his life, actually felt a measure of stability.

Trevor turned out to be an extraordinary companion. Beneath the ice cold, bureaucratic exterior raged passions which Roy, even with his prior experience, found astounding. Released from the constraints of his official life, stripped of the suit and the public persona, Trevor—when he chose—could be as wild as a satyr. Roy, who thought he knew it all, found that in fact he didn't know the half. Trevor taught him so much about the pleasures and possibilities, the techniques and titillations of the flesh, Roy realized that he—along with his old-time customers—had been strictly amateur.

But Trevor's lessons were not only sensual. His interest in Roy's education was equally intense. They went to films, plays and galleries together, and discussed endlessly what they had seen. Trevor brought home a constant stream of books—the emphasis on painting and art history—to be read and analyzed. One fall, the young man found himself enrolled in several non-degree courses at the University of Victoria, in all of which he did well.

Roy was not only enchanted by his new existence but hugely enriched by it. Learning, growing, sharing with Trevor a life not only of the body but of the mind, he felt like a real, whole person. Expanding to a degree he would not have deemed possible, Roy evolved in two years from an emotionally stunted hooker into a young man of richness and promise.

And then it all went to ratshit.

IT WAS NEAR the end of their second year. Over breakfast one morning, Trevor said, "I have to go to Ottawa tomorrow."

"Oh?"

"Civil servants' conference. A fucking bore, but there it is."

"Can I come?"

"Best not, ducks. Too many people who know me there. Ambitious cunts with prying eyes. We'd have to have separate rooms and the whole thing would be just too tiresome. Ottawa is tedious, anyway. You won't be missing much."

"How long will you be away?"

"A little over a week. But don't worry—I'll be back in plenty of time for our anniversary."

The next evening Roy drove Trevor to the airport. By this time their public image was so well established as to be second nature. Roy, wearing grey slacks and a quiet sweater, helped the older man with his bags. When they parted, they ever so briefly touched hands.

"I'll see you in a week then," Roy said, adding, with only the barest hint of irony, "Uncle Trev."

"All right, David, in a week. But I'll phone tonight." Trevor smiled, gave his lover a shrewd nod and was gone. Roy was alone.

DRIVING BACK ALONG the Pat Bay Highway toward Victoria, Roy, felt a surprising lift of the heart. Until that moment, the prospect of a week without his companion had seemed gloomy. Accelerating, he found himself smiling, realizing with only a fleeting guilt twinge that not only was he not sad—he was excited.

Instead of heading straight home, as promised, Roy turned the BMW in the direction of downtown. What did he have in mind? He had no idea. But he knew he wanted to do something different, something to give a whiff of the exotic to what—he finally admitted—was beginning to seem suspiciously like freedom.

Intuition, or perhaps fate, guided him to a parking lot in the centre of town. A five-minute stroll from there brought him to something that looked interesting: The Green Parrot, a little bar sandwiched between a French and a Greek restaurant, on a street running up from the harbour.

As soon as he went in, Roy knew he was in the right place. The Green Parrot was subdued, by no means a flaunting drag queen of a bar, but clearly gay. The lighting was low, discreet but not dismal, the walls decorated with framed haute couture designs and photos of movie stars. The Green Parrot was a place Roy would surely have discovered in his early days in Victoria, had he not been a street bum. Since then he'd been the exclusive property of Trevor, who shunned such hangouts. Now, drinking in the ambience, his eyes wandering hungrily over the attractive customers, Roy found himself overwhelmed by one simple emotion: He was home.

ROY DID NOT go back to his real home that night.

Not five minutes after his arrival at the bar he met a handsome young man named Marcel. And young! God, he—Roy—was young too: something he had almost forgotten in his two years with his aging protector. An hour and a few drinks after their meeting, Roy was driving his new friend home to Esquimalt.

It hardly occurred to him that he was being unfaithful.

The next day he didn't get back till noon. As soon as he walked in the door he realized the house seemed somehow different, less friendly and comforting—and it also reminded him of something. Then it sank in: despite all the obvious differences, this was eerily like returning to his parents' house in Brantford.

Eeghhh!!!

But he didn't waste time on introspection. Now all he could think of was Marcel—his full name, improbably, was Marcel McGinty—and the exciting time they'd had together. Later, having changed into sexy attire, stuff never permitted in public since the advent of Trevor, Roy once more headed downtown.

It never crossed his mind to check the answering machine.

ROY AND MARCEL had three wonderful days together.

The guy was no great shakes as a lover, so it was Roy's turn to be teacher. But Marcel had a nice little apartment and was expert at whipping up tasty snacks, which they gobbled between long sessions in bed. All appetites were deliciously abetted by a seemingly endless supply of marijuana, which Marcel used as casually as candy, lighting their joints with an engraved gold lighter, which—he laughed—was a gift from an old queen with more money than sense. Thinking about his own older companion, Roy's only reaction was a snigger: at last he was having fun with someone young.

On the third evening, after eating and smoking up a storm at Marcel's, Roy conceived a brilliant, sexy and utterly daring notion. "Hey, gorgeous," he giggled. "You wanna see a bed? You wanna fuck in a real bum-beautiful bed? Sexy—you just come home with me."

In less than an hour the BMW pulled up in the quiet driveway of Trevor's place. Marcel whistled in awe as he got out of the car. "You live *here?* Jesus, lover, your boyfriend must be loaded."

"Yeah—and ancient!" Roy laughed. "So fucking respectable he hasn't even come out yet."

The bed Roy had promised Marcel was in fact his patron's. King size, with a mattress deep and delicious, strewn with pillows and cushions and multi-hued throws, overlooked by a bronze figurine of a monstrously erect Pan, it was a sort of gay-rococo temple, an ultimate, sensual denial of Trevor's super-straight exterior. Roy never actually slept here. This was his master's domain, a haven only shared for one purpose. That accomplished, Roy was summarily ejected to his own quarters. So it was with perverse excitement that he introduced this forbidden shrine to his cute young lover.

They had stupendous fun in Trevor's decadent bed. They came up for air, smoked, had a huge messy meal and smoked some more; then, with the boundless energy of the young, whooped off back to bed and had at it again.

It was in the middle of their second session—surrounded by food mess and marijuana butts, and humping like hogs in the very heart of the holy-of-holies—that Trevor walked into the room.

AT THAT MOMENT, Roy was on top of Marcel, pumping lustily, both with their rumps toward the door. The first thing Roy was aware of was iron fingers biting into his shoulders. Then he was literally hurled across the room.

He did not even feel the impact. By that time his head had

twisted around and he was already making acquaintance with horror. For what he saw in the eyes, in the face, in the entire stark demeanour of the figure looming above him, was his own doom.

There could be no pleading, no reasoning, no possible compromise with the engine of retribution that Trevor had become. Roy's transformed demon-lover was now advancing with an intent that could only be described in one word.

Murder.

"Bitch!" Trevor whispered, like the breath from a tomb. "Whore! Slut! Puking, cunting bitch! I'm going to kill both of you!"

Which was exactly what began to happen.

The first blow from Trevor's sharp, shiny shoe caught Roy squarely in his naked groin. The pain was like nothing he had ever felt: a fiery dagger that ignited in his gut and exploded in every single nerve end of his being. His mouth snapped wide in the rictus of a silent scream. Mercifully, he blacked out, but the relief was short. In what must have been just seconds—crotch feeling as if it had been sliced in half—he re-emerged into wretched awareness.

For a moment everything was a crimson blur, but this cleared, allowing him to see moving shapes and to hear chilling sounds: thumping—retching—mewling shrieks. At first Roy thought it must be he who was doing this. But then his eyes focussed and he saw what was really happening.

Pretty Marcel was being murdered.

The naked boy lay on the floor. Above, in a sort of dancing crouch, hovered Trevor. Marcel's shrieks occurred each time his assailant landed a kick on his already blood-soaked head. And now, with every blow delivered, Trevor himself began a monotonous, mad incantation: "Die bitch—die, dirty bitch—die ... "

Somehow, ignited by horror and despair, Roy managed to get up. His balls felt as though they'd been crushed in a vice. Violent nausea flooded through him. He swayed, beginning to dry-retch even as he staggered toward the slaughter.

"Stop!" he croaked, in a coarse bark. "*Stop!*"

Trevor did stop. But only long enough to lay a vicious blow across the bridge of his former lover's nose. This time Roy's scream was anything but silent, and he landed once more in a heap upon the floor. This pain had its own special brand of anguish, but it also produced the saving grace of rage. Roy lay still, as the pain was slowly supplanted by the new emotion.

From across the room, the sound of blows had resumed. But now there were no more shrieks. Marcel was unconscious—if not already dead.

Understanding this, Roy finally realized that his own time was swiftly running out. Summoning his last strength, he struggled to his feet. Trevor, on the other side of the bed, was busy dealing death with the intense absorption of the insane.

Roy had no idea what he was going to do. Then, as he came around the bed, he was confronted by the figurine of the grinning Pan. With no awareness of decision, he reached out, and somehow the statue was in his hand. It was a foot tall, made of heavy bronze, and his fingers found a firm grip around the legs. He didn't exactly lift it, simply let natural momentum carry the thing forward at the end of his arm. Then, without aim, or even conscious thought, arm and statue were rising, arcing up, descending in a fluid but purposeful curve.

Trevor still seemed utterly absorbed, but at that moment his head turned. He glanced up, directly at the grinning Pan. Their eyes seemed to meet—lock—then the statue struck.

It was the erect phallus that hit first, penetrating the man's temple with a sickening crunch. There followed a time of complete stillness and silence. Trevor did not alter his expression. The intense, mad concentration remained, but now it was fixed—like a moving picture frozen to a still—while sense and meaning slowly departed.

For a measureless time thereafter the tableau held: Roy and Trevor, turned into a bizarre statue themselves, magically conjoined by grinning Pan, whose great organ seemed to be spurting its seed directly into its late owner's brain.

Then it disintegrated. Trevor's muscles, released from command, at last acted like the dead meat they had become, dumping his body in a heap upon the floor. There followed two sounds: first the clatter of the statue as, breaking from its deadly connection, it struck the floor and rolled; then, immediately, the low, final wheeze of air expelled from the corpse.

That was the end of it.

ROY FELT A sigh, eerily reminiscent of the last sound that had come from Trevor, escape from his own throat. He felt like fainting, but a deeper urgency prevented it.

Marcel.

With a cry, Roy stumbled across the body of Trevor and went to Marcel. The boy was lying in a corner, curled up like a small animal, his bloodied head twisted grotesquely. Roy was convinced that he was now in the company of two corpses.

Then Marcel whimpered, the sound low but unmistakable.

"Marcel—Jesus—*Marcel!*"

Immediately Roy was down on the floor, cradling the boy in his arms. The eyes fluttered open. "Shit!" Marcel muttered petulantly. "What the fuck have you been doing to me?"

It was some sort of miracle.

The punishment Trevor had inflicted on Marcel had indeed produced a multitude of lacerations: his entire body showed the evidence of the beating. Probably he'd never be quite so pretty again.

But no bones were broken and, gory as it appeared, most of the blood had come from one bad gash on Marcel's scalp.

For all Trevor's insane rage, his ability to inflict damage was much less deadly than it seemed, whereas in his own case, one horribly fortuitous blow had silenced him forever.

So, as it turned out, the one intended for death had survived, the one determined to be slayer had been slain, and the one responsible for the whole mess—Roy—had become the only killer.

Murderer!

That's what everyone would say.

For who would believe that this was an act of self-defence, let alone an attempt to save another?

In the hours that followed, Roy acted like a strangely efficient automaton. Although his nose and balls were swollen, and it pained him to walk, he managed to drive Marcel to Emergency at the Victoria General Hospital. Afterwards he took the boy to his apartment. By then it was 4:00 A.M. They said not a single word about Trevor. It went without saying that they would never see each other again.

Roy got back home at dawn. The house was serene, giving no hint of the baroque tragedy that had so recently occurred. He let himself in. In the hall the first thing that caught his eye was the blinking light on the answering machine.

There were 10 messages.

Every single one was from Trevor.

Starting on the day of departure, unnoticed by Roy during his time of careless debauch, was a chilling record of surprise, anger and finally desperation—the last being short and simple: "David—David! For Christ's sake—are you bloody *dead?* That's it. Fuck the conference! *I'm walking out of this hotel and getting on a plane right now!*"

That was it. Trevor's last words, recorded the day before, mere hours prior to the boys' fatal last liaison. Even as they arrived at the house, this had been waiting, a stark warning—had anyone had the brains to take notice.

Realizing this, overwhelmed by the bitter irony of everything, Roy slumped down by the telephone table. In front of him the answering machine light blinked: *on—off—on—off—fool—fool—FOOL …*

Right there on the floor, overwhelmed by exhaustion, he slept.

FROM THE INSTANT his eyes opened, staring at the still stupidly blinking light, Roy knew his world had irrevocably changed. And something else: he had finally tuned in to his instinct for survival. His first action was to erase the contents of the answering machine. Then he went into Trevor's room.

The body lay there, face frozen in its final manic leer. A tiny trickle of blood came from the hole in Trevor's temple. The only other blood was crusted upon the rampant brass phallus of Pan.

Surveying all this, Roy's only surprise was his own reaction, which seemed completely calm. Looking at the remains of the man who'd saved his life, become his lover, master and almost his killer, Roy found he didn't feel anything.

Except a resolve to avoid the consequences of this madness. No doubt his calmness came from desperation. But never mind. It would do. It was now Friday. Trevor wouldn't be expected at work for at least three days. And visitors never came here.

Roy had breakfast and then went out into the garden. It was very secluded, surrounded by fences and high hedges: a private place for very private people. At the far end of the property there was a dense stand of rhododendrons. Their big shiny leaves made a pleasant contrast to the deeper green of the thick hedge behind.

Roy pushed through the rhodos to the rear. Here, between bushes and hedge, was a dim tunnel, its floor matted with a heavy coat of dead leaves and needles. He knelt and began clearing the leaf mulch, stacking it carefully to both sides, until there was an area of exposed earth about six feet by four.

Finally he fetched a spade from the garden shed and began to dig.

AFTER THE BURIAL he set to work on the house.

The first thing was Trevor's room, but not just to remove evidence of crime. Obsessively, the man had portrayed himself to the world as straight. So—straight he would be remembered, meaning that no one would think about—or search for—an acquaintance who was gay. Roy stripped the baroque bed of all exotica, putting the too-pretty stuff in plastic bags. Everything else—clothes, books, pictures, videos—anything giving the merest hint of Trevor's secret lifestyle, also got bagged.

The bronze Pan already was at rest with its owner under the rhododendrons.

His own bedroom Roy revamped completely, removing all traces of its true occupant, resulting in a bland spare room that might have been occupied by no one at all. Which, actually, was the character he'd been playing for two years: David—no one at all.

Finally Roy went through the entire house, leaving everything as neat and respectable as a church vestry. A reward of this effort was a small discovery: abandoned behind a sofa cushion was the engraved gold lighter of Marcel McGinty. With relief, Roy pocketed the thing and then forgot it. All of this brought him to the end of Saturday.

On Sunday morning, before first light, he locked up carefully and drove away. He found a dumpster and got rid of the bagged-up stuff from the house. Then he drove down the Pat Bay Highway, arriving in time to catch the 7:00 ferry to Vancouver.

Once on the mainland, he drove to the airport, leaving the BMW in long-term parking. The dull overcoat he'd worn over his own bright clothes he left in the car. Finally—his old self for all the world—he used his last money to catch a bus downtown. And that was the end of that part of his life.

Except for the dreams.

They began the very next night.

JOSEPH STOOD AT the window of the house on Dallas Road, gazing at the purple and green and crimson extravaganza of sunset over Juan de Fuca Strait. Behind him sat Roy, a shadow in the encroaching dark, his last words drifting across the intervening space like water drops in a still pool.

"I was pretty clever, I guess. It was like someone else took charge for a while. But that cold bastard fucked off real quick, I can tell you. And all I was left with were the nightmares."

"I can imagine."

Roy sighed, years of pent-up anguish expressed in a single sound. "But Joe, I didn't mean anything like that to happen. I swear."

"Of course!" Joseph said quickly. "Of course, I know that."

"And if I hadn't tried to stop it, he would have killed us both."

"That's obviously what he intended. But—Christ—Roy, *sweetie*— why haven't you told me all this before? I would have understood. I love you! Why didn't you share it with me?"

Roy rose and moved agitatedly to the window. He leaned his forehead against the glass, rolling it from side to side. Finally he said, "That first year back in Vancouver was miserable. Oh, I survived all right. Two years as Trevor's kid had left me real attractive and super-healthy. And I never again went near coke. But I guess I'd grown up more than I realized. Because everything seemed—so hollow. I know that must sound fucking hypocritical, from someone who only wanted to be a whore. But there it is."

There was a long silence. "So what happened?"

Roy unexpectedly laughed. "What happened was the best piece of luck of my life. One night I got beaten up."

Roy was appalled. "You call that *luck*?"

"Of course," Roy said quietly. "Don't you remember, sweetie? It was because of that that I met you."

IN FACT, JOSEPH remembered only too well. Mere hours before, watching Roy sleeping, he'd recalled how his partner had looked at their first meeting.

It was spring in the late 1980s, and he'd been on the mainland in North Vancouver, visiting his half-sister and her husband: a straight, churchgoing couple who lived in constant terror that his sexual orientation might somehow be revealed to their kids. He left early and decided he just had time to make it to Horseshoe Bay for the last ferry. Taking a short cut to get to the Upper Levels Highway, he swung around a bend—and straight ahead was a figure standing right in the middle of the road.

Joseph braked desperately, swerved, missed the figure, hit the curb and almost ended on someone's manicured lawn. Cursing uncharacteristically, he reversed back onto the road to find the cause of the trouble, the idiot, still standing there.

It was a man, that much could be seen. Though his back was turned, something else was apparent: he was weeping. Realizing this, Joseph's anger drained away. This person was clearly so overwrought as to be a danger to himself.

"Excuse me," Joseph said quietly, "I don't know what's the matter, but if you keep standing there you're going to get yourself killed."

The sound of Joseph's voice seemed to cut through the man's hysteria. The weeping stopped and he turned so that his face came full into the light.

Joseph gaped. All he managed to say was, "Oh!"

He found himself looking at a miracle. A broken angel.

And it was love at first sight.

"I COULDN'T TELL you then the real reason I was bawling like that," Roy said. "But when I got beaten up at that party—just before you found me—the shock brought the whole ghastly 'Trevor' thing flashing back. It'd all been bottled up, I guess, waiting to explode." He grinned ruefully. "You must have thought I was a hysterical nut."

"I knew that you were hurting. I just wanted to make things right. That's all I've ever wanted with you, Roy."

"I know, sweetie. I know."

"I'm so glad you finally told me." Joseph meant this, but also was starting to feel impatient. "Roy, I'm so sorry about your terrible experience. Of course you have to know that none of it—*none of it*—could ever make any difference to how I feel about you ... "

"Thank you."

"So, my dear, I think it's time for the rest."

"Rest?"

"For fuck's sake, Roy, what in hell has all this to do with what's been going on here today?"

ROY WENT TO Joseph immediately and hugged him. "Thanks for cleaning up that shitty mess I made, sweetie."

"You're welcome."

"And since you did, you'll know where this morning's paper is. Could you get it, please?"

Without a word, Joseph fetched it and thrust it into Roy's hands. The younger man found the classified section. "There—the obits!"

Joseph fumbled for his reading glasses. "Who? Someone we know?"

"That kid I told you about. Who was with me when Trevor—got killed. He just died."

"How do you know it's the same person?"

"It's him, all right. Marcel McGinty. There can't be two in Victoria. And the age would be right. It says, 'of complications due to AIDS.' And—yeah—that would be right too."

"That's terrible! It's always so sad, dying like that. But why would you … ? Oh, God—you'd been seeing him?"

Roy banged the paper down. "Jesus, no! I told you, I've never seen him again. What do you take me for?"

Joseph drew a deep breath. "All I know, Roy, is that you've had me nearly out of my mind with worry all day. So, okay, since you haven't been seeing Marcel—why is it that his death seems to have made you crazy?"

Instead of answering, Roy began searching through the *Times Colonist* again. At last, he thrust it forward. "Here—read that!"

The paper was folded to a column called "Across Canada." Roy's finger jabbed at a place halfway down. Under the title "Ancient Accident Victim" was a short paragraph:

> *The remains of an ancient accident were found near Grand Forks, B.C., earlier this week. A pickup truck with 1951 plates was discovered by a youth while swimming in Christina Lake. It was totally submerged and contained the bones of one 25- to 40-year-old male, yet to be positively identified. The truck apparently plunged into the lake some time in 1951. Highway 3 was later diverted to a safer route away from the water. Officials believe this is why the mishap has remained so long undiscovered.* CP

Joseph read the paragraph once. Then he read it again. Finally he shrugged. "I don't understand."

Roy took back the paper and sat down, composing himself. He said quietly, "After you went to work this morning, I got up and made breakfast and sat down to read the *Colonist*. The first thing that caught my eye was that piece I just showed you. Well—after what happened to me—anything like that, about old bodies being discovered—it has to make you think. I got to wondering what it would be like if—his body was ever found. But then I wished I hadn't. So I opened the paper to another place, which happened to be the obit section. And right there, sticking out like a blinking light, was the name Marcel McGinty."

Joseph stared. At last he said, "A weird coincidence, all right. But I still don't see what that's got to with you trashing the house. What on earth made you do that?"

Roy felt around in his pocket, extracted a small object and placed it on the table: a cigarette lighter. "I was looking for this."

"Why?"

"Take a good look."

Joseph did so. It was old and scratched, but had been expensive, a gold Dunhill. On one side were engraved letters which Joseph could only just make out.

Marcel McGinty.

"As I told you," Roy said quietly, "I discovered that while I was cleaning up Trevor's place. It was still in my pocket after I went back to Vancouver. Somehow I couldn't throw it away. It seemed like—a kind of warning charm, a reminder of how much trouble can happen if you're really stupid. I still had it when I met you. But, as time passed and the old, bad shit faded, the point of keeping it faded too. I didn't ditch the lighter, simply lost track of it. But then today, when I saw Marcel's name in the paper, my mind played a weird trick: I recognized the name, but I thought I had to be wrong. His name had really been Marcel McLeish or Marcel Magruder or something—

anything—else. I remembered the lighter, and then just *had* to find it, to prove it one way or the other. Well, I searched and searched and—as you can see—I finally found the fucking thing."

The final part of the tale had taken them into the all-forgiving dark. Joseph moved almost reluctantly to a lamp and switched it on. Momentarily, the light felt as blinding as a spotlight, and Joseph felt naked. He said, "But all that business of dashing about in town. When I saw you from my office. What were you doing then?"

"What do you think? I was coming to you, of course."

Joseph blinked. His first instinct was to laugh in disbelief, an urge only curbed by the utter sincerity on Roy's face. "But, Roy, you walked right by."

Roy looked embarrassed. "By the time I found the lighter I was so worked up I was hysterical. Everything from the time of Trevor came rushing back: killing him, disposing of the body, it all suddenly seemed more real than in years. Evil stuff done by a horrible little cunt! Somehow I'd ignored all that, letting the good life with you make me forget it. Realizing *that* made me feel so horribly guilty, all I wanted was to confess. To tell you I was sorry for letting you think all this time I was an okay person."

"Oh, God—*sweetie!*"

"So I rushed out of the house. What I meant to do, I think, was to come down and tell you you'd better ditch me."

"Christ! What stopped you?"

Roy smiled. The expression was so sad, rueful and true that Joseph's heart felt as if it might explode. Roy said, "You did!"

"*Me?*"

"All these years with you. All the love and good times and companionship we've had together. All the growing and sharing: fuck it, Joe, it's made me sane. I couldn't just throw it all away. By the time I got downtown to 'fess-up, it was already starting to seem ridiculous.

As I passed your office I was suddenly scared you'd see me, and how would I explain? In a minute I changed from a crazy bitch into someone who felt like a right schmuck. So—I just kept on going and ended up at work." Roy paused, shrugged. "So that's it, hon. The rest you know."

"Yes."

And then, causing in Joseph a reaction of almost equal parts irritation and relief, Roy gave a dazzling grin. "Oh, by the way— with all that's been going down I forgot to tell you. I finished the hanging. We open tomorrow, and it's going to be *très* fabulous!"

It was very late that night before they finally got to bed. Roy— perhaps symptomatic of catharsis—was instantly asleep. Joseph lay in the dark, listening to his partner's easy breathing, trying to calm his own still-turbulent thoughts.

Everything he'd learned of Roy's hidden past, even the most gruesome details about the fate of Trevor, none of it made the slightest difference to his heart. Whatever his lover had done—and the worst was clearly innocent of intent—was in the past. Roy had grown into a fine, sensitive, caring man, someone with whom Joseph was all the more determined to spend the rest of his life.

And so, as his spirit calmed and his mind at last prepared itself for rest, only one small nagging image remained: a quiet garden with high hedges and rhododendrons—and a leaf-strewn bower that concealed a grim secret.

FOUR

He was walking on a country road holding hands. There was a person on his left and one on his right, and each hand he grasped was strong and warm and marvellously comforting. But they were also huge and high up, apparently the hands of giants. He discovered that, instead of walking, he could swing on the hands and be wafted along. So he did that and the giants laughed, swinging him back and forth, higher and higher, as they moved through the sweet and flowering land. This continued for an eon, while a wondrous fact slowly emerged in his brain: *This is my mother and father. At last they've found me! And now—and now ...*

"... claim it at the cashier's desk in the snack bar on deck four. Will the owner of a small red purse please claim it at the cashier's desk in the snack bar on deck four. Thank you."

Jack opened his eyes. For a moment the final dream image, from which the mechanical voice had snatched him, was superimposed upon reality. Heart-stoppingly sweet, his parents' merriment still sang in his head, behind the talk-buzz of the ferry. Then it was gone, squished between the cracks of the waking world, a dead echo from a tragically unreachable land. There was a fading memory of connection, of union, so complete that it gave golden meaning to all life.

Then even that was gone, leaving such desperate emptiness that his urge was to plunge into the nearby ocean and vanish into oblivion.

Fortunately two factors—ingrained self-preservation plus a thick plate-glass window—put paid to that caprice. That too departed and Jack was left feeling drained and foolish.

Why on earth should he be having such bizarre dreams—especially in the daytime? Considering this, he realized that the key to the puzzle might be in his own hand: his left hand, actually, unconsciously toying with the thing that had brought him upon this unlikely quest. From his pocket he drew forth the wedding ring that he'd retrieved from the drowned truck, along with its cargo of old bones.

He held the plain gold band up to the light. It looked as new as the long-ago day it had been bought. On the inside, the engraved initials stood out clearly. *J. R. D. D.*—Johan Reddski and Doris Day: Johan, called Johnny, who half a century ago had made a journey to tell his good news, creating grief instead of pleasure, death instead of fulfillment; Doris, with the name of a film star but the vocation of nurse, who'd planned to marry Johnny but waited in vain for his return.

Who perhaps was waiting still.

But that last notion, Jack mused glumly, was romantic bullshit. He was a guy in his 40s, a police officer, for Christ's sake. A Mountie. If the sentimental object of this exercise was to track down some pining old dame to let her know her lover's heart had been true—then he'd better rethink his priorities, get out of the Force and be a goddamn grief counsellor.

That last thought was absurd enough to make him chuckle. But he didn't feel amused. Fuck it, why was he *doing* this? Was it his own need for connection? Could all this—including dreams of parents he'd never known and until recently never thought of—be part of some clichéd mid-life quest for identity?

Oh, come on, Jack, get real, he thought, shoving the ring back into his pocket. *All this is is a human-interest story, no more. A small puzzle to add spice to a trip that you're taking alone because ... Why? Because Margie can't get away right now, of course. Okay—but also because...?* Well, yes, perhaps because he still hadn't really decided that he wanted to be with her.

But thinking about that, he discovered that in fact he wasn't too worried. He and Margie were going to be all right. Surprised, he realized he was fairly sure of that now. As to the rest, the less obvious reasons why he was undertaking this odd journey, well, he'd just have to work all that out as he went along.

He leaned back in his comfortable seat. The BC Ferries vessel, *Spirit of Vancouver Island*, on the run between Tsawwassen and Swartz Bay, was vast: a veritable floating highway between the Lower Mainland and Vancouver Island. Jack, on his first visit, found himself as impressed as any tourist.

In awe, he saw that the ferry was moving through what looked like a canyon. High cliffs rose like stone citadels on either side, leaving a gap—barely wide enough, it seemed, for the ship—through which tidal waters flowed with the force of a great river.

Impressive though this picture was, even more intriguing was the presence in the water of great creatures. Fast-moving companions to the ship, they sped through the narrow pass, parallel to the ferry and just as swift. "Killer whales! Orcas!" He heard these words whispered all around. There were at least half a dozen, the largest upwards of 20 feet long, looking like giant dolphins; magnificent outriders keeping company. Every now and then one would dive, to appear again, leaping and broaching with an audible smack upon the waves. This caused the watchers to "Aahhh" themselves with delight. Jack found himself doing it too.

Instead of returning to his seat, he left the lounge and sauntered out onto the open deck. Leaning on the rail, he watched the whales, now departing. The sea was calm and the wind brisk. All around was blue ocean, bluer sky and the ever-changing outlines of rocks, islands and peninsulas.

After the whales finally vanished, Jack closed his eyes, took a deep breath and let the air drift out again slowly, to merge with the wind's brisk slipstream. Right then he realized that he actually felt damned good: if not completely at peace, certainly nearer to it than in a long time. Sadly, closely following, came an extra niggle of perception: that this pleasant sensation was perhaps only a reflex of being on vacation—a trick of the light, of the breeze, of the balmy coastal weather.

Gazing down the long sea lane toward the terminal at Swartz Bay, watching the mountains of Vancouver Island rise in ever-decreasing distance, he realized that he'd better enjoy this peaceful time. For it might just be short-lived.

EMILY MULLER SAT in her secret garden. It was the end of a clear, bright and absolutely still afternoon. The sun, though well on its westerly slide, was still strong enough to be hot, and Emily had retreated to the shelter of the pond-side umbrella. Beyond that welcome shade, the crisp light glowed off a brilliant palette, a host of blooms not yet diminished by summer's advance: Emily's three-dimensional tapestry, tended with infinite care, in the cool centre of which its creator now rested with soil-darkened fingers and the satisfaction of work well done.

Unfortunately, however, her heart was not quite at peace.

It was a week since the news that had changed her life, by giving notice of its imminent conclusion, and, in that time, she had begun to reconcile herself. The original numbness had passed. Also—the outraged feeling of unfairness. What remained was plain regret for fate's crude foreclosure on her future. Still, she would not permit that emotion to linger, aware of the folly of ruining the short time remaining with pointless pining for what could not be.

So what she had was a fairly sound philosophical acceptance of her fate. After all, she'd been given two-thirds of a century, almost triple that of her own mother. Never having known love or marriage was not something she regretted. And the fact that her only family consisted of one unknown child—some stranger who could never mourn her passing—was something she'd come to terms with years ago.

Finally, her own life had brought much success, satisfaction, art—and a beautiful garden. In which she knew she would have been at peace.

If only she'd been alone.

AFTER THE DISCOVERY of the body under the rhododendrons Emily had not immediately known what to do. There was a first moment of horror when, realizing that the "stone" was in fact human remains, she had dropped the skull and backed off. However, this reaction had been followed by a surprising and countervailing thought: this could be me.

All sensation of fear and disgust then evaporated, to be replaced by sorrow at the lost loneliness of the thing she had cast down. So she had bent and retrieved the skull. There was no lower jaw, which was why she had mistaken it for a stone. Without hesitation, Emily wiped away more earth. Now the teeth were revealed clearly, firm and strong and not a single one missing. Then, abruptly, she realized something else: the teeth had fillings.

Emily was so surprised she had almost dropped her find again. So, what had she been thinking? Well, naively, that she'd made some sort of archeological discovery; that—for instance—her garden was on the site of an ancient Native burial ground. But ancient Natives did not have amalgam and gold tooth fillings.

Her perceptions were forced to a sharp turn. A chill spread inside her. For folk modern enough to have visited the dentist did not get planted in backyards, not unless the planting had been a secret. Surprisingly, Emily's chill became something more complex: fascination and curiosity. She brushed at the skull to remove the last earth, detaching a chunk from a depression to the rear of the left eye socket.

Which was when she found the hole.

It was squarely in the middle of the temple, a hole the size of a loonie, obviously too large to have been made by a bullet. But it hadn't been caused by decay either. This damage—revealed after the earth was removed, so Emily's digging couldn't have caused it—had to be the result of a blow. The fatal blow that had caused the owner's demise.

So there it was: Emily's companion in her quiet garden could only be the victim of murder.

It was merely the automatic reflex of a law-abiding citizen that had sent Emily hurrying across the garden in the direction of the telephone. She'd entered the house and was in fact reaching for the phone when something made her stop: a vision so shocking that she withdrew her hand from the phone as if stung.

What had arisen was a premonition more disturbing than any buried body: squads of policemen striding heavy-booted through her peaceful domain, digging up her beds, trampling through her flowers, imposing the brutal machinery of investigation upon her garden and her life.

A life whose span was now reckoned only in months.

And the chaos of the police wouldn't even be the worst part. For with it would come the inevitable publicity: reporters calling at all hours; TV cameras hovering and spying; perhaps even the fact of her own disease exposed, turned into some dreadful soap opera for public display.

The awfulness of this vision made Emily almost physically ill.

She sat heavily, gazing at the phone as it were a viper, feeling as if she'd just peered into an abyss. God, even leukemia hadn't made her feel as bad as this.

Why had she been about to bring upon herself such ruin? Simply to reveal a secret that was obviously very old; predating, at very least, her own 15-year occupation of the house. After a while she understood what she had to do.

She went back to the end of the garden, where her find lay exposed beside the newly disturbed earth. Then Emily experienced her first moment of nervousness. She glanced quickly about, but of course the high hedges provided complete safety from prying eyes. She felt foolish, then angry. Already her unwelcome guest was affecting what was left of her life.

When she went to replace the skull in its resting place, Emily discovered something else. At the bottom of the hole was what looked like a tiny, perfectly formed human arm. She reached down and grasped the limb, which was actually metal and a part of something larger.

Curiosity vied with her need to get this business over, and the former won out. She used her spade to loosen more earth, revealing the jawbone that was a mate to the skull. With surprisingly little emotion, she placed the jaw by the skull, even feeling—but not acting upon—a tidy urge to fit them together. A little more digging and she could move the object attached to the arm. She levered it back and forth, and finally the earth relinquished its prize: small but quite heavy. She dragged it out and set it on the ground.

It was a foot-tall bronze statuette: a man figure with goat legs and goat horns, holding musical pipes. Pan. It also possessed a monstrously disproportionate phallus that jutted, bizarrely, six full inches from the tiny satyr's groin.

Emily's reaction to this last discovery would have given pause even to those who knew her best. She smiled sourly at the great organ, contemplating the perennial male fantasies it embodied. "You *wish!*" she whispered, for only Pan and the rhododendrons to hear.

Through dirt and tarnish, and despite the absurd phallus, Emily could see that her find was well crafted. No Rodin, to be sure, nor yet a relic from antiquity. This was a modern creation, but skilfully sculpted. Emily's own taste ran to paintings, but her knowledge of art led her to understand that such a work would not come cheap.

So why had it been abandoned?

She contemplated the statue. From her position, its jutting sex organ was so prominent it partially obscured her view of the skull that lay beyond, shattered temple-bone gaping at the sky. Once, twice, Emily shifted focus, from bronze uber-organ to skull hole and back—then she got it.

Pan had been the murder weapon.

Emily's wave of disgust was followed by relief. Having solved the puzzle, she could finally get on with her plans. She set skull and jaw-bone carefully back in the hole, spading in earth till they were nicely covered. About to replace the statue, she paused. Though grotesque, it was a fine work. Even if it was the murder weapon, that didn't make it evil in itself. Every esthetic fibre in her being rebelled against burying it like old garbage. So—somewhat in the spirit of a curator—she tucked it neatly away in the garden shed. Returning to her task, she replaced the rest of the soil, at last carefully repairing the top carpet of mulch and leaves. When it was all done, it was difficult even for her to see where the disturbed place had been. Finally she went in and wrote a careful description of her find, its location and her reasons for conceal-ment. With this she included a meticulously drawn garden map. She put it all in an envelope bearing the message "To be opened only after my death." This she placed inside her will.

All of this had happened two days earlier.

NOW, AS SHE sat in the shade of the umbrella, realizing how elusive was the peace she'd expected, she found herself seriously wondering if she had done the right thing.

She knew that, in the short time left, there was no way she could open her sanctuary to invasion. That was beyond question. But she was aware of an odd niggle way at the back of her mind, which logic could not quite neutralize: it was almost as if the ancient remains in the garden—absurd as such a notion might seem—were calling to her.

Of course, not for a moment did Emily think this was actually happening. She didn't believe in spirits, certainly not any kind of entity aware enough to desire communication with the real world. Yet there was something—less than a belief but more than a mere fantasy—that murmured of a psychic imbalance brought about by the violence that had once occurred in her quiet sanctuary. Whether or not this was romantic nonsense, the facts were these: when she had been unaware of the garden's other inhabitant she had known tranquility; now that the veil was lifted, this was no longer so.

Since the traditional remedy—passing off the problem to the appropriate authorities—was not available, and since she couldn't just forget about it, something else would have to be done. But what?

She thought a long time but no solution appeared. However, she did come up with a direction, which at least would give her an activity for the time being: the presence of her companion must remain a secret but the least she could do, for her own peace of mind, was to attempt to discover his or her identity.

How this could be done without giving away the secret itself, she had no idea. Whether her task was feasible was even more uncertain. But until the inner need receded, or a better idea came along, this would have to be her occupation.

So much for peaceful last days in the garden.

THERE WERE VERY few people in the chapel when Joseph and Roy arrived. Because the time and place of the service had been in the newspaper obituary, they'd expected a larger turnout. But, with their own appearance and that of the minister, there were only eight people to pay last respects to the late Marcel McGinty.

Roy had at first found the idea of attending the young man's funeral strange and appalling. So Joseph had tried to explain. What he found most distressing was not what had happened in the past, but the damage that the secret of it had so nearly done. The need now, he said earnestly, was to restore the sane and normal pattern of their lives. An appropriate start would be to treat Marcel McGinty just like other friends who'd passed the same way: honouring him by being there to say goodbye. Far from being strange, such an action would be a sort of absolution for them both.

Put that way, Roy had to agree.

When they arrived they sat at the rear of the small chapel. At the front sat an older couple: a heavy, stiff-faced man and a pale, red-eyed woman. Marcel's parents, probably. Immediately behind was a younger woman whom Roy had little trouble in recognizing as the dead man's sister. She was accompanied by a husband and a teenaged daughter, both of whom made scant effort to hide the fact they wanted to be elsewhere.

The casket seemed lonely and cheap. They were thankful that it was firmly closed.

The pastor was a middle-aged man with placid eyes and a manner as smooth and automatic as a player piano. His suit was pale, and his sermon matched it. Joseph had been to gay funerals which, though sad, had yet contained a measure of love, camaraderie and even defiance, but it didn't happen here. This service was for the benefit of straight family members, abrim with evasions and hypocritical solemnity.

Catching himself in these bleak thoughts, Joseph brought himself up short. The family were only doing their best, for God's sake. At least they hadn't abandoned their flesh entirely. At least they were here. All too often the Marcels of the world were shuttled out of it alone.

Mercifully, the service was short. There was apparently no reception. When it was over, everyone just melted away.

THAT NIGHT AT dinner they were unnaturally silent. As he was serving dessert, Joseph abruptly put down the spoon and leaned across the table. "Roy," he said quietly, "I really am sorry for suggesting we go to that damn funeral."

Roy shrugged. "It wasn't so bad, I guess."

"But—remember I said I thought it'd be good for both of us?"

"Well, it was!" Roy grimaced. "Don't get me wrong, sweet thing, as an experience it was pure shit. But that was okay because we were together. And I'll tell you something else: when I saw that poor guy's coffin, I thought, *Jesus, that could be me.* Then I thought, *If it wasn't for Joe, it probably would be.*"

"Oh, Roy ... "

"Well, it's true. It was a mean little service. They couldn't even tell the truth about who Marcel really was, for God's sake. But it was still okay. It reminded me just how fortunate I am."

"We're both fortunate! But this is what I wanted to tell you. Being there made me feel a bit guilty."

"For fuck's sake, why?"

Joseph sighed. "Because I have so much, a life that's truly blessed. Because—dear Roy—I'm so damn *lucky!*"

"You're feeling guilty because you're lucky?"

"I'm not explaining it very well. Think about Marcel's parents today. Okay, they hadn't abandoned him. At least they were there.

But that service. Jesus, they used the poor guy's death to deny everything real about his life."

"Agreed. So?"

"I couldn't help thinking about my own mother, remembering how great she was when I was growing up. How she accepted me— everything about me—so I wasn't fucked up, like so many people we know."

Roy chuckled. "That's my darlin'. The only straight gay guy in town."

"But that's right!—if that means I'm happy about myself. And most of that is probably due to my mom."

Roy's eyes widened in comprehension. "Who you haven't seen in …?"

"As you know—a very long time."

"But I always assumed that must be because you felt the same as me. I haven't seen my shits since I left Ontario. Which, darling, is just dandy. But—sounds like you really care about your old duck."

"I do."

"Then—excuse me, sweets—but it seems like something pretty strange is going on here. What happened?"

Joseph looked perplexed. "Nothing did."

"What made you stop seeing her?"

"I never intended to. Before you and I met, I used to go up-Island fairly regularly."

"So it's because of us?"

"No. I told you, my mother totally supported my lifestyle."

"But you never took me to meet her. So I naturally thought … Well—why in hell don't you see her?"

"I don't know."

Roy's eyes narrowed. "Sweetie—I just bet you do. That's what this guilt shit is all about. Listen, it sounds to me like your ma's a sweet gal. And I know you're a sweet fella. But you two sweeties never see each other. So now, simple ol' me has got to wonder just why the fuck that might be."

Joseph grinned. "For a charming airhead, you do sometimes have a way of cutting to the chase."

"Thanks, Einstein. Stop stalling."

"Actually what I'm trying to do now is think. Years ago, my mother and I used to be very close. But then—it sort of went wrong."

"What happened? Oh, but, excuse me, this 'charming airhead' forgot. You said nothing did."

"Well, I'm wrong. It had to be something."

"No kidding!"

"You made your point. I'm trying to remember. And you know— I've never taken time to put this together before—but I think it may have all started when I learned something. You see   one day I found out that all my life my mother been lying to me."

"What about?"

"My dad."

JACK HAD DISCOVERED his lodging simply by driving around. When he reached Victoria it was quite early so he had plenty of time. Though he'd never been to the provincial capital before, it was soon obvious where the tourists hung out: the Inner Harbour area with its ritzy hotels, gift shops, picture-postcard views—and scarily inflated prices. So he'd driven a bit, finding an alternative to the main route out of town, the original highway, which still boasted some older but well-kept motels. In one of these he found a neat little room with 1950s decor, a lot of varnished wood and, most importantly, a phone. That, as it turned out, was the easy part.

Much harder was the task he'd set himself. Being a policeman, Jack had from time to time been involved in searching for missing people. But such investigations had generally been recent and specific, aided by the full resources of the police machinery. In this case, not only was he on his own, but the trail—assuming there even was one—was about as cold as it could be.

Fifty years cold.

However, Jack told himself, the simplest mode of investigation was still best; to wit—the telephone. He went out and got a pepperoni pizza and a six-pack: not the most healthy fare, but as a cop he knew the efficacy of comfort food when facing a long, dull and potentially frustrating task.

As it turned out, in the Greater Victoria area there were nearly 90 listings under the name of Day. There was no Doris, but several D. Days. These he tried first, just to get the ball rolling.

He had a simple formula. If the person who answered the phone sounded like an older woman he'd ask if she was Doris Day. If a younger person or a man answered, he'd say that he was searching for a lady, in her 70s, once named Doris Day, and did they have such a person as a relative? Like much regular police procedure, it was as straightforward and mundane as that.

As it turned out, his D. Days were all home but all turned up blank. Most were men, one a teen, one a woman in her 20s. None had ever heard of his Doris Day.

Jack didn't even pause. From the outset he'd decided that the only way to do this was with brisk calm, as if he were doing a routine shift. In short, no attitude. With such possibility of defeat, these precautions were wisest taken in advance.

For the next two hours he went at it solidly, moving down the list. While most of his calls were answered—those that weren't he marked to try later—he still had no joy. A couple of folk old enough to remember Doris Day the film star thought he was kidding around. One person alluded to an obscure politician named

Day who'd had a Doris-joke made up about him. But nobody had heard of his quarry.

At 10:00 the lateness of the hour gave Jack a thoroughly welcome excuse to take a break.

BUT HE DIDN'T put down the phone. Instead, with an odd twinge of nervousness, he dialled a more familiar number. After the second ring, Margie came on the line.

"Hello?"

"Hi, Margs, me."

"Darling! *Hi!*" With those two words, so warm that he could almost feel the essence of her bubbling through the line, all trace of nervousness evaporated. He now knew for sure that if there'd been any uncertainty in this relationship, it was only in himself. All his problems were over. Or maybe not quite.

Guiltily, he remembered there was another reason why he could be feeling embarrassed. He hadn't told his lady—or anyone, come to that—the real reason for his trip to Vancouver Island.

Which was absurd. Well, no, which was understandable—if one accepted the macho notion that tough guys didn't go around sorting out lost loves. But even if some people viewed it in that unflattering light—he preferred to think of it simply as a policeman's puzzle—Jack knew the real folly lay in keeping secrets from the one person he most needed to trust.

So when she asked what he had been up to, he told her everything.

After he'd finished there was a pause, so long he began to think that he'd made a big mistake. "You still there?" he said nervously.

"What? Oh, darling, of course. I'm just—well, kind of amazed."

"You think I'm being stupid?"

"No, darling! I think it's wonderful. You're wonderful. I just never realized you were such a romantic."

"For Christ's sake, don't spread it around."

She laughed. "Don't worry. So—how's it going?"

"What?"

"The search, dummy."

"Nothing yet, but it's early days."

"Well, just promise. The minute you do find her, you let me know."

"I notice you didn't say if."

"That's right."

"The reason I came to this damn island is that it's the only lead I have. Reddski's sister said that Doris was working here as a nurse."

"Yes. I was there."

"But 50 years ago, for Christ's sake. She may not be here anymore. She may not be anywhere. She may be dead."

"Are you telling me—or yourself?"

"I'm just saying—this is probably a wild goose chase. Don't expect too much."

Margie said quietly, "Oh, you'll find her, all right."

"How do you know?"

"A feeling."

"Ah!"

"But my feelings have always been pretty damn correct."

"Really?'

"Well, darling—think of the one I've always had about you."

THE NEXT MORNING, he got going again. First he first phoned the numbers that hadn't answered last night, disposing of several: then on down the list.

In two hours he'd reached the three-quarter mark. Just 15 fresh numbers to go. Not even a sniff of a positive response. By noon Jack's voice was growing hoarse; he began to feel considerable respect for people like telemarketers, who talked on the phone for a living—he was as exhausted as if he'd spent a hard night on patrol.

And now, despite his mental preparations, the hopelessness of the task was seeping through his defences. *Why in hell are you doing this?* a sly voice began to whimper after each negative response, which now seemed almost inevitable. At that point there were five names left on the list.

He put down the phone, intending to knock off for lunch. Then he thought, *fuck it*, and picked it up again, deciding to at least finish this first run before taking a break.

This time, on the first number he dialled, and in answer to his very first question, the voice on the other end said, "Doris Day? Well, of course I know her. She's my aunt."

JACK WAS SO stunned he actually gasped. The phone voice said, "What's the matter? Are you all right?"

"Oh—yes," Jack said hastily. "I've been looking for Doris for a long time. So finding her—if she *is* the person I'm looking for—is a bit of a shock."

The voice, a woman who didn't sound all that young herself, said, "What do you mean, if she is the person?"

"Day is not an uncommon name. The actual woman I'm looking for would have to be older, someone who's been on Vancouver Island a very long time, and who was once a nurse. Is there the remotest chance that that could be your aunt?"

The woman's voice grew warmer. "In fact, it could. My aunt was a nurse for many years. Right here, too. Why are you looking for her?"

The reason for the quest was too personal to be discussed with a stranger over the phone. So Jack had ready a plausible story. "I believe she was an old friend of my family. I was asked to look her up, and give regards, that sort of thing."

"Oh, how nice," the woman said. "My aunt will be so pleased. She's wonderfully bright. Remembers everything about all her old friends. Who am I talking to?"

"My name's Jack Marsden. I'm from Christina Lake. I just arrived in town last night."

"Well, welcome to the Island, Mr. Marsden. I'm Violet Day."

"Hello, Mrs. Day."

"Miss," the lady said briskly. "Doris is my aunt by blood not marriage, and like her I never married. Aunt Doris is my father's sister. But let's not bother about all that on the phone. You should come out tomorrow and talk to her yourself at the party."

"Party?"

"Yes, you really timed it right, Mr. Marsden. Tomorrow we're giving her a birthday party. Tomorrow Aunt Doris will be a hundred years old."

FIVE

Anita sat in her usual comfortable chair by the big picture window overlooking the ocean. Her hands were busy with needles and wool, but she hardly glanced at them. Under her fingers—from which encroaching stiffness had not yet robbed all of the skill—the knitting grew: slowly, yes, but still even and strong.

Anita was gazing out at the magnificent view that the window afforded: the bay, the broad seascape beyond, Salt Spring Island in the middle distance and the sawtooth silhouette of the mainland mountains, crouching on the very rim of the world. This was her favourite view. But today, for all the attention she paid it, she might as well have been looking at a blank wall.

This is where the foolishness ends, she said to herself. And though she'd done it on many recent occasions, this time it was different. It was as though all past resolutions had simply been rehearsals, for an opening night that had finally arrived. So—here it was: audience seated, overture playing, curtain rising. At last the show was about to begin. If what she had in mind could be called a show.

More like a show*stopper*.

Anita smiled faintly, wondering why she'd chosen to put her thoughts in such theatrical terms. But it actually wasn't mysterious, just a way of keeping reality at arm's length with fanciful terminology. The choice of those particular terms also wasn't strange. Anita had always enjoyed the theatre. And no verbal ornamentation could disguise the central fact: she really had made the big decision.

Now there was no turning back.

Having finally accepted this, Anita switched her attention to the comfortable reality of her immediate surroundings. Beside her was a cup of tea, now cold, a saucer containing her 10 o'clock pain pill—and her precious letter case.

To her left slept ancient Mrs. Findley. Farther off in the lounge a bridge game was in progress, the four players, all in their 80s, intense and silent. Equally quiet, because he was dozing over one of the large-print murder mysteries that the mobile library delivered each Thursday, sat wafer-thin Tim Turnbull. In the polished hallway, on noiseless white runners, an aide glided by.

Silence. Of all the qualities of Arbutus Lodge, this was the most touted and prized. When Grace had surveyed the place after her mother moved in, that was the first thing she talked about. "Oh, the peace and quiet, Mother! So much nicer for you than living with our raucous little family."

Of course, that was just Grace's snide little way of reproach. After Anita's health had got to the point five years ago that she could no longer cope, Grace had demanded that her mother move in with her. There was certainly plenty of room in the rattling pile in North Van that son-in-law Tom's bloated lawyer salary allowed. But "raucous" the family certainly was not. Grace had seen to that. In fact, the distinct lack not just of noise but of any sort of joy in her daughter's home was a big reason—though not the major one—why Anita had steadfastly refused the offer. It was the silence—the one thing she actually disliked about Arbutus Lodge—that had made her think of Grace now.

Relaxing in the knowledge of her big decision, Anita now began wondering what her reaction would be.

One thing was certain: she would not blame herself.

Grace had always been a beautiful child: not sweet but clever, not loving but hugely manipulative. Most importantly, Grace had always been a ruler, a control freak. From the time she had emerged from the womb, she had demanded her own way. Whatever she decided to do, she would do. More annoyingly, whatever she decided other people should do, she'd have them do, no matter what.

Anita's own personality was strong, so she had not allowed her life, or Grace's, to be entirely ruined. But it had been a battle, not helped by the fact that she was a widow whose only ally was Grace's older sibling, a boy as mild as she was strong. Both mother and son had to struggle for independence from Grace. They'd both survived, but Anita wasn't sure how much the female battles had contributed to the path eventually taken by her son. Probably very little. But what maybe would not have occurred was the estrangement that had finally grown between them.

As for Grace, estrangement didn't come into it, since nobody could get close to her in the first place. At 17, the instant she finished high school, she had left home, a certain relief to those remaining.

For years Anita scarcely heard from her. Then, out of the blue, she received an invitation to her daughter's wedding. Tom Weber, Grace's chosen, was 15 years her senior, a recent partner in a prestigious Vancouver law firm, his face firmly turned to the warm wind of wealth. So the reasons Grace snagged him were obvious enough. Tom was a good lawyer, a plain, quiet man, overwhelmed by his stunning young wife and apparently only too happy to be ruled.

After the opulent wedding, Anita saw Grace and Tom only occasionally. Five years into the marriage, Grace had her first child, a girl, and for a time Anita travelled regularly to see them. These visits afforded some of the happiest moments of her life: the only times, as she recalled later, when the empty place that had been so long in her heart almost completely filled.

Two years later, Grace gave birth again. A boy. Just one problem. Along with her second child Grace also got religion, and not just any religion. She now became a bossy, preachy, fundamentalist Christian. Grace, the ruler, had finally chosen to be ruled. Not by just anyone, but the biggest kahuna of all, a God as intolerant and tyrannical as herself, giving her an excuse to "lord" it over everyone even more crushingly than ever.

One visit with this born-again harridan had Anita scurrying back to Vancouver Island, vowing never to return. Of course she did, but rarely. The stunned, obedient persons of son-in-law and grandchildren filled her with pity. She loved them but couldn't help them. For her own sanity, the best she could do was to stay away.

Her son, however, was quite another matter.

From the time he was very little, the boy had been as quiet and affable as his sister was the opposite. Mother and son were close, made even closer by the alliance of having to stand up to Grace. But it had been so much more than that: he, after all, was her first child.

Her love child.

When Anita had met George Gillespie it was quite obvious she was pregnant. By then—such were the attitudes of the times—she had had to quit her job and was looking forward to a bleak future, not only as a woman abandoned by her lover but as a single mom. George had changed all that.

George Gillespie was what then had been called "a goer." What he liked he went after and what he went after he almost inevitably got. Minimally educated, he'd gone to work as a carhop in Victoria's first A&W drive-in, and by the time he was 25 he owned his own A&W franchise. By his early 30s George was well on the way to riches, which was when he decided it was time to take a wife. Anita never did quite understand how this turned out to be her.

They had met under the most embarrassing circumstances: in George's own restaurant, when she'd somehow misplaced a purse and been unable to pay her bill. Then—the minor miracle. What began as an apologetic encounter with the manager (George) somehow concluded not only with the cancellation of her bill but the request to share a much finer meal on a future occasion. Of course, she thought she knew only too well what he wanted, but something about George made her accept anyway. Which had led to the biggest surprise of her life. What George Gillespie really wanted was a wife and what he finally decided he wanted in that department—even pregnant with another man's child—was Anita.

She didn't love George, not as she had the other. But, considering what real love had accomplished, maybe that was a good thing. So they were married. Three months later her son was born. And here was the remarkable thing: George was as proud as any real father could be. He acted as if the child were his own, and there grew between them a bond such as few natural parents achieve.

So Anita, though still not in love, grew very content, and achingly grateful to the man who had brought so much goodness into her life. It took a long while—so long that for a time she feared that George was infertile—but at last they had a child of their own. Her daughter was born just two days after her son's eighth birthday. Less than two years later, on his way home from a business meeting, George had been hit by a drunk running a light and killed instantly.

So, as seemed to be her fate, Anita found herself once more abandoned by the man in her world. But now she had money, respectability—and two children to raise. She cried bitterly over the loss of her kind and loving husband, though it wasn't utter desolation, as it had been with the other. Anita got on with what turned out to be a full and happy life. A life that now, through isolation and loneliness—her own stupid fault, she fully acknowledged—plus encroaching debility, was rapidly growing untenable.

A life that, she remembered with relief, was soon to reach its right and proper conclusion.

"GOOD MORNING, ANITA. How are you doing this morning?"

Anita emerged from her reverie to focus on the person who had arrived by her side. Meg Lordly, the administrator of Arbutus Lodge, was smart, attractive and the antithesis of the image implied by her name. Far from being bossy, she was quietly kind, and her skills at care, management, diplomacy and, above all, sweet sympathy were legendary. The existence of "Meggie"—as she was fondly called—was the single factor that made Arbutus Lodge a cut above most comparable establishments. So if Anita had any regrets about what she was planning, it was the bother it might bring to Meg. The manager would no doubt hold herself responsible, the consolation being that she was also the one who would actually understand.

"You're knitting again," Meggie said, retrieving a ball of wool that had fallen to the floor. "Pain a bit better today?"

Anita smiled. Who didn't when the sun of Meggie shone? "Maybe a little," she lied. "Thanks for asking."

Meggie smiled. "My job, dear. Getting better is yours."

She was winding the excess wool that had spilled from the fallen ball. Leaning to replace it on the bed, her arm bumped Anita's writing case which was positioned somewhat precariously on the side table. Anita's heart leaped as it teetered. Meg reached swiftly, preventing the case's fall, ignorant of the flood of emotions that had overwhelmed Anita: anger for not foreseeing the accident, frustration at not being able to stop it, fear at what might be revealed by the fall and, finally, horror at the consequences of discovery.

Meg. having no inkling of the significance of what had almost happened, completely misconstrued Anita's anguished expression. "I know it's terrible, dear, feeling so helpless. I also know you're in more pain than you ever let on. Next time the doctor comes I really think we should get him to increase your meds."

Anita managed to nod, in sweet knowledge that soon she'd be through with meds—not to mention the ever-growing country of pain that drugs never really vanquished—for good. And at last, when all the well-meant palaver was done, she found herself once more mercifully alone, free to pursue her own thoughts.

Unsurprisingly, they now settled on the object that had been the cause of her shock: her writing case. Specifically, she began to review her recent resolution to keep the case always near her person. This had seemed a sensible enough precaution, to protect her secret from prying eyes and fingers. Also, kind hands were ever busy, maintaining cleanliness and order, attempting to slow the galloping entropy in this haven for the decrepit; unguarded, her precious case might be moved or mislaid. Finally, since declining manipulative skills might soon make her plans physically impossible, it had seemed wise to be always in a position to practise and test.

Strangely, it had never occurred to her that keeping it close might prove hazardous in itself.

But the danger had passed so, composure recovered, Anita prepared for her usual routine. First she checked the room. Everyone was either dozing or immersed in their own affairs. No one paid her the slightest attention.

Reassured, she began her daily exercise. Carefully she leaned across and placed a hand on either side of her writing case. It was not large; it held only a small writing pad, pen and pack of envelopes. But it was solid, made of teakwood with a lot of fancy inlay in ivory and pearl, which also made possible its secret.

The revelation of this was simple enough, if one knew the trick, but it also took coordination and dexterity. Nothing that a normal person—even a child—wouldn't find easy, but formidable for anyone with encroaching arthritis. Knitting kept Anita's hands as supple as possible, but it couldn't halt the progress of the disease. So, to make sure she wasn't caught out, Anita practised her special task at least once each day.

Now she carefully lifted the case onto her lap, opening the lid and removing the contents, as if preparing to write a letter. Then, with a final cautious glance about, she began her exercise.

The inside of the case was plain, the only decoration being a line of brass studs around the bottom, echoing a similar pattern on the outside lid, all very elegant and artistic. But one of the inside studs was not just decorative. When Anita pressed, it gave a crisp little click. At the same time, she slid her other hand under the case and put pressure at a certain place on one end. For a moment nothing happened. Anita's face grew anxious. She pressed the stud harder, putting extra pressure on the outside place. This time her lower hand began to move. With a tiny squeak, from underneath the case, a panel slid slowly outwards.

As soon as this happened Anita became quite still. For a moment she stared fixedly at the odd transformation. Then, suddenly, her hand jerked, making the panel slide in and vanish.

This last movement caused pain, and Anita's face contorted in a silent but all-too-telling spasm. But it passed, replaced by an expression of huge relief. In the fullness of time, this also was transformed—into something almost resembling joy.

EMILY AWOKE TO a brilliantly beautiful morning: a leaf-dappled glow falling across the foot of her bed whispered of the dew-fresh joys awaiting in the garden. But for a while she just lay, sluggishly content, immersed in the essence of the sweet new day. Abruptly, as was her habit, she got out of bed. It was then that she had her first inkling of change.

It was not pain she felt. Not even the tiredness that had followed the "flu"—which had turned out to be the onset of her disease. No, this was different. She took a deep breath, walked about, stood still again, eyes closed, trying to figure out what she did feel. Only one thing emerged, a very odd metaphor indeed: the impression was that her whole body was coated in a fine film, through which all outside stimulus must travel before reaching her senses; as if, in all perceptions, she was one subtle generation removed from where she'd once been; everything a slightly blurred copy of the original.

Even in the shower the feeling persisted, making the water pulsation less vibrant, the soap smell less pungent, the vigorous after-towelling feel as if it were being administered to another person. At breakfast things were similarly odd. Finally, irritation masking growing anxiety, Emily pushed it all aside, forcing herself to focus on the task she'd set herself the previous day.

The quest to discover the identity of her disquieting garden guest could start, she had decided, quite close to home. That in mind, later in the morning she put on a sun hat and set off on foot for the village. Five minutes' walk brought her to the local post office. This was a wooden structure, actually quite old but recently refurbished in fake, though not too garish, frontier style.

Jewel McBride was a round, pleasant woman, who'd been post-mistress at Cobble Hill for as long as Emily had been resident. The McBrides were a family with roots going back to the earliest times. This, plus her job, made Jewel a natural source of information. She was also down-home friendly and a good talker—an obvious place to begin the identity search.

No one else was in the post office when Emily entered, which was good. She didn't want to make her errand seem too obvious or important, so she first asked for stamps.

Moving to fetch them, Jewel said, "Lovely summer, so far."

Emily nodded, her voice casual. "I think so."

"Wonderful for gardening."

"It certainly is."

"Joan Scully tells me you keep a lovely one."

"She's very kind."

"Yours is one of the oldest houses around here, you know," Jewel said. "When I was young it was a real eyesore. But then a lot of places were a bit ragged back then."

Sensing an opening, Emily said, "Well, I'd heard it was old, but I didn't realize it'd been around *that* long. I suppose it must have had a lot of owners."

Jewel's reply was interrupted by the clang of the doorbell.

"Hi, Jewel. Mornin', Emily," came a beery voice, instantly recognized by Emily as Joan's husband, Fred. Fred Scully drank too much, but he was a pleasant enough fellow and good to Joan. Showing no hint of impatience, Emily made some small talk while he concluded his business. No other customers arrived so, after Fred had given her a not too politically correct pat and ambled off, Emily got back to the matter in hand.

"We were talking about my house," she said. "Did it have a lot of owners?"

Jewel shook her head. "Actually, no. Not many at all."

"Oh?"

"The original place must have been built just after the turn of the century—the 20th century, I mean. You have to remember to say that now, don't you?—by the Gregorys. They were one of the first families around here. Settled just after the railway came through." She chuckled. "And related to mine, I've heard, in more ways than I care to tell."

"So—these Gregorys owned the house a long time?"

"Oh, for always. They built it. Children took it over. One of the grandchildren, Luke Gregory—a cantankerous old fart, if there ever was—lived in it alone forever. He was still there, scratching along, letting the place go to wrack and ruin, even after I started working here. But he finally died and the house was sold."

"When was that?"

Jewel scrunched her brow. "Let me see. I started here in '75—no, '74—and we reorganized the sorting room in 1980. Old Luke was still on the route then, but not long after that he kicked it. That must been—about 1982."

"I bought the place in '88."

"So—between then and you, let's see ... " Jewel closed her eyes briefly, scanning a mental route list. Then she nodded to herself, smiled in satisfaction and said with quiet finality, "Just one!"

To cover her excitement, Emily pretended to look for something in her bag. When she could trust herself to sound casual, she said, "So he—or she—must have been the last owner before me. Would you happen to remember the name?"

Jewel shook her head. "No. Except that it was a man, I do remember that. Just a minute, I can find out."

She disappeared into the back, and Emily realized she had a problem. Inevitably, Jewel was going to ask why she wanted to know about the previous owner. But then came a stunningly sensible realization: the shock of her garden discovery had made her paranoid beyond all sense. For heaven's sake, no one could possibly know the true reason for her inquiries. She could make up any old excuse she liked.

This belated wisdom brought great relief. And when the postmistress returned, she didn't even ask right away why Emily wanted the information. She just said cheerfully, "Yes, I was right. It was a man. His name was Trevor Devereaux."

Jewel didn't know much about Trevor Devereaux, other than that he had lived alone, and restored the house and garden. "He didn't do much of that stuff himself, though."

"Oh?"

"Well, he was one of those bureaucrat types. Bigwig down in Victoria, as I recall. He had a whole bunch of contractors doing renovations and working on the grounds and fences and plantings before he even moved in. After that he kept to himself. Which is why—busybody that I am—I remember so little about him, I suppose. Why are you interested?"

Freed from her earlier paranoia, Emily was unfazed. "Oh, you know academics," she smiled. "Even retired, we can't stop poking into things. I got to thinking—I've been here for years and I hardly know a thing about my own little house, or who lived there or anything."

Jewel nodded, cheerfully. "I wish I could tell you more. But, as I said, Mr. Devereaux was very private. I think I heard that for a while he had a relative living with him, but I can't even be sure of that." She glanced at the clock on the wall. "Goodness, where did the morning go? Anything else I can for you do, before I close for lunch?"

Emily headed for the door. "No. Thanks for your help."

Jewel followed Emily so that she could lock up behind her. But just before she closed the door, she said, "Oh—one more thing I just remembered about Mr. Devereaux."

Emily stopped, feeling a prickle at the back of her neck. "Oh?"

"It was a rumour going around at the time."

"What was it?"

Jewel's expression was amused, skeptical, but without guile. "Well, I realize you can't believe everything you hear—but the story was that Mr. Devereaux didn't just sell up and move away."

"So—what?"

"The story is he *vanished*."

JOSEPH COULDN'T SLEEP, so he decided to go for a walk. He passed Roy's room quietly, but there was little need for stealth. The younger man was sprawled face down, blissfully unconscious. As Joseph slipped through the kitchen, the clock said 2:50. Letting himself out, he checked that he had his key and was reminded of the time, two days before, when he had arrived home to find the house in a shambles. That in itself had turned out to be unimportant. What was subsequently revealed, however, had been deeply disturbing; which, no doubt, was why he was now having so much trouble getting decent rest.

Joseph walked out the front gate, crossing Dallas Road and heading along the cliffside walk. The air was midsummer still, the sky a star-specked hood. A low-slung moon trailed a silver slick on the blackness of Juan de Fuca Strait.

He walked for a while, soothed by the exercise, enjoying, despite inner turmoil, the sensation of his body gliding through the crisp gloom. He came to a place where the land bulged to form a park. Here were small trees, slanted by the prevailing winds, flanking an open sward with benches. This was one of the most popular walks in the city; only in this deepest trough of night could Joseph's presence have been so completely solitary.

He sat on one of the benches, gazing out at the dark water. His focus fixed on a faint cluster of brightness in the far distance: a cruise ship drifting east, heading for Vancouver or the Inside Passage to Alaska. He watched the lights distractedly, his thoughts having returned to the place where they now seemed irrevocably trapped. In his mind, by some arcane logic, two things had become intertwined: the ancient saga wherein his lover had become a killer, and the even older story of his relationship with his own mother.

The first of these was the most worrisome, yet it was not the actual deed that preyed upon Joseph's mind. The perpetrator, after all, had been little more than a boy, caught in circumstances beyond his control, defending his own life and that of another. Knowing Roy, Joseph was absolutely convinced of the truth of that. What concerned him was not what had happened but its still-potential consequences, prompted by the same thing that had freaked out poor Roy: the discovery of the remains in the lake, a location so remote it would seem the bones would be lost forever.

Yet, by a quirk of fate, they had been discovered. After half a century. So, how much more likely was it that a body, stuffed into a shallow backyard grave, would eventually come to light. If that happened, there'd be little trouble establishing its identity, since Trevor had owned the property and there would be a record of his disappearance. After that, despite Roy's precautions, it was not impossible that a link might be made between the two of them.

Joseph knew full well the infinitesimal chance of any of this. It was simply the possibility that haunted him. Despite an unorthodox private life, he had put all his energy into creating a world that was quiet and unremarked upon and, above all, safe. To have this kind of shadow hanging over him was more than he could bear.

So what was to be done?

The worst thing was that he had no idea. Save for the unthinkable notion of Roy turning himself in, there seemed to be no solution.

Except to wait and hope, possibly for the rest of their lives. Also unthinkable.

Damn!

With this conundrum circling ever more tightly in his brain, Joseph finally realized that he'd better let it go. These concerns were merely theoretical, but they still had the potential to drive a person crazy. Luckily—or unluckily, depending on the point of view—there was one sure way to be diverted from a worry: replace it with another.

Joseph did have another concern conveniently to hand: his newly rekindled awareness of the sadness, the utter absurdity, of the situation between himself and his mother. How could it have happened? More important, how in hell could he have let it go on so long?

His real appreciation of the situation had come crashing home after the funeral of poor Marcel McGinty. He could still see clearly the bemused look on Roy's face after he'd tried to explain his long neglect. He remembered the all-too-tactful remark: "Excuse me, sweets—but it seems like something pretty strange is going on here … "

That was putting it mildly. Yet somehow it had never occurred to him just how completely he'd abandoned the one person who had truly cared for him. What could have made such emotional amnesia possible? Well, the trigger to that process was at least clear: as he'd told Roy, the falling-out he and his mum had had, following the astonishing revelation about his dad. The fact that George Gillespie was not his real father at all.

Of course, such a discovery would be a shock for anyone. But, since he had perished before Joseph was 10, only the sketchiest of memories of the man remained. And after that Joseph and his mother became close in a way that otherwise mightn't have been possible. Friends, confidants, actual allies against his own sister, Grace, who was a born candidate for Ruler of the Western World. When—to the relief of both—Grace had moved out, Joseph and his mother had been perfectly content together.

For a while, anyway.

At that time they lived in Duncan, a town 60 kilometres north of Victoria. His mother had grown up there and, after George Gillespie's death, she moved her family back. Duncan was okay but, in those days, no great place to be gay. Joseph was discreet and had never actually been bothered, but the older he got the more confined he felt. The fact that his mother accepted his sexuality was wonderful, contributing vastly to his emotional stability and making him, as Roy never tired of saying, the "straightest gay guy around."

But, as Joseph reached his late 20s, broader pastures beckoned. First, he got a transfer to his bank's main branch in Victoria. Then, blaming the arduous commute, he revealed to his mother that he'd found himself an apartment in the city.

Which was when it all went wrong.

The first surprising thing about his mother's response was its stubbornness. She seemed unwilling to grasp that he was actually leaving. She thought he was teasing. When he'd finally convinced her otherwise, she pretended that his decision was no more than a whim. In reaction, all the anguish of his life poured out: a gay man, stuck in a small town, where he couldn't come out even if he dared, living in circumstances that made it impossible to have any kind of relationship.

This last confession prompted an even more unexpected reaction. "I don't see what you want with relationships. I thought you were happy here with me."

He sighed. "Of course I'm happy, Ma. But I'm a grown man. Sooner or later I've got to have a life of my own."

"A life without me, you mean."

"Why do you put it like that? I just mean—well—a home of my own. With maybe, sooner or later—you know—a partner."

"So it's a partner you want?"

"Well, of course! Doesn't everyone? And—look, I'm sorry—but I'll never find one living at home with my mother."

He hadn't meant to put it quite so strongly. But it seemed to do the trick, for his mother blurted, "All right, go on! If that's what you want. Go and find your damn 'partner.' Go away and leave me." Then, after a pause, she added, "Just like he did."

Joseph stared, astonished by her last phrase. "Do you mean Dad?" And when she just looked at him in a confused sort of way, he continued, "Oh, come on, Dad didn't leave us. Not in any way he could help. He was killed, for heaven's sake."

After a pause she said softly, "I didn't mean him."

"Then who are we talking about?"

In reply to which, in a sort of compelled monotone, low but very distinct, she said, "I'm talking about your *real* father."

And then it all came out: how his mother had been pregnant when she met George Gillespie, how he'd married her anyway and loved and treated Joseph like a real son, how George was the best thing that ever happened to both of them—a saint, oh, yes. But throughout these revelations, startling and sad as they were, not one more reference was made to the one person who, presumably, had started this whole chain of events, the man who, by the fact of his leaving, Joseph was now supposedly emulating: his astonishingly revealed biological father.

When the story was done, with no further mention of this shadowy personage, Joseph said, "So, Ma, who was he?"

Which was when he got his biggest shock. For all that greeted him was silence.

"I mean this man who made you pregnant. Did you love him?"

Nothing.

"Well, where did you meet him?"

Nothing.

"At least tell me his name."

Still nothing—nothing at all. To all further questions and pleas the same response: dumb silence. Having revealed one astounding, life-altering detail, that Joseph's father was someone completely other than the historical record, his mother refused to follow up with a single word on the subject. And although it was tempting—indeed he did try—to think that this was all a trick, a punishment for his abandonment of her, in the end he couldn't believe it. Whatever else, his mother wouldn't stoop that low. He knew her too well. So the only explanation was something much simpler: the shock of his news had brought forth not a lie but an unintended truth, something she'd never meant him to know, a part of her life that had caused her such grief, or shame, that she refused to revisit it again, even to help her own son.

Only one reference was ever made to the devastating blow his mother had delivered that night, and not until the next weekend, when he moved out for good. As Joseph paused at the door, very quietly, almost to his back, she said, "I'm sorry. I wish I'd never told you."

Hardly a week after he'd set up his new place, his mother visited. She cried and apologized for being so stubborn and selfish. She loved him. She really did want him to have a life of his own. She just missed him, that was all.

He told her he understood and that he loved her and missed her too—all of which were true. Yet now things were different. They both knew it. Not because of what had been said, but because of what, apparently, could not be.

Because Joseph's real father was never mentioned again.

After that, it seemed everything changed. Not obviously, not immediately, but subtly and incrementally. Being in the city, alone in his own place, brought not only freedom; a whole layer of personality, repressed, or perhaps merely delayed, by the living with his mother, now had room to grow. This did not mean a change in his outer demeanour; he had no need to express his sexuality in any new flamboyance. Apart from the conservative persona required by his bank job, with which he'd always felt quite comfortable anyway, he simply felt no urge for the more colourful excesses favoured by some of the gay community. But still, the inner Joseph was now quietly glowing and, above all, free.

But that new freedom meant something else: he saw less and less of his mother. After a while, without apparent intention, they seemed to drift into a paler relationship, which, by infinitesimal stages, evolved into no relationship at all. Joseph could not remember any actual decision to stop seeing his mother, nothing so upfront and honest. No. What had happened, as he now sadly admitted, was much more insidious, a slow evolution into a life that had no place for the person who had loved him longest, with no understanding that the change was happening, hence no need to examine the situation, let alone do anything about it.

Abandonment by default.

JOSEPH STOOD AND walked down to the cliff edge, gazing at the rocks and gentle swell below, with an expression that would have alarmed an observer, had one been abroad in this deep end of the night.

But although his look might have been mistaken for anguish, it was in fact resolve. Despite the appearance of desperation, his stance was the result of relief: release, as from a long, long confinement.

Then—like some druggy idiot, as he recalled later—he actually cackled aloud, for the solution to this heavy half of the double bill of angst that had lately rocked his tranquil world was so simple that just by acknowledgment it was halfway to done.

For God's sake—all he had to do was go see her.

The eastern sky had a distinct pre-dawn glow when Joseph arrived back at the house. Pausing only to remove his runners, he flopped straight into bed. Aglow with the relief of decision, he slid into sleep, being wrenchingly awakened, it seemed a mere heartbeat later, by a raucous alarm on a dazzling day.

Feeling as if he'd been hauled through a wringer, yet more content than in a very long time, Joseph shoehorned himself out of bed. Passing Roy's room, he saw that his partner was snoring softly and, incredibly, had apparently not moved a muscle. Joseph grinned and moved on to the kitchen.

While waiting for his tea water to boil, he was already making plans.

ANITA LAY WIDE awake. The light was off but a full moon hung in the clear sky, the blue-white glow streaming through the window so bright as to almost give the sensation of day. When Julia, the night nurse, had come around earlier she'd wanted to close the curtains, but Anita had stopped her, claiming she loved the moonlight, and that it would not spoil her rest. Unmentioned was the fact that she had no intention of sleeping anyway, that she was especially enjoying this peaceful moon—since the sight of it would be her last.

The angle of the light did not find her face, which lay in safe and secret shadow. But it did illuminate much of the bed and a wide square beyond, reaching to the open door of Anita's small, private room. It also threw into sharp relief her bedside table, the water glass on the table, the clock and, comfortingly close, her writing case—the blessed instrument of imminent release.

The clock read a few minutes before 11:00, so there was still plenty of time for remembrances and peaceful contemplation before the deadline: an hour late enough that her efforts wouldn't be interrupted, but leaving sufficient time for the results to be irreversible.

That was the most important thing of all.

In a mildly euphoric way, Anita had seen herself using these last hours to recall the happier moments of her life. Inevitably, *he* would claim a disproportionate share of such thoughts; *he* who had caused her greatest happiness, yet whose faithlessness had also been the instrument of her worst misery. But that was all right. After all, she'd kept his memory on a leash for so long that, even if it broke free now, she doubted if it had the power to harm. And even if it did—not for very long.

Anita had also expected to think about her children: the sweeter times when they had been little, before one had grown tyrant and the other had turned—or been turned, she couldn't forgive herself for that—away.

But now, as she lay in the moon-drenched night, her mind clear, her body free of its usual jazz combo of small agonies, she found herself thinking not of family, but of someone who'd played a late and relatively brief role in her life: Simon Stanfield, the sweet old bad actor.

He who had given her the writing case. In fact, honesty made her admit he hadn't actually given it: more like lumbered her with it, and by chance.

Simon, as he'd never tired of relating, had been trained in England. "At the Rose Bruford School, don't you know: patronized by dear Larry Olivier," he was forever saying. But unlike "dear Larry," Simon's talent had been distinctly limited, his meagre assets his somewhat stagy looks and his undeniable charm.

Arriving from England in the 1950s, Simon had settled in Toronto, becoming part of the small acting community there. He'd plugged away, getting small parts and commercials, looking for the "big break," which in Canada then meant the Stratford Festival or some TV work, and which never came. Liked as a person, he gained the undeserved reputation of being unintelligent. In fact, he was simply one of those sad souls, sprinkled through all the arts, cursed with the desire to create but little feeling for craft. However, Simon was a sticker, remaining, struggling and semi-starving, in an unforgiving profession for over 30 years. Finally he ended up in Vancouver where, having weathered enough to become a usable character, he at last began to get some steady work. This led to a stint with a young company in the town of Chemainus, on Vancouver Island, and this was where his path had crossed Anita's.

Anita was fond of live performances and had patronized the

Chemainus Theatre since its opening. She would take friends to dinner there, or just go to a show by herself. On one of the latter occasions, following a spirited revival of *The Importance of Being Earnest*, she got chatting with an acquaintance and when the talk ended she realized she was alone in the foyer. Then the performers appeared, homeward bound, and Anita recognized the actor who'd played the Reverend Chasuble. Anita said hello and told him how much she had enjoyed the show and particularly his part. This delighted the actor, leading to an invitation to coffee.

Thus began a friendship which, though intermittent and quite platonic, became an interesting part of her life. Anita soon realized Simon's acting limitations—Chasuble was the best thing she ever saw him do—but she was charmed and genuinely warmed by the man. For his part, Simon seemed astonished and flattered, acknowledging, when they knew each other better, that he had few real friends.

Friends were all Anita and Simon would ever be, but it was a relationship which grew surprisingly important. She saw him act in several shows on the Island and—combined with semi-reluctant visits with her daughter—made trips to Vancouver to see Simon perform, or just to see him. As they got to know one another better, he would come to the Island for return visits. Totally at home with Anita by then, Simon would bunk on her couch, and they would walk and dine and watch TV and chat whole weekends away.

She and Simon got on together, Anita realized, like two old girlfriends. This didn't mean he was like a woman; being an actor didn't make him gay, though he might have been. In all likelihood he was just neutral, or past being interested. What he did have was a woman's sensibility, which allowed them a rare level of communication.

Simon had a makeup case, which for an actor was natural enough. What was unusual was the case itself, an exquisitely inlaid wooden box. He always had it with him, whether he was working or not. When Anita commented on this—it was late one evening after they'd had long talks over a not-meagre amount of wine—her friend had become uncharacteristically grave.

"There's something you should know about me, dear heart," he'd said. "Ever since I was young I've had an absolute terror of being old."

She had laughed. "Goodness—join the club. Growing old frightens everyone."

He shook his head with surprising heat. "No, dear, I didn't say growing old—I can stand that. I said *being* old."

"Being, growing—what's the difference?"

"Anita, sweetie, the difference is everything in the world. Growing old is unavoidable. It happens to us all, and with luck it can happen with some kind of grace. Being old is very different. It's the end result of the process—the 'sans teeth, sans eyes, sans taste, sans everything' result, as the Bard so aptly put it. The filthy, undignified wind-down of the whole sad shebang that can sometimes drag on for years. Well, dear heart, all my life I've been determined that such a fate will never befall me."

She'd stared in incomprehension. "How can you stop it?"

Wordlessly Simon rose and fetched the article that had begun the conversation. "You were asking about my makeup case, wondering why I always take it everywhere? Okay, I'll show you. But you have to swear to keep this a secret. Do you swear?"

"Of course, if you think it's so important."

"And another thing. If you don't like what I show you, or don't agree with my plan—there'll be no arguments or reproaches. Just say so, and we'll never speak of it again. Agreed?"

Intrigued, Anita agreed.

Simon upended the case, leaving its contents on the table. He brought it back empty, showing her a row of ornamental studs on the inside. One of these he pressed firmly, *click*, and a small panel slid out from underneath.

Behind the panel was a shallow depression, a secret compartment large enough to hold jewellery, or some small, precious object. Its contents, however, were not riches. Revealed was a strip of cotton batting and underneath that a slim paper packet. Simon removed the packet, opened it, then slowly—a trifle theatrically—upended it over his open palm.

Anita wasn't sure what she'd expected, but what appeared were perhaps a dozen plain white pills. Feeling a certain sense of anticlimax, she said, "What on earth are those? Aspirin?"

Simon smiled gravely. "The Aspirin of the gods, my dear. Seconal."

"Seconal?"

"The most powerful of barbiturates, don't you know. These are super-strength. Got 'em in Mexico—where they don't bother with doctor's prescriptions—years ago. One puts you out for a night, two for a day, while half a dozen … "

He didn't finish. He didn't need to. It was all instantly obvious. For anyone who couldn't face the idea of being marooned alone in decrepitude, here, in Simon's innocent-looking case, was the solution.

Lying now in the moonlight, looking at the case and thinking of Simon, Anita was struck by the irony of how things had turned out. Because less than a month after revealing his secret, her friend had made his final exit entirely without its help, courtesy of a sudden and massive stroke.

This had happened on a fine evening in the middle of Anita's own living room. One moment Simon had been chatting, stepping briskly to fetch another glass of vino; the next he'd dropped like a stone, as if felled by an invisible poleaxe. Anita dialled 911 and medics arrived swiftly, but she'd known he was dead.

Simon didn't have family in Canada. If there were English relatives Anita had no way of finding then. As for friends, it seemed that she was it. So Anita arranged the funeral, announced the death in the Vancouver and Toronto papers and, it seemed, was the solitary mourner. Simon had few possessions, little in the bank and no will. Finding no one to claim the trifles her lonely friend had left behind, Anita wound up with them by default. Simon's personal things she burned, his clothes went to the Salvation Army. His makeup case she kept—because it had been his and because it was beautiful.

For a long time she all but forgot its secret.

Now the moonlight was almost gone. The clock on the dresser said a few minutes after midnight. So deep was the hush that Anita could hear the soft squeak of the nurse's footsteps approaching from the far end of the corridor. In a moment she would poke her head in for a last check, and that would be it.

And so it turned out. The nurse appeared, shining her discreet light in the direction of the bed. Anita pretended to be asleep and the girl departed.

Free at last.

Now that the time had come, Anita found she was quite calm. Slowly, deliberately, she eased herself up on her left elbow. The effort caused a chorus of miseries to mutter through her joints, but this only spurred her on. At last she was ready. She would clasp the case with her right hand, slide it off the dresser and help support it with her left as she brought it onto the bed. This was the most hazardous part. If she lost control and the case fell, not only would it make a horrific racket, but there would be no way she could retrieve it.

When she reached for the case she didn't try to move it immediately. She made herself pause, taking several breaths and preparing for the real agony that would explode when she made her big move. At last, as ready as she would ever be, Anita gripped the case with her right hand, slid it forward, and twisted her other arm around as it crossed the crucial gap. This resulted in a riot of tortured nerve ends. Anita all but screamed aloud.

But the case successfully made the trip, landing with a soft thunk on the bed. Afterwards, with it secure under her throbbing hand, she leaned back, panting, eyes tear-damp, as the pain slowly ebbed.

Now all she had to do was open the panel and extract the contents, a move rehearsed earlier today. The water glass was comfortably close. Once the Seconal tablets were in hand, the final act would only require a moment.

Anita meant to take the lot.

After downing the pills, she would close the secret compartment and return the case to the table. So, when they found her, no one would know the truth. With luck it would be assumed that she'd simply passed away in her sleep. No recriminations or embarrassment. Most important: nobody would be held responsible.

Now all Anita had to do was get on with it, and she was completely ready. She lay back, relaxing, preparing.

It was then that something frightening occurred. Into her mind, without warning, and so powerful that it could not be blocked or ignored, came an image: a single, shattering memory. This recollection was ancient, but crystal clear, as if imprinted yesterday. It was *him*: Johnny. His fine, strong, hopelessly loved and half-century-missed face, in that last aching moment, as he'd grinned at her—oh, so sweetly, so believably—from the window of his departing pickup.

Three days he'd be gone, he said. Just long enough to drive to his parents' farm in the Interior, break the news about their marriage, then return. She'd pleaded to go too, to meet his family. But no, they were strange and old-fashioned, he said. Catholic and foreign-born. It needed to be broken gently. Especially the fact that he wasn't going back to the farm. That definitely had to be done alone.

So she'd let him go. Naively believing those words, uttered only so that he could get what he—what all men—wanted, she'd given herself to him. He'd promised to marry her and love her forever, then he had run off, never to return. And later, after all the heartbreak and betrayal, what had she done? Why, spent the rest of her days pining for the fool, poisoning her life with denial and regret. Finally, as if this wasn't enough, she had driven away the one good thing that Johnny had left with her: his son.

To whom only once, in spiteful anger, had she revealed a mean morsel of the truth.

Faced now with the image of the one she'd denied so long, the one she'd expected this night to elude, exhausted by her physical effort and betrayed by her own fatal memories, Anita had no hope of suppressing the tide that welled up inside. From awful depths it came, with unstoppable force. Her body was wracked with a storm of sobs, harsh and relentless, which made every arthritic joint shriek in protest.

However, despite her heaving chest and shaking limbs, and the hot tears that seared her cheeks, Anita suffered her torment in complete silence. No alert was sounded, no official presence arrived to subvert the course of fate.

After a while the storm abated. Exhausted, Anita lay back. Only after a very long time did her brain resume function. But when it did, tortured and harried as she'd been, there was no lessening of resolve.

And so, having survived the final test, Anita lay quiet, grasping her precious case and waiting for a last small portion of strength, all that would be needed to provide relief forever.

SIX

J ack realized he should have known that it could never have been that easy. To search for a person, the only lead being that she was a namesake of Doris Day, a star whose fame had itself long receded into the movie vaults of history, was unrealistic enough. But to have expected, after half a century, to find that individual simply by making a few phone calls was in hindsight beginning to seem sadly deluded.

By this time it was late and he was feeling exhausted and not a little stupid. He got himself a beer, drank half of it in a few gulps, then sprawled on the bed, wondering what the fuck he was going to do now. He dragged out the ring and examined it. The relic glimmered in his hand, a taunting message from yesteryear, inspiring not a single new or clever idea.

What in hell did he imagine he was doing anyway? Here he was, a policeman, for Christ's sake; solid RCMP jock, veteran of 21 years of no-nonsense cop life, in the midst of a quest that might be the plot of some romantic chick movie. Hardly surprising that it hadn't even occurred to him to contact the local law, to enlist the police apparatus in his search. Well, of course it hadn't; whatever the wisdom of this enterprise, one thing he didn't need was to become a laughingstock.

He put the ring away, finding himself with only one concrete thought: right now he wished that he was back home putting the make on sweet Margie. Which was definitely the most sensible thought he'd had all day. So he hauled the phone onto the bed and called her. "Jesus, girl, I wish like hell you were with me," he ended up saying.

Her presence came drifting through the phone like warm summer. "Me too, darling. No luck with your search then?"

So he told her everything that had happened, culminating with the fiasco of the century-old Doris. Margie laughed hard and that made him feel a lot better. Nevertheless he said, "I reckon I'm gonna pack up and head back tomorrow."

Margie's reaction was unexpected. "Well, Jack, nothing could make this lusty lass happier than to have you sashay into her bedroom tomorrow night. You know that."

"But   ?"

"Well, doing this—this sweet and funny hunt you're on—it's such an unlikely thing for you that I think somehow, deep down, it's something you must need."

"Why?"

Margie laughed, but without humour. "Darling, I wouldn't even try to tell you that. You'll have to work it out for yourself. But, much as I'd love to have you back, I think, since you've gone this far, you should really keep at it a bit longer. "

"I guess you're right."

Suddenly Margie gave an odd little squeak. "But listen, copper, you got me so involved I forgot the news."

"News?"

"Yes. I got my vacation pushed forward. I finish at the end of the week. So—what I'm thinking now is since I've never seen Vancouver Island, and since I miss my old copper something cruel, maybe Doug and I should pop ourselves on a plane and come join you."

The surge of elation that hit him then was so intense that he actually cackled like an idiot. "It's terrific. How soon can you get here?"

"Saturday. Soon as I can get a flight. I'll let you know later in the week. Okay?"

"About as okay as it gets."

"Thanks, Jack, you're sweet. Oh—before I hang up there's something else I wanted to tell you. An idea that might help find Doris."

"Shoot."

"Well, maybe you're looking for the wrong name. I mean, just because Doris didn't get to marry Johnny doesn't mean she never married at all. In fact, she most likely did. So why not find out if her name is on a B.C. marriage certificate some time back then? Go to the archives, or wherever it is you find such things. Then, if you discover that she married, you'll know who it was, and you'll have a new name to carry on your search. What do you think?"

"That you're a genius. That if you were a cop you'd probably be my boss."

The next morning he got going right away. The BC Archives, he'd ascertained, were downtown near the legislature, beside the Royal BC Museum. He found the place easily, discovering that the archives were on the lowest floor, approached by a walkway through a garden of native plants surrounding an ornamental pool. They were entered through a heavy wooden door, inside which all was quiet and warmly serene. There was a small vestibule with an inquiry desk manned by a uniformed attendant.

Jack approached the desk, standing behind a neat-looking woman in her 60s who had just preceded him. She was renewing her visitor's pass, something Jack realized he also would need. The procedure seemed simple enough, involving little more than the presentation of satisfactory ID. As her application was being filled out, the woman smiled apologetically at Jack. "Sorry to keep you waiting," she said. "These things only last a year, and mine always seems to have run out just when I want to use it again."

"That's okay. I'm in no hurry."

The woman gave him a quick smile, at the same time looking a trifle surprised, an expression that swiftly passed. Her completed card was produced and, apparently well versed in the procedure, she was already signing the visitors' book as Jack went to commence his own registration.

Then something unexpected happened. As the woman finished signing and turned away, heading for the door to the archives proper, she stopped dead. This was so sudden that Jack almost cannoned into her back. Starting a ritual apology, he realized that she was quite unaware—she seemed to have fallen into a dead faint.

Training and quick reflexes came into play. Jack took a single step, his arms shot out, and he had the woman supported before her buckling knees could deposit her upon the floor.

The woman seemed to have hardly any weight at all, lifting her was like holding up a child. Jack took another step and leaned down so he could see her face; she opened her eyes, looking so startled and afraid that Jack almost dropped her again.

But he didn't. Instead, feeling her returning strength, he half let her go, at the same time assuming his practised, authoritative-but-reassuring cop face. "It's okay, Ma'am," he said. "You're okay now."

Then the woman surprised him once again. Her fear vanished entirely, replaced by an almost beatific smile.

"Yes," she said, staring deep into his eyes. "I know, dear. And I'm just so glad it's you!"

EMILY HAD BEEN about to ring the bell when Fred Scully opened the door. He was evidently on his way to work and though his face had its usual flush, his eyes were clear and sober. He was cheerful and, Emily noted, remarkably presentable.

"Oh, hi, Emily," Fred rumbled, his beery voice filled with such genuine goodwill that, as usual, Emily found herself liking him, despite the mess he continued to make of his life and Joan's. "I'm just off for another day of torment," he continued. "Joan's here. We were just talking about you." Fred grabbed Emily, but not in his usual mildly lecherous manner. "Emily, Joan told me your—ah—bad news. Rotten luck, old girl. I'm sorry, so very sorry." He squeezed her arm and hurried out, leaving Emily not knowing whether to laugh or cry.

She pulled herself together, moving toward the back of the house, calling as she went. "Joan, hi!"

Joan was in the kitchen. The big woman moved quickly to her friend, enveloping her in a fierce hug even before her first greeting. Emily sat while Joan poured her tea, finally saying, "I saw Fred as I came in. He was—very kind."

"Well, I thought you wouldn't mind me telling him." Joan placed the tea in front of Emily. "And my poor old guy was actually quite devastated."

Emily smiled gently. "Yes, I could see that. I was very moved."

"Hon, he likes you. And in spite of everything, he's a sweet and thoughtful man. If he'd only cut back on the booze a teeny bit, I think we could be very happy." She laughed, more with resignation than bitterness. "But that'll happen, right? Enough about us. How are you?"

Emily told Joan about the odd feeling she'd experienced earlier, of all her senses being at a slight remove from any outside stimulus. This had been alarming, since it was probably a harbinger of things to come. Though her first instinct had been not to mention it, she was telling Joan because, though still determined to keep her illness private, she was equally resolved to hold nothing back from her friend.

Joan looked pleased, and seemed to understand that that was all Emily wanted to say, so the talk moved on to other things. After a while Emily said casually, "I've decided that this summer, I want to do some research on my house."

"To find out when it was built?"

"Oh, I already know that. Jewel McBride said it was around 1905. No—what I'm interested in is the people. Who lived in it. Their history. That sort of thing."

Emily had spent some time contemplating whether to tell her friend about the bones in the garden. In fact, wanting to share her strange knowledge with at least one soul, she'd been sorely tempted. But she had to admit that asking Joan to keep such a secret would be unfair: too much unasked for responsibility.

"For instance," Emily continued, "I'd like to find out about the last owner, the one who renovated the house so tastefully and started my beautiful garden. Now that must have been one fascinating person."

Joan looked thoughtful. "His name was something French, I think. But I can't remember what."

"Actually, I do know that much. It was Trevor Devereaux."

"Of course. Now I remember."

"That's something else I found out from Jewel."

"She would know, wouldn't she? Being postmistress and living round here forever. What else did she tell you?"

"Not much. She said he kept to himself."

"Well, that I can vouch for. In all the years he lived across the street, I doubt we spoke 10 words."

"So you don't remember what he looked like?"

"Only that he was an older person, I think, but not old. Silver hair, anyway. Sort of severe looking. Neat and really distinguished. That's about all."

"Jewel said she thought he was a civil servant in Victoria."

"Yes, I think I heard that too. But hold on, I heard something else, come to think of it."

"What?"

"That the man just up and disappeared."

"Yes. Jewel told me that too. What do you know about it?"

"Not much. I just recall the house was empty for a while. Then this rumour went around about something strange happening. You know small towns and gossip, you can't take it seriously. Anyway, it didn't last. Nobody knew Mr. Devereaux so it was hard to miss him. I doubt if I would have thought of him again if it hadn't been for an odd little piece in—I think—the *Times Colonist*, a while later."

"What did the paper say?"

"Oh, it was just a general piece about the dangers of foreign travel. How more and more Canadians seemed to be getting mugged and even murdered abroad. Among the examples, it mentioned our Mr. Devereaux who, they said, had gone on holiday and vanished. Evidently, the only clue was his car. It was found abandoned at the Vancouver airport."

Thinking of the quiet bones in her garden, Emily gave an inward grimace. If their owner was whom she suspected, then the airport car must have been a red herring; the "dangerous travel" for poor Mr. Devereaux had occurred no farther abroad than his own backyard. But she just said, "Well, that's very interesting. Thanks."

"You're welcome. Not much use in the research on your house, though."

"Perhaps not," Emily said quietly. "But every little bit helps. And something I've always found with research—you often can't tell which information will turn out to be the most important."

And those were the last words they spoke about Trevor Devereaux.

At home Emily found herself, almost without conscious voli-tion, in the garden. The fact that her guest—her *companion*, as she'd almost come to think of him—was no longer an anonymous stranger but almost certainly a respected civil servant, thought to have van-ished abroad, was actually somewhat welcome. For although Emily held no belief other than that the bones were just inanimate stuff, she couldn't quite dispel the sensation of loneliness that their dis-covery had invoked. Not only had a life been ended here; an entire persona, a history, had been summarily capped, thrust away beneath the silent earth with no one to know or care. That thought—more than any nonsense about actual spirits—had begun to haunt her. So the idea of the lost one having a life, and of herself, still, if temporar-ily, among the living, learning about that life, somehow made Emily feel considerably better.

She now knew his name and even something of his business. Sketchy though this was, it was a start. In Emily's imagination, the lost soul was being coaxed from the shadows, revoking its imposed state of non-being. This was not an exercise in ethics, morality or even logic. It was just a mind game. Little more than therapeutic poetry, and pretty cheap and sentimental at that. But for her it was necessary. It brought relief. Considering the oblivion yawning in her own near future, the notion of bringing to some poor spirit, even within the frail fabric of fantasy, the gift of acknowledgment, was something that Emily found almost mystically sweet.

This was all well and good. But what she did not feel, she discov-ered, was any lessening in her actual curiosity. If anything, its intensity grew. Inevitably, that led to another question: what was she going to do next? One line of action presented itself. It probably wouldn't be hugely fruitful, but it was the only thing she could think of. So well before mid-morning she was heading south in her little Subaru.

When she left home the sky had been slightly overcast, but as she came down from her beloved Malahat Mountain Drive, through the green chasm of Goldstream Park, she emerged into sunshine. Victoria, due to its location between mountain chains, enjoyed better weather than many parts of the region, a fact that often made it the butt of not-unenvious jokes by those living nearby. Emily, for her part, considered the marginally cooler climate north of the Malahat a small price to pay for the rural peace of Cobble Hill.

She was thinking of none of this, however, as she drove south on Highway 1, which eventually became Douglas Street, ending in downtown Victoria. She had again become aware of the strange cushioning of sensory input that had overtaken her earlier. It was quite subtle now, little more than a lessening in the familiarity of driving, and she had managed to put it aside entirely by the time she reached her destination.

Only when she went to sign in did she realize that her visitor's pass must be hopelessly out of date. But the process of renewing it was routine. She knew the attendant on duty at the desk, an older fellow, pleasant but renowned for his persnickety attention to detail. The man recognized her too, greeting her familiarly. "I'm afraid my pass has expired," Emily said.

"Yes, it certainly is a while since you've been in," the man said. "Well, we'll soon get you straight."

He fetched the form and she produced her ID and dutifully set to work. Presently the outer door opened, letting in another customer. Glancing around casually, Emily noted that the newcomer did not have the appearance of the people—students, academics or scholars—who typically frequented places like this; he was fortyish, tall, muscular and good-looking, an image more easily associated with sports bars than musty archive stacks. But immediately she felt embarrassment at the cliché. Heaven knows, there was hardly such a thing as a "typical" anyone anymore.

Still, there was something more interesting than the non-academic appearance of the man. Somehow he seemed familiar and it took a moment to figure out why. When she did, Emily was a trifle shocked—it was because the man quite markedly resembled her own father.

It was a tribute to Emily's knowledge of the archive rigmarole that all of this took place while she was busy filling out the form. At the same time she even managed to smile politely at the man himself. "Sorry to keep you waiting," she said, indicating her task. "These things only last a year, and mine always seems to have run out just when I want to use it again."

"That's okay. I'm in no hurry," he smiled, and Emily was freshly intrigued.

Normally, even if a person possessed a superficial resemblance to another, it diminished with the actual use of the features. But in this case the smile heightened the likeness, taking Emily right back to when she was little, a time when her dad would have been about the same age as this man right now. A trifle perturbed now, Emily collected her pass and turned, but, as she did so, an extraordinary idea came into her mind.

This was something that never in her life had she even vaguely anticipated. Now it burst upon her, so shockingly that she stopped in her tracks. At the same time there arose from inside a rapidly spreading numbness, akin to the sense-dampening she'd experienced earlier but swift and cruel. This was accompanied by a roaring in her ears and the onset of actual darkness which, starting at the periphery of her vision, proceeded to obliterate the world. Emily experienced a fleeting sensation, not of falling but of floating free, as if the shock of intuition had released her from all earthly bounds. She had an instant of euphoria, of pure, unsullied grace.

Then there was nothing.

"OH DEAR, I'M really sorry to have been so much trouble."

"Nonsense. It's no trouble at all." Jack deposited a cup of tea beside Emily, putting down his own cup and taking a seat. They were in the museum coffee shop upstairs from the archives. Physically, Emily was feeling almost completely recovered. Her mind, however, resembled a train wreck.

After the strange occurrence below, when she'd fainted dead away, consciousness had returned almost instantly, to reveal that she was in the arms of this stranger. Even more surprising were the words that she'd heard issuing from her own mouth. "I'm just so glad it's you." What had that been about?

Well, of course, the trouble was—and it made her want to hide her head as she realized it—she now knew perfectly well. Despite her fainting spell, her thought sequence before and after was quite clear. When she'd originally seen this man he'd reminded her of her father, so later, in that first instant of re-emergence, finding herself staring into those hauntingly familiar features, she'd momentarily thought that's who it was. Natural enough. Certainly no cause for embarrassment.

But she *was* embarrassed. As she sat sipping tea, one part of her mind marvelling at how easy, normal and even relaxed she'd begun to feel in the company of this stranger, another part was wrestling with something else entirely: not just the fact that she'd fainted, nor that this had caused the sort of unseemly commotion she abhorred. Not even that she had mistaken the man for her parent. No, the basis of her unease was something else, something more.

Something she did not—or could not, or would not—let herself remember.

She sipped her tea, forcing herself to concentrate on the person who was sitting opposite.

"I've just realized," the man was saying, "that in all the excitement we never actually introduced ourselves. I'm Jack Marsden."

Both relieved and amused by the mundaneness of this exchange, Emily told him her name.

Jack extended his hand across the table in a quaintly formal gesture and Emily took it. His grasp was warm and strong. Somewhat disquieting, however, was the hint of sternness and practised interrogation with which he regarded her. "You know, I'm still not entirely comfortable with not getting you proper help. Are you sure you're okay?"

Emily withdrew her hand. "Yes, thank you—as okay as I'm ever going to be." Damn! She hadn't meant to say that, hinting at things she had no intention of sharing with this stranger. Hurriedly she added, "For someone of—my age, I mean."

I Ie smiled. "You don't look very old to me." And then, as if he'd overstepped some mark of propriety, he quickly continued. "So—Emily—what brought you to the archives today?"

"Oh, research." Emily realized that here was yet another thing she didn't want to talk about. So, before he could say, "Research on what?" she continued, "And you? Are you doing research, too?"

"I guess you could call it that. Actually it's a bit of a long shot. I'm trying to find someone—er—a relative. But I've been having trouble, and I only know her maiden name. So I thought—it was my girlfriend's idea—that if I could find the record of this woman's marriage, it would give me another avenue to follow."

"Good idea. When was she married?"

"Well, it would have to have been some time after 1950."

Emily shook her head. "Ah!"

"Excuse me?"

"I'm afraid you've come to the wrong place."

"How's that?"

"In this province marriage records are only made public after 75 years. So unless your relative was married before that time, you won't find it in the archives." Jack looked somewhat more than routinely gloomy, so Emily added, "You could possibly get your information somewhere else. At the provincial registrar's office, maybe. Though I couldn't say offhand what their access and privacy policies are."

"Thanks," Jack said. "I'm new at this sort of thing, which must be pretty obvious."

"We all have to start somewhere … "

Emily trailed off. She'd been looking at Jack, wondering who he was trying to find, and why, since she was a relative, he knew so little about her. Then, triggered by this speculation, something else happened. It was like a bright light turning on in her head, an explosion of understanding: no, recollection. What had finally come back was the thought she'd had just before fainting.

In fact, she realized that this could even have caused the faint. Had she not been sitting now, it might have happened again. As it was, she gave a hard gasp.

"What's the matter?" Jack said quickly. "Are you feeling bad again?"

Emily shook her head, but the shock of her idea was still reverberating and so was the understanding of why her mind had suppressed it, for the notion was wild and foolish—and agonizingly possible.

The extraordinary thought was this: perhaps Jack Marsden had the look of her father for the simple reason that he was actually a relative. Her son?

When Emily, just days before, in reaction to the news of her fatal disease, had told Joan the bizarre story of her birth, and how she had given her own baby up, her assertion that her subsequent life had been free from all thoughts of the child was not precisely true.

Certainly, she'd never consciously wanted children. At no time had she longed for the patter of tiny feet, to provide purpose, fill a void, or otherwise give flavour to her neat and cosily academic existence.

Even in her briefly promiscuous youth, sex had seemed a poor reason to become tied to another demanding human being. And she'd not needed either the security or the psychic immortality supposedly conferred by offspring.

And yet, at the very deepest level, there had always been an awareness of—what? Absence? Not exactly. Incompleteness? Thinking of it now, all Emily could come up with was a feeling, at once despised and irresistible, that, from the very onset, this moment, whatever its portent or conclusion, had been inevitable. So without giving herself the chance to ponder, or to let timidity pull her back from the brink, she said, "Marsden. That's an interesting name, English, of course, but not common around here. Are you from Victoria, Mr. Marsden?"

"Jack, please!" he said quickly. "No, I live in the Interior. Christina Lake."

"A very lovely part of the country," Emily said, and then, before the frightened part of her brain could pile on yet another platitude, she took the plunge. "Do you have family? In Christina Lake, I mean."

Jack shook his head. "No. Well, Margie—my girlfriend—and her son are there. But my ex-wife and daughter live a bit farther away. In Winnipeg, unfortunately."

"Which means you don't get to see your child very often?"

"Not as much as I'd like, no."

Emily tried to look concerned. But she had other fish to fry and now that she had started, she wouldn't let herself be sidetracked. She took a deep breath and, trying to make her voice as casual as possible, said, "And the rest of your family—your parents—are they a long way off too?"

Jack nodded. "Even farther, actually. Ontario."

"Ah!"

"Though, to be honest, that's not a great hardship. I've never been very close to my folks."

"I see."

Emily's face, which she was trying to keep impassive, must have registered at least some of her excitement, because Jack reacted as if she'd actually voiced the question that engulfed her, or as if he'd read her thoughts. "Mind you," he said, "I'm not sure that's surprising. That we're not close, I mean."

"Oh?"

He shook his head thoughtfully. "We never really got on. Not from the time I was a little kid. Later, after I'd left home and gained more perspective, I wondered if it really would have made one hell of a lot of difference."

After a pause Emily asked, "What?"

Now Jack looked startled, as if he were being asked to explain something she already knew. He said, "Why, I meant if they'd been my real parents—if I hadn't been adopted."

Emily sat as still as stone, but her heart had begun to pound painfully. And though she felt no return of the earlier faintness, she was glad she was safely sitting. After a bit she tried to take a sip of tea, but her hand quivered so badly that she dared not. So she lowered her head and closed her eyes, hoping desperately for the reaction to subside.

And yet at the same time she was exultant. This was without doubt the most extraordinary confluence of her life. Nothing as important had ever happened—would ever happen—again. This was a moment that, by all laws of probability, she should have entirely missed. As it was, this returning, realigning, reuniting, this full turn of the life-wheel—had actually come to pass.

Flesh that was her flesh, flesh that had been sundered, forgotten, rendered into irrelevance by ignorance and uncaring; against all odds that flesh had reconnected. Blissfully unconcerned about the conscious plans of both parties, their bodies had somehow travelled to this point of contact, unerringly homing in upon the commonality of their genes. All of this ran through Emily's mind in less time than it took her to decide that she really shouldn't yet risk trying to take another sip of tea.

So instead she said quietly, "Jack, tell me—what's the date of your birthday?"

Jack told her. After that, Emily actually *did* faint again.

SEVEN

Joseph decided to phone the number he had for his mother at the earliest reasonable hour, and the least likely to draw attention to the appalling lapse of time since his last contact.

In fact he had called this number only once before, five years ago, when his mother had moved into Arbutus Lodge. And even then he hadn't actually spoken to her. Previous to that she'd written him a note, briefly explaining the move and relaying her new address and phone, but containing no hint that she ever expected him to visit. Unreasonably put out by the implication that she knew him so well, he'd called the number anyway. He got the Lodge office and said that he was the son of a new resident. The woman on the other end had sounded pleased, wanting to put him through to his mother right away. But in the end he'd chickened out, simply giving his name and phone number—"in case of emergencies"—and lying that he would call back later.

Emergencies? Right! Like to let a crippled old woman's self-absorbed, asshole son know that his mother had croaked, finally relieving him of the last vestige of need to ever bother about her again.

Joseph pulled himself up short: that kind of thinking was something he'd studiously avoided in the past. Now it was even more important not to fall into the guilt trap. Recrimination could so easily, he well knew, become a substitute for action.

So act he did. Just after 8:00 he picked up the phone and got straight through to the Lodge office. When he stated his name and asked to speak to his mother, the person at the other end didn't seem in the least fazed that this was the very first call he'd made in years. Instead, she just said, "Oh yes, Mr. Gillespie, but I'm not sure whether your mom will be up yet. I'll just send someone to check. Hold on."

It was as simple as that.

But not quite. When the woman came back on the line, she said that Mrs. Gillespie was still sleeping, which was unusual but a good thing, since her arthritis had been giving her bad nights of late. They didn't like to wake her, but as soon as she roused herself they'd be sure to let her know he'd called.

On the spur of the moment, Joseph told her not to do that. He preferred to come personally and give his mother a surprise.

The woman sounded surprised herself, leaving Joseph to think that she well knew the extent of his delinquency. "Oh, she *will* be thrilled," she said. "Will you be here today?"

Faced with the brutal immediacy of what he seemed to be doing, Joseph hesitated. "I'm not sure. What are your visiting hours?"

The woman chuckled. "Goodness, Mr. Gillespie, this isn't a prison. We like to think of it as a real home. We don't have hours." She might have added that if he'd ever actually visited the place, he'd know that. But she said, "Any time will be just fine."

"Thank you," Joseph said, adding somewhat pathetically, "you've been very helpful. Goodbye."

Hanging up, he realized that his heart was pounding.

Despite his hesitation when asked about the timing of his visit, he realized with relief that this was due merely to nervous excitement. His determination to see his mother was still as strong as ever. The only question now was when. He poured himself more tea, put bread in the toaster and began seriously to consider when exactly he would go.

His first idea was simply to throw on clothes, get in the car and head out. At that thought his heart sped up again, and his whole body experienced an anticipatory tingle. But his old cautious nature prosaically reasserted itself. This was the middle of the week, for heaven's sake. His appointment calendar was chock-a-block, accentuated by the rescheduling of several customers who had been cancelled due to the big drama with Roy. That that event had also been the catalyst to bring him to his senses, vis-à-vis his mother, was all very fine, but a reawakening of filial feeling was no reason to neglect his clients.

So, he just couldn't just go right then. On the other hand, he didn't intend to let work become an excuse for putting off what now had become of overwhelming importance. Really, the answer was pretty clear: by the time Joseph had started his second piece of toast, his plan was complete. Instead of his usual power walk to work, he'd take the car and leave it in a nearby parkade. Then, as soon as his last appointment was done, he'd get the hell away and be out of town comfortably ahead of the rush hour. That would put him over the Malahat and in Duncan by 5:00. And 20 minutes later ...

Yes!

Sitting at the breakfast table, morning light enveloping him like the glow of new-kindled life, Roy's gentle snores chuckling comfortably down the hall, Joseph sighed with satisfaction, feeling a weight lift in a region he'd hardly known existed. At that moment, for the first time in longer than he could remember, he felt completely whole.

ANITA MOVED TOWARD the light.

In fact, she seemed to have been doing this for some time. She couldn't understand where she was, or what she was doing, or even the significance of the light itself, though in some small corner of her awareness there was an understanding that what was happening was very important.

This moving, this journey, which seemed to have been endless, did not involve physical discomfort. This was surprising. In some dim memory, it seemed that for a long time, her whole world had revolved around pain. But there was no pain now. No physical sensation at all. Just a marvellous buoyancy of thought that bore her seamlessly, causing her whole being to vibrate in time with the pulsing brightness that drew her inexorably on.

And then, as time passed, without surprise, she realized she did know what was happening. Of course! With that knowledge came joy, ecstasy so radiant and pure that, had it been possible, she would have screamed aloud with pleasure.

For now she knew the truth: she was dying. She was finally embarked on the wondrous journey so long anticipated.

To him!

How long had it been? An age. An eternity of despair. A bitter eon since that never-to-be-forgotten moment when he'd stolen himself from her life.

The wonderful one. The loving, lying logger. Her own lost Johnny.

But now the waiting, the longing, the pain and regret—all were over. She knew where she was headed; this going toward the light was just a beginning. Beyond, waiting—as he'd always waited—was her best love.

Now it seemed that up ahead the quality of illumination was changing. At the very centre of the light field appeared a small region of shifting colour. Featureless white was drifting into palest blue, a solidifying area that gradually took on the shape of a rectangle, higher than it was wide.

A portal.

Just as she'd been expecting.

The non-physical nature of this non-place again prevented her crying aloud, but bliss was carolling in Anita's brain, she whom Johnny had always known as Doris, so it didn't matter that there was no voice. Anyway, now she was almost at the portal. Around her, above and below, the great entrance loomed. She was passing through, and now she could hear something. An actual physical voice. It was calling her name.

"Anita. *Anita!*"

I'm coming! Darling, I'm coming, Anita cried in her mind. Certain that she knew who had called, she looked about but could not see a soul. Then she laughed as she understood why: she couldn't see because her eyes were closed.

So she opened them.

She was lying in a place filled with light. But this was not the radiance of the heavens; rather it was the brisk glow of morning in a perfectly ordinary room.

Her room.

Beside her loomed a figure, but not that of a man and certainly not any lost love. In a scramble of returning consciousness she recognized Meg Lordly, the kindly administrator of Arbutus Lodge, hovering by her bed. "Goodness, dear, you were in a doze," Meggie smiled. "The nurse said you were sleeping late, but for a moment I almost thought you'd—left us."

Anita gaped at the woman as understanding brutal as ice water sluiced her brain: she was alive. This was followed by a second deluge: bitter disappointment. But before that could take hold, yet another emotion overrode all else: horror.

So it had all been a lie. A delusion. Simon Stanfield's magic pills must have been old. Or maybe they weren't Seconal at all, just fakes some Mexican conman had palmed off on her foolish friend. In any case, here she was, awake, compos mentis, already beginning to feel the throb of her arthritic joints—and doomed to stay this way into some unbearable future.

"Damn!" Anita said.

"What, dear?"

"I—er—didn't mean to sleep so late," Anita began, then her hand knocked painfully against something hard. Wincing, she glanced down—to discover her writing case still where she'd placed it before taking the pills the night before.

And it was … undisturbed. Secret compartment closed. Most importantly, not returned to the table to cover her tracks, as planned.

Which could only mean that after the pain and exhaustion of getting the case onto the bed, plus the emotional storm induced by her unexpectedly powerful recollections of Johnny, while waiting to regain strength for the final deed—she'd instead fallen asleep.

And that had to mean—she hadn't taken the pills at all.

Anita laughed.

It was a joyous, spontaneous explosion, and though it caused a harmonic tremor of miseries throughout her whole frame, for a while she couldn't stop.

"Goodness," Meggie said, "you *are* in good form today." She leaned across and picked up the writing case. "But it's lucky this didn't fall off in the night and wake up the whole shop. Well, no harm done. I'll put it back on the table." She did so, smiling indulgently. "By the sound of that laugh, my guess is that today you're feeling a bit better."

Anita had stopped laughing by now. The echo of the movement still sang a sickening pain-song in every nerve end. But joy at her reprieve was such that the agony was a sort of anthem, a hymn to the knowledge that she had not, after all, lost her means of exit.

"I am feeling better," Anita said. "For a minute there I didn't think I was, but yes, I am."

The understatement of the year.

Meggie, as was her habit, stayed and chatted for a bit. Anita made automatic responses but had no idea what was said, too consumed with raw relief to think of much else.

Later, an aide arrived and helped her dress. It was always a slow and painful process but today she endured it with a light heart, and was soon ensconced in her favourite chair in the lounge. When her morning meds arrived, a residue of euphoria tempted her to ignore the pain pills, but she wisely resisted this foolishness: with the endgame still unplayed, she was going to need every bit of strength and agility her besieged old carcass could muster.

For the rest of the morning and then through the long afternoon, Anita went slowly and patiently through her usual routine; reading for a while, taking a long lunch in the pleasant dining room, socializing with a couple of friends and one of her favourite nurses, knitting, napping: anything to pass the time, and to give the appearance of a very ordinary day.

Her writing case was where Meggie had put it, safely on the table by her bed. No more clandestine rehearsals for the opening of the secret compartment were needed. She could do it, she knew that. Last night's ridiculous failure weighed on her mind a little, but not overmuch. Considering what might have happened—the case falling off the bed, the discovery of her pills, the vanishing of all possibility of release—she was aware that she had been vastly lucky.

So with equanimity and a light heart, Anita went about her routine and waited. At last the afternoon was over. Supper came and went: Anita managed a creditably hearty meal, considering that it was her last. Immediately after supper, feigning a headache, she obtained assistance to get to bed early.

Once there and safely settled, the last request she made to the departing aide was for her writing case to be put on the bed beside her: after all, since not a soul knew of its secret or her intentions, why on earth not?

Once alone, she opened the hidden compartment. Removing its contents took only a moment. Soon she had the precious pill packet safely stowed beneath her pillow. That was all there was to it. Without haste, she closed the compartment. During no part of the operation did anyone even pass her door. So, when it was finally done, this monumentally important act, it turned out to be so uneventful that Anita was almost disappointed by the sense of anticlimax.

Almost but not quite. Mostly she felt satisfaction. Cautious triumph. Soon, when things quieted down—as early as possible but not so early as to cause undue concern—Anita would put out her light. But just before that she would take the pills.

Then, in the safe and blessed dark, the journey that last night had only been a frustrating dream would become reality.

JOSEPH HAD INTENDED to be out of the office by 4:00.

However, it turned out to be not quite so simple. His final client for the day, an old customer who did a lot of business with the bank, was in the midst of a complex deal and it took Joseph a good hour longer than anticipated. He wasn't ready to depart until well after 5:00. By the time he'd edged, crawled and cursed his way out of the parking building and was finally nosing up Douglas Street, now thoroughly stuffed into the belly of the evening commute, it was getting on for 6:00. So much for a swift exit from the city.

But the woman at Arbutus Lodge had said there were no fixed visiting hours and Joseph reminded himself not to get in a fret. He still had plenty of time. His mother did not even know he was coming. When he did arrive she'd probably be less than thrilled anyway;

he mustn't let his refurbished filial feelings blind him to that. Early or late, what did it really matter?

Creeping along, waiting to reach the relative freedom of Highway 1, he nevertheless couldn't stop a simmering feeling of unease. He tried to tell himself that this was simply delayed shock, a reaction to the excitement of his mother-epiphany and the dramatic step he was taking in an attempt at reconciliation. He tried to reassure himself that it was simply an attack of nerves.

Somehow he couldn't quite believe it.

By the time he neared the end of the freeway north of town, traffic was really zipping along. The freeway itself ended at a set of lights, beyond which the road narrowed before climbing around the mountains. By this point most of the commuter crowd had peeled off, so he should be able to maintain a good pace for the rest of the trip. With luck, he might even reach his destination by 7:00.

The last lights were green as Joseph's car approached. He was in the outside of the two through lanes, just one car was in front, Joseph 30 metres behind. It looked like they would both make it through the green but the amber flashers that signalled an imminent light change came on. The car ahead speeded up. Joseph did too. Suddenly he became aware of another car—an old but swift Porsche—passing fast on his right and squeezing in front at the last moment. People did that all the time at this intersection. "Damn idiot!" Joseph muttered, as the Porsche passed not only himself but also the vehicle ahead, cutting in so hair-raisingly close that, in reaction, he hit his own brakes, convinced that there was going to be a crash.

The Porsche shot by, honking and sashaying its cheeky ass. The car it had cut off blared its own horn in fury and followed fast, but Joseph was the one most affected by the near-catastrophe. His instinctive but needless application of his own brakes was much faster than his recovery. For several seconds he continued to brake, then came a crash—from behind.

His car bucked violently as it was shoved forward. Joseph's body jerked. His head snapped forward, then back, saved from deadly whiplash only by the solidly mounted headrest. For a frozen instant it seemed as if the whole world was about to explode.

Then, as swiftly as it had begun, the rear-end assault was over. Instinct must have guided Joseph's hands, for later he had no memory of getting his car onto the shoulder. Next thing he knew he had stopped and there was someone tapping urgently on the window.

"Sir—sir! Are you all right?"

Joseph shook himself. The window tapper was a young woman. Fumbling, he lowered the glass.

"What an awful thing!" the woman said. "Are you okay?"

"I think so. How about you?"

"Oh, I'm fine. I tried not to hit you, but when you braked like that I just couldn't stop in time. I'm terribly sorry."

"No, it's my fault," Joseph said. "I thought there was going to be an accident and I guess I sort of panicked."

They continued in that manner, each taking the blame, a polite Canadian dance that ended with damage assessment—remarkably little to either vehicle—and the exchange of addresses and licence numbers. When it was over, the woman, still apologizing, got into her car and drove off. When Joseph turned the ignition key of his own vehicle it refused to start.

By that time the clock on the dash said 6:45. If things kept going like this, Joseph realized, his mother would soon be in bed and asleep. That thought brought a fresh wave of irrational anxiety. But he squelched it, trying to concentrate on the problem at hand.

In all likelihood the car trouble hadn't actually been caused by the accident. Lately he'd been having difficulty starting with the engine hot, a problem that usually righted itself when it cooled. So, feeling easier, but still giving a curse that he'd forgotten to bring his cellphone, he settled stoically to wait.

Then he realized something else: dummy, he'd just passed a Shell station. They'd certainly have a pay phone. With a sigh of irritation but also relief, he walked back to the station, which took all of three minutes. "Thank you for using Telus," the idiot automated voice chanted, then his call went through. The phone at the other end began to ring. It rang and rang. At last, darkly convinced that it wasn't going to be answered, he was about to hang up when the ringing stopped. A woman's voice said, "Arbutus Lodge. Good evening."

Joseph didn't say a word. So sure had he been that he wasn't going to succeed that he was momentarily struck with dumb surprise.

"Hello," the woman said. "Are you there?"

Joseph coughed, spluttered like a fool. "Yes," he said at last. "This is Joseph—er—Mrs. Gillespie's son, Joseph. I'm on my way up from Victoria, but I've had a small car accident. If I arrive in about an hour do you think that would be too late?"

Suddenly he was sure she would say not to come, and he was relieved and glad and disappointed and guilty, all in the same giddy instant. But the cheerful voice on the other end said, "Oh, no, Mr. Gillespie."

"I'm too late?"

She laughed. "Sorry—I meant, no, it's not too late. An hour from now would be just fine."

"I see," Joseph said lamely.

"But, wait a minute," she continued. "I've just remembered. I saw your mom a while back, and I think she may have been on her way to early bed. Do you want me to check?"

"Oh, yes. Thank you."

"Okay, hold on."

There was a clatter as the phone went down. Joseph, waiting, refused to let himself speculate further about a single damn thing. This emotional roller coaster was really too exhausting. If the news was that his mother was asleep, he'd turn around and come back tomorrow. It was really quite simple. After all these years, what the hell could one more day matter?

The phone was picked up again. "Your mother's light is still on," the woman said. "Shall I tell her you're on your way?"

"Ah …!" Joseph replied, with all the decisiveness of a dithering fool. His instinct was to tell her no, that he wanted his visit to be a surprise, but he was also worried by fears that he was actually hedging bets, retaining a last chance to change his coward mind. Finally he was saved by a simple equation: it was better that his mother be ignorant, surprised if he did come and not disappointed if he didn't leaving the onus for correct action entirely on himself.

"No, don't tell her," he said at last. "But I *will* be there. Just as soon as I can."

"All right then. We'll expect you when we see you."

"Fine. Goodbye."

He hung up and headed back. Now all that was needed was some co-operation from the damn car.

MEG LORDLY WAS exhausted.

What was supposed never to happen at Arbutus Lodge had happened yet again—for the third time this month—and, naturally, it was she who had ended up carrying the slack. On this occasion it had been the usually reliable RN, Stephanie, who had unaccountably failed to appear at shift change. So Meg, who had started at 8:00 in the morning, had to fill in, and all her administrative chores had piled up, keeping her at her desk hours after what was supposed to be quitting time.

It was her own damn fault, of course: her good will, huge energy, attention to detail and genuine love for a vocation that enriched the lives of so many older folk all meant that she also found it impossible to restrict herself to mere management. Whenever one of the nurses or aides needed help or couldn't handle a situation, it was Meg who was called upon: get someone up, calm someone down; soothe, explain, confide, chat, encourage, reassure, patch, pacify and entertain; this was part of her ongoing routine. The old darlings—all of whom she loved dearly—thought of their Meggie variously as friend, daughter, nurse, servant, confidante, and sometimes even parent, but they made it clear they depended on her entirely, ensuring that on most days she was cheerfully run ragged.

What with the absence of one staff member, the death of one of the residents—a regular but always sad occasion—plus several of the small emergencies that always seemed to come in clusters, today had been even more hectic than usual. For Meg it had involved 11 hours either at her desk or on her feet, with barely a pause for a nibble or a cup of tea. Now, as she finally finished the last piece of paperwork and rose, preparing for escape, the remaining energy seemed barely enough to carry her to her car.

She put on her jacket and hadn't reached the door when the phone on her desk started to ring. *Damn!*

Meg had no obligation to answer. If the phone rang long enough, one of the night staff would respond. Meg knew this but paused anyway, the insistent sound nagging at her well-honed sense of duty and order. Oh, well—how long would it take? She sighed, returned to her desk and picked up the phone. And recognized the voice on the other end right away. It was the man who had called earlier in the day, the son of Anita Gillespie: the son who lived only an hour away, but in five years hadn't come to see her once.

This morning he'd sounded uncertain and embarrassed—as

well he might, considering his appalling record. But for his mother's sake Meg had been professionally neutral, giving no hint of her awareness of his delinquency. Still, he'd sounded intelligent, and she had an idea he knew exactly what she was thinking. The reason for his call, astonishingly, was that he intended to visit. Meg hadn't disguised her delight, telling him how thrilled his mother would be. She'd also asked to give Anita the good news and was disappointed when he'd said he wanted his appearance to be a surprise.

Later, during the long and demanding day, the impending visit had often come into her thoughts. Of all the residents of Arbutus Lodge, Anita was one of the most pleasant and, though she lived with much pain, had the fewest complaints. Affable to everyone, she nonetheless possessed a quiet substratum of melancholy.

Anita did have a daughter, a creature of demanding demeanour, whose rare visits seemed to cause less pleasure at their advent than relief at their conclusion. After Meg had known Anita a while, and they'd developed a degree of intimacy, she got the feeling that, even more than the ever-present pain, what really haunted the old woman's life was loneliness. There had been some sort of falling out in the family, long ago—that much Meg had pieced together. What had occurred was never revealed, but Anita seemed to be haunted by a deep sense of loss, aggravated, if not necessarily caused, by the absence of her son. Meg's feeling was that she blamed herself for the situation.

Despite all this, the old lady had always been surface-cheerful, among the most stable of Meg's charges. So it had been with vague disquiet that she had viewed her friend in the last weeks. For Anita had changed.

This was subtle, noticeable apparently only to the administrator herself, but it was definitely there. What illogically worried Meg was that this change seemed to be for the better. If anything, Anita was more resigned, more serene: paradoxically, in inverse proportion to the disease consuming the last shards of her comfort, she appeared increasingly at peace.

It was a sad fact that folk with arthritis, despite the cruel attack from their immune systems, could sometimes survive in agony for a very long time. Anita was one of these, with a constitution that might well force her to endure years of torture. Yet lately, the worse things got, the less she seemed to mind. It was all very puzzling.

In the last weeks, these concerns had been increasingly on Meg's mind, so that morning, when the surprise call had come from the long-lost son, she'd almost seen it as the answer to an unconscious prayer. More than anything, Meg would have loved to break the good news about the visit. But she'd been told not to, so she couldn't; of course, this was wise, since nothing could be worse than the crushing disappointment if the prodigal should change his mind.

Busy as Meg's day turned out to be, the promised arrival of the son stayed with her. As the hours passed and no one appeared, she reached the sad conclusion that he wasn't coming after all, an emotion mitigated only by the knowledge that Anita herself had been spared the disappointment. It was only much later, settled in her office, tiredly wrestling with the last tag-ends of bureaucracy, that she'd finally forgotten the worrying business. But then, when she actually heard that voice again on the phone, it all came back.

She resisted the irritated urge to demand an explanation from the idiot, which was fortunate, since it turned that out the cause of his non-appearance was a car accident. He wanted to know if it was too late to come now, the answer to which in most circumstances would have been a brisk "Yes." But, having found with relief that Anita's light was still on, she couldn't resist telling him to come anyway. *Come. Just come, damn you! Come and get it over with*, she'd thought, receiving assurance that he would be there in an hour.

Once more, he declined permission for news to be given that he was coming.

Having hung up the phone, her own work done, there was nothing left but to leave. Meg would have loved to hang about, a happy spy when the meeting finally took place, but of course that was ridiculous. So she packed up and, fatigue descending upon a body that was beginning to feel older than her charges, headed for her car.

She reached it, got in and started the engine. But she didn't drive off immediately. Happily, or was it a bother, she couldn't quite decide, she'd begun to have another thought ...

THE CLOCK ON the table said 7:30.

A few minutes ago someone had come along the corridor almost to Anita's door, giving her a small start, but then retreated without looking in. Since then, apart from the faint snores of ancient Mrs. Leoni in the next room, canned laughter from the lounge TV and the distant, lonesome bark of a dog, there had been blessed peace.

Now it was time.

After stowing the little pills safely under the pillow, inches from her hand, Anita had been comfortingly aware of their presence. At last the moment had arrived to let them do their work.

Well—almost arrived. Remembering the recent near-visit, she decided to play it safe and wait 10 more minutes. By then the interval needed for her clumsy hands to perform their last, vital task would surely be free of interruption.

Tonight there would be no slip-ups. Tonight she felt coldly purposeful and very clear. The turmoil of emotion that had exploded after the savage flashback to Johnny, and the subsequent exhaustion that had derailed the previous night's intentions, were thoroughly over.

This time the job would get done.

Anita lay comfortably, the misery-chorus in her joints muted by the extra pain pill she'd taken to ensure maximum mobility, her mind, blessedly, a near-blank. To keep it that way, to give her thoughts a simple point of focus—thus guarding against any repeat of last night's problems—she kept her eyes steadfastly upon the clock. This was a sturdy article with a face large enough to be read easily from the bed. Its sweeping second hand moved in a stately arc, which Anita now counted eight times. At the commencement of the ninth circuit, she reached beneath the pillow and took out the paper packet. By the middle of the tenth she had positioned this securely in her left hand while, with the stiff but determined fingers of her right, she pried open the flap.

She now raised the packet, peering inside. There they were: a heap of small white blobs, about a dozen, looking just like Aspirin.

Release. Peace at last.

But now the moment had finally arrived, Anita felt no exultation. No apprehension either. Not even relief. What she felt—all she felt—was a numb resolve, the solitary focus of her retreating world. This steadied her as, very carefully, she poured the pills from the packet into the cupped palm of her left hand, poked the empty packet back into the writing case, slowly returned it to the table and prepared to complete the operation.

Her plan was safe and simple. She would take a couple of pills, wash them down with water from the glass on the table, then take a couple more, repeating the process until all the Seconal was consumed. Only one modification was allowed in this careful procedure: the first time she would take just one pill, making sure that it could be easily swallowed before increasing the dose.

In fact, there was no trouble at all. Although slightly larger than her regular pain pills, the first tablet slid down easily, helped by just a small gulp of water. With relief, Anita took a deep breath and was preparing to transfer two more pills to her mouth when brisk footsteps sounded in the hall.

For a moment she couldn't move a muscle. She just sat, frozen, while the footsteps rapidly approached. Only at the last instant did the fingers of her left hand close over their tell-tale contents—and a split second later a face appeared around the door.

It was the administrator, Meg Lordly.

"Hello, dear," Meggie said brightly. "Well—I see you're still awake."

Anita didn't say a word. Shock, guilt and fear erupted with a mind-bending jolt so fierce that it was all she could do not to shriek aloud. Fortunately, she didn't. What did occur was that her whole body convulsed, and though some water spilled from the glass in her right hand, her left snapped even more tightly around its secret.

"Oh, I'm sorry," Meg said. "I didn't mean to startle you."

Anita, whose mouth was alarmingly agape, managed to shut it. Shock evolved into something more manageable: self-preservation morphed into useful rage, so that even though her left hand burned with the knowledge of its forbidden cargo, the rest of her could don the convincing disguise of annoyance.

"I was just going to sleep," Anita snapped.

"Of course you were. I'm so sorry, dear. I didn't mean to disturb you." Meg's manner was cheerful, but even in her shocked state, Anita sensed that the visit was not as casual as it seemed; the younger woman was hiding something.

She knows! Anita suddenly thought. *She's found out what I mean to do and come to stop me.*

But the panic caused by this notion evaporated as soon as it arose. For the feeling from Meg wasn't that. Rather, what she was hiding seemed more akin to embarrassment—no, not exactly that either—nervous anticipation. That was more like it.

"I was just on my way home," Meg said, with almost a stammer, "and I—well, seeing your light on, I—I thought I'd say goodnight."

"Oh," Anita said, her composure now recovering rapidly. "That's nice. It's a surprise to see you so late."

"Yes—well—I was just passing so I ... Goodnight, again."

"Goodnight."

Meg smiled, uncertain and now definitely embarrassed. She turned as if to leave, then swung back again. Smiling even more uncertainly—almost foolishly—she hovered in the doorway.

What on earth was going on? Anita had now become so intrigued that her own surprise and fear were quite forgotten. For heaven's sake, was the woman going to leave or not? Finally, it became obvious that Anita herself was going to have to say something.

"Was there something else, dear?" she asked.

"No," Meg replied, and then, quickly, "Yes!"

"Oh?"

But having committed herself thus far Meg didn't say another word. For several moments, as Anita stared, Meg just stood there, an array of conflicting emotions washing across her features with such speed that the result was almost comical. She herself seemed to become aware of this. She gave an embarrassed cough, closed her eyes, sighed, which apparently marked the formation of resolve, and came back into the room. Moving to the bed, she stood looking down. Her eyes then shifted to the glass of water, still clutched in Anita's hand. She took this, placed it on the table while gazing at it intently, as if searching its depths for confirmation of something and, at last, with obvious effort, she switched her gaze to Anita.

Meg then sat on the bed, taking the hand that had held the glass in her own. Anita's other hand, the contents of which should by now have started their fatal work, lay still on the covers, safely closed and as far from the regard of either woman as if it were invisible.

Meg said, "Anita, I came by to tell you something. And I must be honest, I was told not to. I was told to let what may be going to happen be a surprise. But I thought—well—if he arrived and found you asleep he might—seeing how things have been between you—he might just leave again and not come back. And if that happened I don't think I could bear it. So I came back to make sure you stayed awake and—I just hope I'm doing the right thing ..."

Anita stared. Finally all she could say was, "Meggie—would you please tell me what you're talking about?"

The administrator said at last, "Your son!"

"What?"

"Your son. What's his name?"

"Joseph."

"Joseph, yes. I just talked to Joseph on the phone. Actually we talked twice today—the last time a few minutes ago. And, well, Anita—he's on his way."

Through a fog Anita heard herself say, "On his way where?"

"*Here!* He had some car trouble—that's why he's so late—but it's okay now." Meggie smiled triumphantly. "So, my dear, if you can keep awake, your son should arrive in about half an hour."

Anita stared—stared and stared and stared—while the words "if you can keep awake" went round and round in her brain. One of her hands, the one still clutching Meggie's, was as cold as ice; the other, with its cargo of death, felt as if it was on fire. From the lounge, the studio audience on the TV gave a distant bray of mindless laughter.

THIS TIME JOSEPH'S car started on the first turn of the key, as if there had never been any problem. *Thanks a lot, bitch,* he muttered peevishly, nevertheless feeling mightily relieved to be on his way. After that, everything seemed to go like clockwork. He was across the Malahat and into Mill Bay in 25 minutes. In another 25 he would finally reach his destination.

A while later, still heading north on Highway 1, he noticed the turnoff to the village of Cobble Hill. The name struck a chord of apprehension; despite growing excitement at the prospect of seeing his mother, he couldn't help wondering at the reason for this unexpected emotion. Then suddenly, with an unpleasant shock, he did remember. Of course, Cobble Hill: the place where Roy had once shared a house with that vile man, Trevor, and where ...

Oh God!

The dreadful happenings in that house, as related by Roy, came back in all their gory detail. Freshly appalled, Joseph wondered how he'd managed to blank out this information and, infinitely more important, how, in the all-too-real present, he was going to deal with the dark legacy from that long-ago tragedy: the yardful of buried bones.

Of course, this problem had struck him before: on the night— it already seemed an age ago—of the original revelation. But the funeral of Marcel McGinty, its harrowing emotional impact, leading in turn to the long-overdue change of heart about his mother, had all succeeded in taking Joseph's mind off Roy's awful secret. But now, as if to spoil the only tranquil moments of what had already been a perfectly horrid journey, it all came crashing back.

Damnation!

Driving along the long, straight stretch where the highway bypassed Cobble Hill, Joseph approached an intersection opposite a small lake, where yet another sign pointed the way to that fateful village. So powerful was the revived mental picture of what had happened there, he was filled with an irrational but overwhelming compulsion. He slowed, made the sharp left turn, and was actually heading along the road toward Cobble Hill village when he shook his head, jammed on the brakes and pulled savagely off to the side.

What was he up to now? What could he possibly accomplish by going to Cobble Hill? What was the matter with him? Oh, God— was this yet another excuse not to see his mother?

Idiot!

In frustration, and without checking his rear-view mirror, he shoved his car back into gear and made an abrupt U-turn, only just avoiding yet another accident and now hardly even caring.

Soon he was back on the highway. No more thoughts, fears or fantasies, he swore to himself. No more sidetracks or subterfuges, no matter how compelling. He was going there. Straight there. To his mother, and that was that.

WHEN HE ARRIVED at Arbutus Lodge shortly before 8:30, there were lights burning but not many. He parked in the visitors' lot and made his way around to the front entrance. This was unlocked, but the foyer beyond was deserted.

Setting eyes on the place for the first time, Joseph was immediately struck by how non-institutional it looked: more like a hotel or fancy spa than what it essentially was, a glorified old folks' home. He was glad of that, relieved that his mother had ended up somewhere nice; then he was appalled at the ease with which the idea of her "ending up" had presented itself. Right after that it struck him how near he'd come to never seeing this place at all—not until it was too late. He stood very still in the middle of the empty foyer, looking about at the ritzy but ultimately sad establishment where his only flesh and blood was spending her declining years alone, and was suddenly filled with such sadness and shame that it was all he could do not to turn and flee.

But then, from somewhere down a hallway that led off the foyer came the sound of laughter. It was no more than canned merriment from a TV show, but it was enough to jolt Joseph from his sentimental spasm. At that point he realized he had no idea where to find his parent. As if in response to his need, from the direction of the TV room brisk footsteps approached. Around a corner appeared a fit young woman who, upon seeing him, stopped and raised her hands in an almost comical gesture of relief.

"Mr. Gillespie?" She moved forward again, with a smile so warm as to almost radiate physical heat. "Well—it has to be you, surely?"

"Ah, yes," Joseph stuttered. "I'm me—I mean, I'm Mr. Gillespie. Joseph! Mrs. Gillespie's ... "

"Yes, yes, yes!" The woman cut him off cheerily. "And I'm Meg Lordly, the person you've been chatting to off and on all day. Well, Joseph, I'm glad you finally got here in one piece. None the worse for your accident, I hope?"

"No."

"Good! And, while we stand here chatting, I'm sure your poor mom's just going mad with anticipation. Come on!" She started swiftly along the corridor, talking over her shoulder. "I know you told me not to warn her. But you were so late I decided if I didn't tell her she'd be asleep by the time you arrived. So, no surprise, I'm afraid." They turned a corner and came to the beginning of yet another short corridor. Nearing a door, Meg turned to him, voice lowered. "Here we are. Good luck."

Joseph smiled thinly. "Thanks."

He started forward, but then there was a sudden touch on his arm. He turned back to see Meg, her face somehow expressing happiness, worry, censure and relief all at the same time.

"I'm sorry, Joseph." Her voice was barely above a whisper though very clear. "But before you go in I must say one thing. I don't know why you've stayed away so long, or why you've come now. I'm just hugely glad you did."

"Yes, well, thanks," he began, but she cut him off with a gesture.

"Please, just listen! Your mother is one of the kindest, dearest and most patient people I've ever known. In all the years she's been here, I have never—*never*—heard a word of blame from her, or of complaint, even though she's been eaten up with pain and," the grip on his arm tightened, "listen carefully now—slowly dying of loneliness. I don't know whether it's you she's been pining for or somebody else, but one thing's certain: though she puts on the bravest face of anyone here, I've not the slightest doubt that your mother's heart is broken. So, when you finally get in there, whatever it is you have to say after all this time, just remember what I've told you." Her grip transferred from arm to elbow and delivered a little shove. "Off you go."

Propelled by Meg, Joseph almost stumbled through the open door. The room he found himself in was small. Upon the bed, propped on a thick pile of pillows, lay his mother. Her eyes were half-hooded, as if warding off sleep, but there was no doubt that she was conscious: the look of excitement and expectation on her face was so intense that it struck him almost like a physical blow.

Also shocking was the change in her. Of course, Joseph had been prepared for his mother to look older, and she did. But it was not this that awed him: it was the feeling that emanated from the bed, as if— and he could only find words for this when he recalled it much later— as if she were someone who was already not quite of this world.

Joseph stood dead still, at first able only to stare. Finally he pulled himself together enough to speak, the words emerging as a sort of comical croak, "Hello, Mother!" was all that he managed to say.

At this point his mother underwent an astonishing transformation. The sweet look on her face vanished, to be replaced by an expression so different that he thought she must be crazy.

"Oh, heavens, Joe." Her voice came out in a weird, dry, cracked whisper. "What took you so long?"

"I'm sorry," Joseph said. "I'm so sorry I haven't visited … "

"I don't mean that!" his mother gasped. "I know why you haven't visited, and I don't blame you. It's my own fault, but we'll talk about that later. I meant—what took you so long getting here tonight?"

Not knowing what to say, half-convinced that his mother was senile, Joseph just gaped. She shook her head in brisk dismissal of the subject, with yet another expression: dire urgency. Her voice came out in a whisper. "Joe—see that she's gone."

"What …?"

"Meggie, the woman who brought you here, go to the door and check she's gone. Do it now, please!"

BEMUSED, AT LAST sadly certain that the person he'd so long neglected had indeed misplaced her faculties, Joseph went to the door as requested, looking into the empty corridor. "Gone!"

"Good! Now come here—quick!"

When he reached the bed he found himself freshly appalled, this time not by the notion that his mother was deranged, but by the brand new understanding that she was not. Now, as she had done, he found himself speaking in a whisper. "What is it? Mother, what's the matter?"

She shook her head violently, refusing explanation, instead pointing with her right hand to the bedside table. "Tissues!"

"What?"

"Tissues! Pass me some tissues, please. Now!"

In a fog of bewilderment Joseph did so.

"Spread them out here."

His mother indicated a place on the left side of the bed, near her waist. Having given up speculating, Joseph simply did as he was told, first placing the tissues side by side and then, after his mother shook her head violently, on top of one another, in a thick layer. This accomplished, he looked at her, wondering what her next strange instructions might be. But now his mother's full attention was upon herself, as she struggled to sit higher in the bed. Instinctively his arms went out to help, but she gave a quick head shake, which stopped him cold, followed by a grunt of pain so intense that it made his stomach clench.

When it was done, she settled back, breathing hard but with increasing control. Finally, looking directly into his eyes, she raised her left fist.

At first Joseph took this to be a gesture of anger at himself, no doubt deeply deserved. Then he saw that the hand was horribly gnarled and knotted, and understood that, far from being shaken in rage, it was being extended in some sort of plea.

"My hand," Anita whispered. "It's been closed so long I can't open it. Please, help me."

He stared, confused. "Mother, I don't know ... Shouldn't I call someone ... ?"

The hand stayed where it was, but his mother's head swung up, so sharply that she gave another involuntary gasp of pain. ""No! No one must know! Don't! *Don't call anyone!*"

"Okay—all right. I won't!"

"Good. Now dear, this is terribly important. Please, just help me open my hand."

IT TOOK A long time.

At first, his mere touch on the grossly swollen joints caused his mother such pain that she could barely stop herself screaming. But she wouldn't let that deter her; each time the pain eased she nodded resolutely and he would start again, at first lightly rubbing, then stroking, then, as the reluctant blood began to flow, actually starting a light massage.

This, surprisingly, began to revive an ancient memory: rubbing his mother's hands years ago, when she was tired and it had seemed no more than a tender gesture to relieve tension. Who could have known that her old small aches would turn into this? Who could have guessed that such a gulf of lost years would separate that time from now? It struck Joseph that his mother's hand was a fitting symbol of their own relationship: diseased, warped into a parody of the thing it once had been, the good love that had been allowed to wither. Here they were, two almost strangers, blood-joined yet all but lost to one another, performing a ritual that one didn't understand and the other couldn't explain: labouring to get open this one poor, tortured hand.

But at last it began to happen.

The first joint of her little finger eased out the tiniest bit, then in the same manner the ring finger followed. At this point Anita's hand, held gently in both of Joseph's, was palm up. He continued his massage and gradually the middle digit began to relax. Then, as if released by a spring, the entire hand opened almost completely.

At that moment Joseph's eyes had been on his mother's face. Feeling the muscles loosen, he glanced down, just in time to see that the palm appeared to be filled with a heap of small white pellets. Then the hand jerked from his grasp, turned over and dumped its contents on the waiting tissues.

Joseph sucked in a breath, his mouth opening with the inevitable astonished query. It stayed like that, wide but silent, as, on some deep level, a jumble of puzzle pieces snapped together at lightning speed. The result of this was an icy understanding; he felt like a sleepwalker who wakes to find himself on the brink of an abyss.

"Mother!" he whispered.

She said not a word. Her right hand swung over and joined her left. With deliberate intensity, jerking and fumbling but with fierce concentration, the distorted fingers worked together to fold up the tissue pile, the obvious intention being first to conceal and then to confine the contents. It took an agonizing time and Joseph, heart in mouth, could only watch helplessly. This was the final act of a drama that his mother had performed alone. And though he had appeared at a possibly crucial moment, it was clear that the conclusion of it was entirely up to her.

Eventually the result of Anita's labours was a solid paper ball, something that she could hold in one hand. Only then did she look at her son. The hand with the paper ball extended toward him, but stopped just out of his reach.

"Well?"

"Well, what, Mother?"

Her breath hissed in annoyance. "Don't be silly, Joe. I can see that you saw. That you understand. That you know! Now tell me—this appearance tonight, out of the blue, what does it mean?"

"Mother—I'm here!"

"Yes, dear, here *now*. But is this just a moment? Is it curiosity? Or maybe a silly guilt reflex that will take you off again as soon as it subsides? If so, I'm glad you came. I'm happy to see you one last time. But if that's all—then you must leave again right now. Walk away and say nothing to a soul about what you've seen. That's the only thing I ask of you."

"Mother ... "

She shook her head resolutely, indicating the crumpled paper in her hand. "Because if you take this from my hand, if you dispose of what was to be my last chance of peace, it will be—like a promise."

Joseph looked steadily at his mother. Eventually he said, "I know."

And extended his hand.

His mother hesitated only a moment more. Then she placed the paper in Joseph's palm. She indicated a door on the far side of the room. "The toilet is in there."

He nodded, moved into the tiny bathroom, threw the paper into the bowl, flushed. He didn't take his eyes off the swirling water until he was sure it had done its work.

When he returned his mother was lying back again in the bed. Her eyes were now almost closed, but her face wore a dreamily contented smile. "I have to sleep now, dear," she said.

"Mother?"

His anxiety evidently penetrated her haze. She shook her head, reached up and patted his hand. "It's all right, dear, I'm fine. I only had the chance to take one. But now I'm afraid I can't hold it off any longer."

"I'll come back first thing tomorrow. That's a promise."

She sighed, drifting. The hand that had patted him dropped to the quilt. "I believe it. And I'll look forward to it … "—her voice was now just a murmur, but it held the conviction of a prayer—"more than you'll ever know."

Feeling numb but at the same time extraordinarily exhilarated, Joseph leaned down and kissed her. Then he made his way across the room. At the door he was stopped by her voice.

"Joe!"

He paused. "Yes?"

"I was just thinking, dreaming, about your father … "

"My father?"

"Your real one. For a moment, as you left, I even started thinking you were him." A laugh drifted across, barely audible but perhaps the single happiest sound that he had ever heard. "But you aren't him, only part of him, the best part. He's not lost but still here, in you, dear Joe. And when you come—tomorrow—I promise I'll tell you everything you've ever needed to know."

EIGHT

"You're quite right," Jack said. "I really can see how anyone who knew your dad would think we must be related."

Emily gave him a small smile. "Nature certainly can play strange tricks."

They were sitting in Emily's elegant living room, she holding a cup of tea and now looking reasonably rested, he nursing a beer. In the perfectly tended garden beyond the windows, afternoon sun produced an idyllic chiaroscuro of colour and light and shade.

Jack was looking at a photo, old but quite clear: a man who, but for the moustache and greying hair, might easily have been himself. He kept staring at the picture, finally giving a bemused head shake. "The likeness is amazing. Truly remarkable. But, as I said, though I don't know anything about my real folks, the one thing I'm certain of is my birth date."

"Which makes you five years too young to be my son."

"And you are an only child, yes?"

Emily gave an involuntary wince. "Oh, yes!"

Noting the reaction, Jack said. "I'm sorry. It's just that I was wondering if you maybe had a younger sister. Someone who still could be my ... "

"Your mother? Yes, I do understand. But I'm afraid that could never have happened."

"Why is that?"

"My mother ... died at the time of my birth."

"Sorry to hear it."

Emily gave a wry little smile. "I hardly need say it was quite a long time ago."

"There's just one other idea. It could be embarrassing, but since we've started on this, I don't honestly see how it can be avoided."

"I know," Emily said briskly. "Of course! And I've thought of it too. You're wondering about the possibility of my dad himself having fathered another child."

"I guess so, yes."

"I'm afraid that's not possible either, not if you're the age you say. You see, two years after my own son was born, and three before you, my poor old dad died of a heart attack."

"Ah! I'm sorry. Well—that seems to be that." Jack stared at the photo a while longer, then put it aside and walked to the window. "Beautiful garden. So secluded and peaceful. It must give you a great deal of pleasure."

"It's my favourite place in the whole world."

"I can believe that." He abruptly turned back. "But I'm waffling. Since you flat refused to let me take you to the hospital, I'm glad you at least let me drive you home."

"You were very kind."

Jack shrugged. "Well, of course, I was dying to see this dad of yours that I so much resemble, especially since I never knew my own. But I have to admit, my interest went a little beyond that."

"How so?"

"It's a just a feeling I had. Could I tell you about it?"

"If you like."

Jack came back from the window and sat again. "I'm a police-man, as you know. I'm okay at my job, but I'm not exactly your usual jock-cop, as my girlfriend keeps telling me, and as you'd know if I told you what actually brought me to this part of the world."

"What's that? Or is it a secret?"

"No. More like a bit embarrassing. Though, in fact, you're some-one I think I wouldn't feel embarrassed telling. But can I go on?"

"Of course."

"Okay, what I'm stuck with here, with you, is not so much a question as a really strong feeling. These things hardly ever hap-pen to me, but when they do it's usually connected with my work. You know, the odd hunches that come when there's no evidence, but actually turn out to be right?"

"I have heard of that."

"As I said, I don't get them often. And that's good, because depending on hunches can really screw up police work. But when they do happen, they're usually quite powerful ... "

There was a pause while Jack seemed to ponder, or perhaps he was just trying to choose words. Tranquilly, Emily asked, "What has this to do with me?"

Jack shook himself, half rose and sat again, scratching his ear in agitation. "I don't know. Maybe absolutely nothing. But let me tell you what happened. After we met, in the way we did, with you get-ting sick and me helping out, and then getting to talk, and that really weird business about us maybe being related, I kept getting this strong sensation that something, somehow, was quite badly wrong."

At that moment Emily was not looking at Jack. She did manage to raise her eyes, however, to find that his expression had nothing of certainty and was anything but accusatory; rather it was discon-certed and, on another level, simply concerned. Quietly, she said, "You believe that I've done something wrong?"

Jack looked pained. "No! I don't mean that at all. I ... actually, I've no idea what I mean. I've just got this feeling," he grinned awkwardly, "plus what's beginning to seem like a somewhat neurotic need to tell you about it."

"Why?"

"I'm not sure. To try to—I mean, if there *is* something wrong— to try to help, I guess. That is, if there was any way I could."

There was a very long silence. Jack and Emily looked at each other calmly, in a way that only after a while began to get strained. Then Emily said, "Jack, you really are a very unusual young man."

He shrugged awkwardly. "Maybe, but I'm not exactly happy about it. And I'll also completely understand now if you tell me to mind my own damn business."

"Perhaps that's exactly what I should do."

"So—there isn't?"

"What?"

"Anything wrong?"

She just stared. At last she said, "You're also unusually persistent."

"I guess so."

"Which I'm perfectly aware isn't an answer."

"So?"

It was now Emily's turn to move to the window. After a moment she said, "Did you mean it, before, when you said you liked my garden?"

Jack looked bewildered. "Yes! Well, I was sort of making conversation, trying to get around to what I really wanted to say. But yes, I do like it. Who wouldn't? It's spectacular, and you're obviously an excellent gardener. Is there some reason we're talking about this now? Apart from changing the subject, I mean?"

Emily kept looking out, her gaze sweeping randomly over flower beds and rockeries, pond and paths and dreaming lawns, her expression no longer tense but edging into something akin to resolve. "Actually, it may just be that it is the subject."

"Your garden?"

"Yes."

"How's that?"

For a while she was quite still, then she gave a sigh and returned to Jack. "Later," she said quietly.

"Later?"

"If we talk about this, we'll do it later. All right?"

"Then there is something to talk about?"

Emily smiled patiently. "We'll talk about that later too."

Jack nodded philosophically. He sipped on his beer and, to fill the awkward pause that was starting to grow, once more picked up the photo of Emily's father.

Watching him, Emily said, "What if it had turned out that we were related? Wouldn't that have been strange?"

Jack put the picture down again. "But we're not."

"No, not unless there's some odd family connection way back that we can't know and won't ever be able to trace. But I like you. You were kind enough to take care of me, and you're also a stranger in town. I was wondering if you wouldn't let me thank you by sharing my sanctuary for a short while and perhaps letting me make you a little supper?"

Jack looked surprised. "Well, sure, that would be great, but are you sure you're up to cooking?"

"Yes, I think I can just about manage that."

"Then I'd be honoured."

Emily smiled. "Such a gentleman. The people of Christina Lake must think themselves very lucky to have you. Well, good." She rose, heading for the kitchen. "Relax, drink your beer, look around. I've got a quite nice collection of paintings, if you're interested in that sort of thing."

She left the room, but almost immediately came back into the doorway. In a completely different voice she said, "One thing I didn't tell you, and I suddenly thought I probably should."

"Yes?"

"I'm not a very sentimental person. Since I gave up my child all those years ago, I confess I've never really thought of him much. And I'd be lying if I told you that I'd had any real regrets. But today, meeting you, for the very first time I think I may have missed out on something."

She gave him a quick smile and, before he could reply, disappeared into the kitchen.

THE KITCHEN WINDOW gave a somewhat different view of the garden, but substantial nonetheless. From where she stood at the kitchen counter, her hands moving automatically over the beginnings of supper, Emily could see all the way down to where the high hedge and the line of big, old rhodos marked the end of her property. From the secret place beneath the enveloping greenery she could almost feel her recently discovered garden guest, with whom she now proceeded to have an internal conversation.

What on earth did he mean? she said, referring to the man now sitting in her living room. *How could he know?* And then, directly addressing the buried bones: *How could he possibly have the smallest idea about YOU?*

Well, of course, he couldn't. He didn't! Although Jack had said he felt something was wrong, he'd also assured her that he had no idea what it was. Only Emily's guilt—no, not guilt, since she had committed no crime—only her nervousness, engendered by a knee-jerk reaction at being questioned by a policeman, combined with the fact that she was indeed concealing something, had led to the absurd notion that Jack actually might have an idea of what was going on.

Utter foolishness.

But then, on another level, she already knew that perfectly well. With the certitude of a well-adjusted and educated mind, and a lifetime inhabiting a sane and rational world, she knew that anything that appeared to be effect without cause was impossible; anything that purported to be knowledge without the mechanisms of communication was simply illusion. In which case any feeling, or hunch, that Jack might have about her situation must be based not on his "intuition" but on subtle signals that she herself was transmitting.

Meaning what? That, subconsciously, she actually wanted him to know? Not impossible, perhaps, but why?

Chop, chop went her knife; clatter, crash went her utensils; hiss, sizzle went the heating pans on her stove as Emily toiled away at making supper for a man she'd met only hours ago, but who, all evidence to the contrary, seemed so much like family that she was beginning to feel she'd known him all her life.

This was strange, at once pleasant and disquieting, and perhaps directly at the root of her desire to unburden. In fact, the more she thought about that, the more convinced she became. Jack was not really related to her, but the family resemblance was startling; he was not her son, but the sensation of kinship was close to alarming. Seen in this light, her urge to confess—no, to share—the secret that had come to haunt her last days seemed not merely natural but almost an obligation.

Emily prepared all the ingredients for the omelette, set the table in the dining alcove, took Jack out another beer and commented brightly on the little Emily Carr that had caught his attention, but most of her mind was centred on what now seemed the only thing of any real importance: should she or should she not give in to this escalating urge to tell Jack the secret of her garden.

Returning to the kitchen, she still had not made a decision. She greased the pan, gave a final stir to the egg mixture and poured it in, adding the already sautéed vegetables. Everything was perfect, the omelette beginning to brown and rise with satisfying evenness in preparation for folding, and all the while her thoughts kept churning ...

Had it not been for Jack's line of work, the decision might have been simple. It was the policeman thing, she now grew convinced, that was the real snag. Emily knew instinctively that Jack was not just unusually honest but also—to use a word that seemed to have grown out of fashion—honourable. This meant that finding a crime had been committed, he would feel honour bound to report it. She had no reason to expect anything less. So, telling him her secret would be tantamount to going directly to the law, except for the extra pain and embarrassment caused by Jack being forced to rat on her.

On the other hand, in the unlikely event that his response to her confidence was to ignore his professional duty, she would know that, by making him pander to her own needs, he'd been put in an untenable position, something she had absolutely no right to do.

Damn!

By the time the omelette was ready to fold, the bread she'd put in the oven was warmed and the salad was ready. She served out everything on attractive plates, pulled a bottle of wine from the fridge and called Jack into the kitchen to open it. He went about this task with such simple good grace that, all over again, Emily was struck by how natural they were together. As they sat to eat, she even took a moment for a wry thought: had she been a generation younger, and possessed of a life expectancy of more than a few months, she might have found herself getting attached to him.

This man who looked like her father, this man who felt like her son, this stranger who was neither kin nor lover, who was in fact nothing to her at all, but whose psyche seemed to nestle alongside her own with all the ease of an old and comfortable shoe.

Double damn!

While they ate they talked about painting. Although Jack professed to know little about art—and less about Canadian artists—he was genuinely appreciative of her collection. Without self-consciousness, and lacking any formal terms, he nonetheless revealed an unusual insight into the fundamentals of painting. Recalling the jock image she'd had when she'd first laid eyes on him at the archives, she was once more put in mind of how treacherous it could be to fall into the trap of stereotyping.

"That Emily Carr of yours," Jack said at one point. "Pretty strong stuff. I think I recognized the way she paints. I guess I must have seen reproductions of her work more often than I realized. In magazines, posters, you know?"

"Yes. She's quite an icon now. Especially in B.C. But when she was painting people weren't so impressed. Her work was original and powerful and immortalized this part of the world, like the Group of Seven did for northern Ontario. I picked up my little piece nearly 40 years ago, by sheer luck. That, and those little Group of Seven sketches left me by my father, got me started on collecting. But there's absolutely no way I could afford what they're worth now."

"You were fortunate," Jack said, adding with unaffected simplicity, "Those pictures are really beautiful."

"Yes, they are." After a pause she continued, "I'm sure you're a good cop, Jack. Probably better than you gave yourself credit for ..."

He grinned. "Thanks. However, I sense a 'but' coming?"

"Oh, no! Well, yes, but all I was going to say is that you seem to have such a feeling for art yourself. Didn't you ever have the urge to take it up?"

"As a full-time job?"

"Well—a serious occupation?"

Jack shook his head emphatically. "No. I've always liked pictures. Sometimes, when I look, I even think I can really see what makes them work, or not work, as the case may be. But as for trying to paint, myself, frankly I've got to say it just hasn't occurred to me."

"Never?"

"Well, maybe just a bit, when I was a kid. But for me, from the time I was young, I always had this urge to get out and find something to do that people needed. Also, I guess, to make me feel that people needed me." He chuckled shyly. "Call it the Little Orphan Annie syndrome. Anyway, by my late teens, my school grades weren't great but they were okay. I was big and athletic, but not good enough at any sport to try for a college scholarship. So, when a guidance counsellor suggested I think of being a cop, I went for it. Got into police college and then the RCMP, and I've been there ever since. Along the way I had a stint of married life and had a daughter, whom I love but don't see nearly enough. But I do have a great girlfriend back in Christina Lake. And one reason, though not the main one, that I came to Vancouver Island was to try to clear my head about where she and I are going. Since I've been here, that at least seems to have worked itself out."

"Happily, I hope."

"Yes. In fact Margie and her boy are coming to join me on Saturday. Flying out … " He stopped short. "Well now, haven't you got me chattering on."

"It wasn't my intention, but it's been a pleasure listening."

Jack grinned. "And I thought I was supposed to be the interrogator. Sorry, that was a cheap hint."

"What?'

"Earlier on, remember, when I said I had the feeling that something was wrong ... "

"Ah—that!"

"You said we'd talk about it later."

"Yes, I did."

"How about now?"

"Do you really want to know?"

"Only if you want to tell me."

Emily thought of the rhododendrons at the end of the garden. In her mind she again saw the secluded spot where, digging for that last elusive root, she'd come instead upon the evidence of an ancient horror.

"If I understood you correctly," Jack said, "you mentioned that your problem, whatever it is, was connected with your garden."

Emily wrenched her thoughts back to the man sitting opposite, the holidaying cop whose entrance into her life had, indirectly, been engineered by her unfortunate garden guest: after all, if she hadn't gone to the archives to research pesky Mr. Devereaux, she would never have met Jack.

"The garden, yes," Emily answered finally. "I mentioned my garden because—it's my favourite place in all the world."

"So what's the problem?"

"The problem? The problem, Jack, is that, having just retired, I expected to enjoy my garden for many years to come, but now I'm afraid I'm not going to be able to do that."

"Why is that?"

"Because ... " Emily paused for a long time, looking at Jack. Then she blurted, "Because I've just found out I'm going to die."

GOOD GOD! WHAT on earth could she have been thinking?

She'd decided, intended, in fact, to tell her new friend the bizarre truth about the garden. But then, at the very last instant, with the words of revelation full-formed in her brain, something had come between.

What?

It was not a mysterious influence; Emily most emphatically didn't believe in such things. It was not nervousness about Jack's reaction; she already knew him too well to be concerned about that. It was not even fear of consequences; having grown exhausted by the whole macabre mess, all she wanted was for it to be over.

But now it was not over. Exactly the opposite. In an irrational moment, with the utterance of one fatal sentence, she'd not merely short-circuited her original intention but opened a brand-new can of worms.

For God's sake, why?

Knowing nothing of the whirlwind of confusion and dismay spinning in Emily's brain, Jack was looking at her with surprise and deep concern. But then he nodded, shook his head, nodded emphatically again, as if conducting an internal conversation. When this pantomime ended, but before Jack actually spoke, Emily had a good idea of what he was going to say.

"I knew it," he said.

Well, at least she had been correct about that. Dully, she said, "You don't seem very surprised."

"I guess I'm not."

"How could you know?"

He looked perplexed, scratched his ear in that way he had, then shook his head again. "I'm not sure. Well, I guess those fainting spells you had were a start. But, no, that's not really what did it … "

Jack got up and walked to the window, pointing to where encroaching shadows were easing the garden into night. "It was, now that I think back on it, it was *that* that gave me the final clue."

"My garden?"

"The way you looked at it."

"Oh."

"Listen. This will sound sentimental, but I can't help it. Well, hell, lately I've been doing a whole lot of weird stuff, so I guess it's not exactly surprising."

Emily blinked. "What's all that supposed to mean?"

"Sorry, I'm talking about what first brought me here to the Island, but that's something else again. What I was trying to explain was this—when we were talking earlier, and you were looking at the garden, I thought I felt in you this awful sensation of loss. At first, now here's the kind of sappy bit, and I hope it won't embarrass you too much, me mentioning it, at first I thought this loss-feeling was to do with your thinking you'd found your son and being sad because you hadn't. But it wasn't your need I was feeling then, but my own."

"What do you mean?"

"What I didn't explain earlier was that all my life, like a good many people in my position, I guess, I've had dreams and fantasies about my real parents, even more as I've grown older. So, when I realized we weren't in fact related, what I was feeling, I know now, was not your sense of loss but mine."

"I see."

"But I was getting *something* from you. Something very strong. And though we don't have a blood connection, it seems that somehow there is one anyway. A connection, I mean. Don't you feel it?"

Emily looked at him for a long time. Finally she nodded.

"Now I think I understand what was going on. Since we do have this connection, what I must have been picking up on was the one really important fact you hadn't told me, this thing you knew you were facing, which must have been particularly in your mind when you looked at the garden. That's the wrongness that I kept on being aware of. It's quite simple really."

And who was to say it wasn't?

Because the garden bones had been so much on her mind, and because it was in trying to research their owner that she'd met Jack, Emily had assumed that this was the secret he'd picked up on. But the bones weren't her real problem at all; she'd simply been using them to mask her deeper concerns. The subconscious signals she'd been giving out had been about something much more basic: her own imminent demise.

Well—why not?

Now Jack was saying, "Emily, can I ask you one more question?"

Emily smiled wanly. She knew exactly what he wanted to know. "The answer is—I have a few months."

"Oh, Christ! I'm so sorry."

"It's leukemia. A fast and nasty variety, I'm afraid. I only found out a few days ago. Apart from something I thought was flu, I've had few symptoms. Not till now. But finally odd things have started to happen and no doubt that fainting business at the archives was part of it."

"And that's why you wouldn't let me take you to hospital?"

Emily shrugged. "Not much point, really."

"I see what you mean."

For a long time after that nothing was said. They both sat quite still, staring out at the last lingering light. Then Jack said, "Do you think I could make a phone call?" And, noting Emily's startled expression, "Oh, sorry, it's just—I've remembered Margie was going to call this evening to let me know about her flight. And since I'm here … "

"Of course," Emily said quickly. "The phone's in the hall. Please, help yourself."

After Jack left the room there was the sound of the phone being lifted, a pause, then low, easy talk. Emily refilled her wine glass and sat, sipping, feeling very calm. She contemplated the fact that, instead of revealing the truth about the old bones, she'd done the one thing against which every instinct should have made her recoil—revealed her own death sentence to a stranger.

She found she didn't care. More than that, she discovered she was glad.

Eventually she sat back comfortably and didn't think at all, aware only that, for the very first time since the day of her fatal news, she felt comforted.

Jack returned a few moments later. He sat down and took up his wine glass as if they'd been dining together for years. "They're arriving Saturday afternoon. Victoria airport at five," he said.

"I'm sure you'll be looking forward to that."

"You bet. To tell the truth, I never realized how much I was going to miss them."

"Well, that's always a good sign."

"Oh, and Margie says hi."

Emily looked startled. "What? I don't ... "

"I told her about you. Nothing about what you told me just now. But about our meeting, and about the family resemblance and about me being disappointed, you know, at there not being a real connection. You see, I haven't been open enough with Margs in the past. My fault. Part of this need I seem to have to protect myself, from God knows what. Anyway, I'd made up my mind to stop doing that. So since our meeting has turned out to be so surprisingly important to me, I thought I'd start a new habit by telling her all about it. I hope you don't mind."

"No. As it turns out, I don't mind at all."

"Great."

They sat sipping in companionable silence. After a while Jack said, "By the way, she says I should tell you."

"Tell me what?"

"The reason I came to Vancouver Island."

"I see. Do you want to?"

"Until a while ago I would have said no, but now, since we've got to know each other, and especially since you were so open with me, yes, I think I do."

"Then please go ahead."

"It's sort of a long story. Are you up to hearing it now?"

Emily smiled and reached out, lightly touching his hand. The contact felt easy and completely right, the mental conflict that had so recently consumed her, in connection with her garden guest, rapidly diminishing. The strange non-connected sensation, which she was starting to associate with her disease, was beginning to creep up on her again, but now it seemed oddly pleasant, a buffer against something which, with the appearance of this unexpected young man, hinted at being an overwhelming joy. She said, "I'm fine, Jack. And now I'm intrigued. Please, tell me all about it."

He shrugged, looking relieved. "Okay. It all started a couple of weeks ago, when I found this ... "

From his pocket Jack produced a small object, which he placed on the table. Bending closer, Emily saw that it was a plain, gold wedding band.

NINE

"So does that mean you're Polish?" Roy asked.

"Well, the name Reddski is Polish. That's what he told my mother." Joseph shrugged. "I guess that makes me half-Polish, anyway."

"Gee, I think it's just so romantic."

"Being Polish?"

"No, you idiot—discovering you had a mysterious dad who just up and vanished. I only wish my bitch-poppa had done the same. Baby, would my life have been sweeter."

Roy and Joseph were having breakfast in their little kitchen overlooking the morning-bright Juan de Fuca Strait. It was two days after Joseph's first visit to his mother, and a day since his return to her, when he'd finally learned the full story of Johan Reddski, his real father.

In fact, after he had known for so long that his actual dad was not the man whose name he bore, and considering his mother's strange silence over the years, the story itself had come as something of an anticlimax: from what Joseph could make out, just one more example of the seduce-and-run game that straight guys so often played as a substitute for love.

Of course, he hadn't told his mother that. So shaken had he been by the dire course of action that his arrival had only just averted that, apart from some heartfelt words of sympathy and regret, he'd scarcely opened his mouth at all.

Knowing the past, his indifference, his inexcusable neglect of the woman who'd cared for him most and loved him longest, he'd hardly yet even dared to think of the awful tragedy which, had it occurred, would have been his fault alone. To protect himself from the guilt, the disgust, the despair that threatened to overwhelm him, Joseph had built a fierce determination never to let his mother out of his life or his heart again. And most importantly, never again to allow her to be lonely. This, he knew, was slim recompense for what had gone before, but it was the only thing he could do.

"I don't really think we can say my dad vanished," Joseph said. "I didn't tell this to my mother, but my feeling is that the guy just took a powder."

"But you said your poor ma's been pining for him ever since?"

"It seems so, yes."

Roy gave a truly heartfelt sigh. "Oh, that's so *sad!*" But then his eyebrows lifted teasingly. "Hey, Joe, if I were to up and vanish like that, would you spend the rest of your life pining for *me?*"

Joseph would have liked to return the banter, but couldn't bring himself to do it. Feeling stupidly vulnerable, tears pricking at the corners of his eyes, he simply nodded. "Yes, I guess I would."

Roy bit his lip and quickly reached across the table, squeezing Joseph's hand. "I'm sorry, sweetie, that was just stupid bitch-talk. You know I'd never leave you in a million years."

His partner's real penitence and concern broke the moment and Joseph managed a grin. "I know that, Roy. I'm just still feeling a little fragile."

"I understand. What are you going to do now?"

"About my mother?"

"Yes. You know, Joe, I'd really like to meet her."

Joseph couldn't hide his astonishment. "Really?"

"Well, of course, sweetie, now that I know you don't hate her anymore."

"I never did hate her. What I felt, or grew into, was rather worse. Indifference."

"Ah! How did that happen? Was it us?"

Joseph shook his head sadly. "I only wish I had that excuse. But no, my mother didn't mind my being gay. She was just mad because I was moving out on my own, and somehow that got mixed up with the way my real father left her. But since I didn't know about that, I didn't understand. Later she tried to smooth it over, but it started something bad between us and bit by bit I sort of drifted away. I'm not trying to justify myself, you understand. But that's the way it happened."

One thing he didn't tell Roy was what had almost been the end result of that drifting. After the fateful night, when his appearance had interrupted what surely would have been her final act, neither his mother nor he had mentioned it again. And they never would. The image of the arthritis-tortured hand opening to reveal its clutched cargo of death was something Joseph would carry to his own grave, but that was something he would have to bear, a small retribution for all the damage done. He intended neither to reinforce the memory by sharing it nor to ease the guilt by confessing it, even to his lover. And the last thing he wanted was to injure his mother's dignity by revealing her purpose, or to distress his partner with the knowledge of it. He needed no public blame himself, since his conscience was capable of providing more than enough punishment for a lifetime.

He said to Roy, "Anyway, I've already told my mother about you."

"Cool."

"And she wants to meet you too."

Roy did a pretend-pout. "Really! And when were you planning to tell me?"

"Knowing how you feel about your own folks, dear heart, only when you were in a really good mood."

Roy laughed, but had the grace to look a little embarrassed.

"If it means anything, I know she'll like you."

Roy seemed pleased, and then Joseph remembered a detail of his mother's revelations that he knew would give his partner a giggle. "Oh, by the way, here's something I forgot to tell you. You know the actress, Doris Day?"

Roy frowned, pursing his lips in a mock-faggy way that he knew Joseph found both distasteful and irresistibly comic. "You mean that old-timey belle who made all those silly movies with the heavenly Rock Hudson?"

"The very same."

"What, she's come out of the closet at last?"

"Goodness, she's probably forgotten where the closet is, Roy. By now the old duck must be in her 80s. No, what I wanted to tell you was about my mother. Her name used to be Doris Day too."

"You're kidding! How divinely chic. How come you never told me?"

"I only found out yesterday, when she was telling me about my real dad. Mother's maiden name was Day—that I did know, of course. But the only first name I ever heard her use is Anita. Her full name is Anita Doris Day, and when she was young, going out with my dad, she went by the name Doris. Evidently my dad loved that. He thought it was cute and romantic."

"Really?" Roy chuckled wickedly. "Sounds pretty faggy to me. Maybe the apple didn't fall far from the tree after all. Perhaps your daddy ran off with some fella."

"Don't be too smart, sweetie. If he'd really been gay I wouldn't be here. Anyway, Doris Day was a huge star in those days, and my mom was flattered to have the same name. But after my dad left, she never called herself Doris again."

"Now that is sad. Why not?"

"Because he liked it so much, that's all she could tell me. And, I got the feeling, because she needed to start a new life. Doris Day, I think, reminded her of romance and disappointment and being taken advantage of, and she was through with all that. She was alone, pregnant with me, and sure she was in for a tough time. But then she met my stepfather, George Gillespie, who turned out to be as goofy about her as she'd been about Johnny Reddski. So it all turned out okay, except that deep down she never stopped pining for the guy who'd abandoned her." *Just as his son had*, Joseph said to himself, then grimly pushed the thought away. "And she never let on to a soul that her name had once been Doris."

"Wow!"

"I thought it'd amuse you."

Roy feigned offence. "Amuse me? I think it's the saddest little tale I ever heard. What kind of airhead do you think I am, rotten beast?"

"Sorry, hon. Anyway, now you know, just promise me one thing. When you finally do meet my mom," he grinned, "please don't go calling her Doris."

They ate the remainder of breakfast in silence. The new exhibition at the Balshine Gallery was a tremendous success and Roy, having worked so hard on the setup, was having a small respite, going in only in the afternoons. Joseph's own business at the bank had piled up, a casualty of recent distractions, but he intended within the next few days to have that under control.

After breakfast, as a further token of getting his life back on track, Joseph put his office shoes in a bag and started out to walk to work. It was another beautiful morning in the park, with vibrant light and glowing morning colours, an almost exact copy of the day, little more than a week ago, when he'd last walked here, blissfully unaware of the explosions that were about to rock his quiet life.

Despite the near-fatal nature of what had occurred, Joseph was hugely aware of how lucky he'd been. His mother was alive, and they still had places to go from here.

That left only the other thing: the long-ago deed done by Roy.

As he thought about this, it was as if a haze—a subtle flattening of hues and perspectives—settled across the morning. Joseph shivered, then a surprising thought struck him: not once, since the initial telling, had Roy so much as hinted at the business again.

That wasn't strange in itself. A killing, no matter how desperate and justified, was hardly a subject for casual talk. But Roy's silence had been more than avoidance of unpleasantness. Thinking back, released from his other preoccupations, Joseph realized that, ever since that night, Roy's demeanour had been as if the whole thing had never happened, as if sharing the secret had enabled him to erase it from his mind entirely.

Well, more power to him.

Joseph couldn't be so handily forgetful, but his problem wasn't with the past. What still haunted his cautious mind was the thought that the past might eventually catch up with the future.

How could such a thing happen? Well, someday the body could be discovered. Also, the fact of Roy's presence at the time of death might be shown. A combination of these two possibilities was, Joseph had to admit, statistically infinitesimal. But lotteries were won on slimmer odds, so, his banker's mind being what it was, as long as the smallest chance existed of the numbers coming up, he could never be entirely at rest.

Something would have to be done.

ON A MORNING so extravagantly lovely it was like a clichéd scene from a romantic movie, Jack came slowly to consciousness. In fact, when he opened his eyes, momentarily having no idea where he was, it was almost as if he were in such a creation:

Pale, bright room; sun angling across flowered counterpane, making golden patterns on antique wallpaper; birdsong beyond window, open wide to morning breeze; beyond, garden overflowing with scents and sounds of summer: move in close on weary traveller awakening at last in paradise—swell music—roll credits—dissolve to action.

Jack stretched luxuriously in the narrow bed, grinning at the image, fanciful and ironic, while at the same time reconnecting gently with the surprising fact of his actual whereabouts.

Scene: Emily's spare room—the morning after.

On the previous evening, after concluding his tale about the quest that had brought him to Vancouver Island and having finished, with only minor assistance from his hostess, a second bottle of good white wine, Jack had come up against a somewhat embarrassing reality. He'd driven Emily home in her own car, so his vehicle was still sitting in the museum parking lot in Victoria. Anyway, he was in no state to drive. It was too late for buses so, short of taking a ruinously expensive 50-kilometre taxi ride, he had no way of getting back to his motel.

This had not bothered Emily. She'd insisted on Jack using her spare room. After all they'd gone through in their short acquaintance, anything else would have been not only churlish but plainly nonsensical. Once he was in bed, unconsciousness had descended with all the swiftness of a movie fade-to-black, and he'd slept like a child.

Awakening now in this peaceful setting, Jack let the ambience soak into the very core of his being. He felt deliciously rested, despite last night's wine; quite clear and fresh—and more thankful for being alive than he had felt in a very long time.

It was then that the major revelation of last evening sickeningly resurfaced: Emily, so newly a friend, whose abode held him in such a comforting embrace, was herself under sentence of death. With this thought, all the pleasure drained rudely from the day. Jack sat up, threw back the covers and slung himself out of bed. Brute energy coursed through his body, itself a rebuke to the dark endgame being played out by his hostess.

Feeling guilty, but also knowing that that was stupid, Jack drifted to the window. Here was yet another view of Emily's garden; flower beds, pond, gentle sweep of lawns, all framed in the distance by a line of rhododendrons, a green fortress against the world's attention.

This paradise was all Emily's creation, and she was about to be summarily evicted. *Damn*, Jack thought, *what a stupid fucking waste*. But he knew it wasn't. In creating this garden, Emily's time had been anything but wasted. In fact, it was a living memorial to her. And if she was not going to spend as much time here as expected, well, that was just the way the world sometimes worked. Death, as Jack well knew, was ultimately a part of life, the only real tragedy being if the departee had nothing in the leaving to regret. That was certainly not the case here.

However, this garden, for all Emily's love and care, could not miss her when she was gone. Jack, who'd known the gardener for only a moment, thought he most definitely would. Standing at the window, staring at the garden and thinking these thoughts, Jack's body abruptly put him in mind of more mundane matters: he badly needed to take a leak.

He swiftly dressed, opening the bedroom door to the almost dizzyingly delectable smell of coffee. As he hurried across the hall to the bathroom, from the kitchen Emily's voice called a cheerful "good morning."

When he entered the kitchen, Emily said without preamble,

"You know, Jack, I've been thinking. What I'd really like is to meet your girl, Margie. Would that be possible?"

"Absolutely. I know she'd love to meet you too."

Emily busied herself pouring coffee and as she handed it to him she said, "I think she must be a very exceptional woman."

"She is, but what makes you say so?"

"If you'll forgive me, because of what she seems to have done for you."

"Ah. Well, you're sure right about that."

"And because it was she who urged you to tell me about why you came to the Island. I wonder how she knew the story would mean so much to me."

Jack raised his eyebrows. "Wow! Last night I must have been drunker than I thought. I'd no idea it made such an impression."

"Oh, yes," Emily said quietly. "More than you know."

That surprised Jack. He was not sure of her meaning. Somehow he didn't like to ask.

The coffee was as good as it had smelled. Emily prepared a breakfast of fruit and cereal and rich toast. For one whose days were deemed to be few, Emily looked remarkably fit. Jack was just considering if he should comment on this when Emily, as if reading his mind, said with a smile, "In case you're wondering, today I feel quite good. Almost as well as you look, actually."

"Terrific! And, yes, I do feel okay. In spite of a bit too much wine last night."

"Oh, that was nothing. A little lubrication for your intriguing tale. Fancy that poor woman never knowing her man was on his way back to her. That was really very moving."

Jack drank coffee and munched on toast and after a while said, "I've an idea that I've come to the end of it now."

"Your search?"

"Yes."

"You're giving it up?"

"Well, it was a pretty long shot in the first place. Let's face it, I don't really know that the woman's actually here. Or even if she's alive. And if I did find her, I've no real reason to think she'd want to hear my news."

"Maybe you're right. But it seems a pity, after all your work. When did you change your mind?"

"I don't think I knew I had changed it until just now."

"Really? You are strange. Oh, sorry. I didn't mean it to come out like that."

Jack gave a dry laugh. "But you're right. I feel kind of strange about it too. As soon as we began to talk today, I think I knew it was over. Apart from Margs, you're the only one I've told. But last night as I was telling it, bringing it into the open like that, I finally realized that, no matter how mysterious and important it seemed, what I'd been doing wasn't a true investigation."

"So what have you been doing?"

Jack looked perplexed and shook his head, as if dismissing the whole thing. Finally Emily said, "I'm sorry, Jack. I didn't mean to put you on the spot."

"Not at all. If it was anyone but you, maybe. But, if you'll forgive me, it's because of your situation, your illness, and the fact that you trusted me enough to tell me, that I need to tell you this. What we've been through, in the short time we've known each other, has somehow made me able to see myself clearly. So—what I've really been up to, as I now see it, is avoiding making decisions in my life by getting involved in a fantasy."

"Oh dear, that sounds terribly Freudian. Is that all there is to it?"

"Not all, but largely, I think."

"And you've only just realized it?"

"I was starting to about the time we met, after I'd spent days chasing wild geese, and ended up, mistakenly, as you pointed out, at the archives. And I hadn't even considered using my own police contacts to help. Know why? Because I knew damn well that if I tried, I'd have been laughed all the way back to Christina Lake."

"That doesn't mean that it was wrong."

"No, just sentimental and unrealistic—and a means of avoiding my real life."

"Or perhaps of making space to think about what you really needed to do with it. Have you thought of that?"

Jack looked startled. "No, I hadn't."

"Didn't you say it was since you've come here that you'd sorted out your feelings, and that's why you were looking forward to Margie coming?"

"Ah, actually, yes."

"Well, there you are," Emily smiled. "More coffee?"

After breakfast Jack said he really had to get back to Victoria. Emily wanted to drive him but he wouldn't hear of it, so she looked up the Island Coach Lines schedule. She took him to the highway, where he could catch a bus that would get him into the city in about an hour, and they arranged to talk on the phone soon. Jack promised to bring Margie and Doug up for a visit when they arrived.

After Jack boarded the bus, Emily sat in her car and watched until it was out of sight. Then she drove back to Cobble Hill, made tea and sat in her garden.

EMILY HADN'T ADMITTED it, but she wasn't feeling as well as she'd claimed. The strange diminishing-of-senses feeling of earlier days was no longer noticeable, which was a blessing. But what had replaced it was, if less spooky, hardly more pleasant: an unfocussed ache, not so much painful as irritating, all through her body, plus a flu-like lassitude. Little comfort that these were both symptoms she'd been warned to expect.

But once she was seated in the reclining chair by the pond, umbrella positioned against the already-hot sun, tea things conveniently near, she didn't feel too bad. Certainly not uncomfortable enough to distract her from the extraordinary thought-tumble that had been in her head since the previous night.

It was Jack's story, his strange, goddamn-nuisance of a tale, that had set her in this state: greatly moved, hugely mystified, weirdly elated and profoundly disturbed—all at the same time.

At the centre of it all was the fact of the bones.

Sometime last night, in the one fitful bout of sleep she had been vouchsafed, Emily had had a dream about bones. Not just the ones of Jack's story, nor even those of her garden guest. Her dream had been of all the bones in the world.

She had been flying high in the sky, miraculously alone and unaided, though this in itself didn't seem remarkable. What also wasn't strange—although she knew it to be vitally important—was her mission: to make an official tally of all the graves in the world. No sooner had the dream commenced when, in it, she realized she had been on this mission for an eternity. It was her life's work. As she flew, graveyards appeared far below. She would swoop down over each small forest of marking stones and invariably she knew exactly how many graves were in each location. She would make a note of the number and fly on. Immediately thereafter would appear another graveyard. Down she would swoop again and the procedure was repeated. Her tally was always correct and scrupulously complete, which filled her with huge satisfaction. So she flew and swooped and counted, understanding one shining thing: here, in this simple task, was what she'd been needing forever—a reason for being.

But then things began to change. Now she began to notice something new: individual graves appearing all over the place. At first there were just a few, scattered randomly between the proper graveyards, so it wasn't hard to count them. But, as she flew on, the numbers of unofficial burials grew; a host of unmarked interments, hidden but horribly known to her, crowded every secret corner of the land. It was as though the dead were actually breeding beneath the ground, swamping the peaceful present with echoes of a violent past, an ocean of death upon which the frail hulks of the living floated. And these bones were uncountable.

She was flooded with grief so intense that it sucked all her strength. She began to plunge earthward, and having reached the surface didn't stop, continuing deep underground. Foul darkness pressed upon her body and she was quiveringly aware of the reason for this fall from grace. She had failed in her mission. No wonder: the task itself had always been impossible. And something else: the secret sea of bones was hidden for a reason, so it might be blessedly forgotten. All she had achieved by her determined tallying of the past was a denial of the future.

Crushing sorrow overcame her. Deep in the cold earth, herself no more than a jumble of the very bones she'd tried to count, Emily wept—and awoke with real tears soaking her pillow.

The emotion of dreams seems to have its seat in a special part of the brain: more sensitive, more extreme, with little connection to the reasoning mind. Yet it will often take information from that mind, creating fantastic scenarios in an attempt to resolve conflicts that filter down to its twilight domain.

As soon as Emily awoke, though her dream still resonated with shocking immediacy and her chest felt heavy with an actual physical ache, she was instantly, and thankfully, aware of having rejoined the real world. She lay still, staring at the patterns that morning light painted on the ceiling, willing her body to relax, while the inner turmoil slowly subsided. Then, although it was unpleasant, and recent enough to retain a horrid odour of despair, she deliberately went over the details of her dream. She didn't relish this, but understood that it had things to tell her, things that would later bear consideration. She went over the dream several times.

Then she got up, showered, dressed carefully and made breakfast for Jack and herself.

IT SEEMED THAT Jack had had a much better night than she had, for which she was grateful. Telling the story of the strange quest that had led him to Vancouver Island had apparently acted as a sort of catharsis. Emily was not too surprised when, over breakfast, he confided that he had called off his search.

Listening to him explain the happy evolution of his feelings that had occurred since their meeting—because of it, he partly implied—brought her much satisfaction. Knowing that one was dying was, it had to be admitted, a truly irksome thing, what the young would call "a bummer." But if the communication of that misfortune could help another being gain perspective on his own life, perhaps it wasn't in vain. Emily told herself that anyway, finding with surprise that she actually almost believed it.

Another aspect, only now coming fully into focus, which was helping Emily in the acceptance of her lot, was the fact of Jack himself. He was not her son: that had been settled and was completely accepted by both. Anyway, it no longer seemed important. Jack was indeed an orphan, but the family he required was in the present, not the past. Emily had certainly given birth to a son, but thereafter had not needed or even thought of him.

And yet …

And yet, somehow the fact of Jack's existence changed everything.

How could that be? It was ridiculous! Possibly a little mad. But it was so. And after she returned from taking Jack to the bus and got herself settled in the garden, Emily began thinking very seriously about that.

She came to a surprising conclusion: she realized that the details of relatedness, or non-relatedness, in this case, didn't concern her. They were irrelevant. How long had she known Jack? Twenty-four hours. Yet if she thought of the essence of the man, how their personalities seemed to fit, it might as well have been forever. So what Jack was, Emily admitted, as she sat in her beautiful garden, in the final chapter of her too-short life, was the essence of the son she would have desired. The fact of having only a brief time left and nothing to lose engendered, Emily discovered, a truly dizzying freedom: one could be the undisputed possessor of any belief that one chose.

What she chose was Jack as her de facto son.

It didn't matter that she'd never wanted such a thing before. She wanted it now. And if that meant she was crazy, well, that was her decision too. No rules but her own.

No one to answer to but herself.

Emily finished her pot of tea, at one point moved her chair out of the sun and sometime later dozed a little. But at no time, including when she slept, did her mind abandon the long and interwoven thought-train that had begun at an identifiable point the previous night: the moment when, instead of telling Jack about the garden bones, she'd blurted out the fact of her own impending death.

At the time, that had seemed ridiculous, an evasion at best. Now she knew it was neither. Rather, what had been operating, on an intuitive level—and that included her disturbing dream—was pure logic.

Accordingly, when Emily woke up from her doze, it was with the first of several decisions full-formed. This prompted her to rise, move into the house and into her den, where she searched out her will. From this she extracted the sealed envelope entitled, "To be opened only after my death" with the info about her pesky garden guest. Without hesitation she carried the envelope to the living room and burned it in the fireplace.

MONTY BALSHINE WAS a thoroughly happy man. Business had rarely been better since the start of the Adrienne Kilgaron exhibition, when three of the most expensive paintings had sold at the opening. He was anticipating a highly successful year. Not, of course, that he took this entirely for granted: after 30 years in the gallery game, he was well aware of just how fast and inexplicably a season could turn around. Still, since the opening little more than a week ago, two more big Kilgaron pieces had sold, plus a Harold Town from a local collection that had come his way purely by chance and fetched a truly spectacular price. Another Kilgaron was currently under option by a Californian who had walked in off the street. So, although professionally leery of over-optimism, Monty let himself have a guarded glimpse of an immediate future that might be quite bright.

One afternoon, in the week following the Kilgaron opening, he sat in his little office checking out New York gallery websites on his computer. Up front Roy was talking earnestly to a couple who had just entered. Monty couldn't hear the spiel but knew it would be good. Roy had developed into so much more than a mere assistant. Since he'd started five years ago, he'd become a real expert; not only on established Canadian painters but on the entire contemporary North American scene. He had a fine eye, was hugely enthusiastic and could talk up a storm; plus he cared, which was the all-important thing. He loved paintings and had a real feel, not just for established artists but for the new ones coming along. His handling of the current exhibition, despite some small domestic problem that had preoccupied him just before the opening, had been no less than inspired. Monty was now seriously concerned about Roy being lured to a bigger gallery, in Vancouver or even down south. To make sure that didn't happen, he had decided to offer him a partnership.

Now, as he sat at the computer, with Roy's quietly authoritative voice murmuring in the background, he found himself thinking that seldom had he felt so good. Even the skin condition that was the bane of his existence seemed in almost complete remission. Monty's hands lay quiescent on the keyboard while his eyes feasted on far-off and expensive art, secure in the knowledge that he could be undisturbed while his partner-to-be ran the ship.

He was so contentedly preoccupied that he jumped when the telephone rang. He answered to find that the caller was an old friend and valued customer. The person in question had not been at the Kilgaron opening which, when Monty came to think of it, was a surprise, but when he learned the reason for the call, he forgot surprise and instead grew very intent. They talked for a time, sorting details, making arrangements. After the call was over Monty sat gazing unseeing at his computer screen, stunned, very moved and more than a little excited.

In the gallery, Roy was still talking, but not long afterwards the people left. He didn't come to the back right away, meaning that nothing much had happened. But that was okay, because Monty had just had a splendid idea that he wanted to go over carefully in his mind, the perfect situation, brought about by his just-concluded phone conversation, in which to broach to Roy the offer of the partnership.

"OLD MONTY IS being *très* mysterious," Roy said.

He and Joseph were sipping wine in their living room while the sun began its evening flirtation with the horizon beyond the Sooke Hills. The sky was streaked orange and purple and cobalt blue, in a picture-postcard display too garish for art but magnificent in its unabashed reality.

Joseph, contentedly relaxed after a good supper and an office day too busy to allow for the contemplation of problems, refilled his glass and let several moments pass before asking the obvious.

"Mysterious about what?"

Roy laughed. "That's the mystery, sweets. I don't know. All he'll say is that he has plans for the gallery and that when I hear them I'll be mightily intrigued. Those were his actual words, would you believe it, 'mightily intrigued.' Sounds like a bad English mystery. But intrigued about what, he won't say. What do you think?"

"That he's going to offer to take you on as partner."

Roy's look of fake astonishment was comical. "You old sly-boots—has he been talking to you?"

"Of course not. Monty wouldn't do that. I just made a perfectly logical assumption. You're really tremendous at the gallery. You've become Monty's good right hand. I'd say he understands that if he wants to keep you, he has to make it worth your while."

Roy sipped, shrugged and finally nodded matter-of-factly. "You're probably right."

Joseph smiled to himself. Roy was nothing if not self-confident. Well, good for him. Considering his rocky start in life, he had developed into an extraordinary talent. Joseph knew that some of the credit for that evolution must go to himself, to the loving relationship that had transformed them both. But he also knew that, had Roy not already possessed the inner capacity, all the love in the world wouldn't have brought it out.

Contemplating Roy's handsome face as the young man mused on his expanding future, and recalling again the breathtaking reprieve he'd had personally with his mother, Joseph knew that he was just a stone's throw from complete contentment. That last gap, however, couldn't be ignored. Above it hung the shadow: the horror that had once engulfed Roy's life, evidence of which still awaited its day of discovery.

This chance, Joseph had to admit, didn't appear to be bothering Roy at all. His confession to the safe, if distressed, ear of his lover had apparently exorcised the shade of Trevor and he seemed to have put the whole sorry business behind him.

Roy's ability to do this was, to Joseph, quite amazing. He wasn't sure whether he found it admirable or disturbing. After all, his partner wasn't morally guilty of anything other than youth and foolishness. And his drastic action, while taking one life, had saved that of another, not to mention his own. Roy had done nothing intrinsically wrong.

And yet …

And yet a faint, annoying flicker on the back burner of Joseph's mind wanted Roy to feel just a bit badly. He was ashamed of this, fairly certain the urge had nothing to do with justice, but was due to the fact that he was worried about the possible discovery of the remains while Roy was not. Joseph finally admitted that what he really wanted was not that Roy should feel guilty, but that he should make just an effort to share his partner's angst.

Which of course was absurd. Especially since it seemed that there was absolutely nothing to be done anyway.

Roy, who'd wandered to the window, suddenly turned back. "Oh, I forgot to tell you. Monty's been asked by a friend, who's also an old customer, to value an art collection."

Sunk as he'd been in thought, Joseph took a moment to tune in. "Oh? Doesn't he do that all the time?"

"Yes, but apparently this collection is special. He hasn't yet said why. Anyway, he's asked me to go along and tell him what I think." He stopped, gave himself a small slap and broke into a huge grin. "Hey! You're right, sweetie! He is treating me like a partner, isn't he?"

Joseph grinned too. "Sure looks like it."

"We're going to look at it tomorrow morning before the gallery opens. Monty's coming by to pick me up at some ungodly awful hour. So make sure I'm up early, sweets, will you?"

Happy to be wrenched from pointless rumination, Joseph duly promised. Time-keeping and punctuality were things that he generally took care of anyway. This was more natural to his careful soul than that of his partner: just one more of the ways they complemented each other.

Joseph set his own alarm for 6:00, but he need not have bothered. Before it went off he was woken by sounds coming from the kitchen. That was a surprise. It seemed that dear Roy really was getting his life together. Well, good! Joseph snapped down the alarm button, called out "Good morning and good luck," turned over and went back to sleep.

ROY WASN'T SURE what woke him so early. When he opened his eyes, the clock on the dresser—which habitually mocked his tardiness—registered 5:40. He was tempted to turn over and let Joe rouse him at the agreed time, but, to his surprise, that actually felt a bit mean: *Christ!* Roy thought, *am I starting to act like a fucking grown-up?* Well, dull as that might seem, it probably wasn't such a bad idea. It'd certainly be a relief to poor Joe, whose quiet life he seemed to have been disrupting lately. So Roy gave an exaggerated lisping sigh, mocking himself even as he did so, and heaved himself out of bed.

In fact he was so early that he'd showered, dressed and had coffee by the time Monty's car arrived. Looking serene and stylish, and feeling a little smug, he wafted out to the car and, with an airy "Good morning, Monts," settled himself in the passenger seat.

They started out, Monty driving in his careful, bumbling fashion. The car was a well-used old Mercedes, warm and comfortable, and before they'd been going five minutes the reaction to Roy's early awakening hit him. One moment he was sitting back, idly thinking how pleasant it was to be moving opposite to the shuffling, office-bound traffic (and meaning to ask Monty where the fuck they were going anyway, that they'd had to start so early) and the next he was sound asleep.

He drifted back into consciousness feeling very good, his body relaxed and snugly caressed by the purr of the car's engine. He realized he must have been dozing for some time because, after a blissful stretch and yawn, he saw that they were on a country road. Well, that answered one question: the goddamn early start. The thought formed to inquire about their destination, but he was just too lazy to bother. He closed his eyes and drifted again. Some while later there was a sudden braking, a lurch as the car changed direction, and another lurch as they came to a halt.

"Rise and shine, Roy, old thingie," Monty said cheerfully. "We're here—and good morning to you."

Roy grinned. "Yeah, thanks for letting me doze."

"Don't mention. Anyway, dear heart, I'd rather have you fresh for this."

"What's this? And, by the way, where in hell are we?"

"This is a stunning collection of mainly Canadian art belonging to my old friend Emily Muller. And where we are is actually quite a ways from hell—Cobble Hill, to be precise." Monty opened the door and began to get out. "I think this is going to be exciting."

The car had stopped in the driveway beside a house nearly hidden by a high hedge. Emerging, Roy saw that a hedge also ran beside the drive and continued to the left of the house, cutting the property off entirely from next door. He began to get an odd feeling, which he was just trying to identify when Monty said, "Wonderfully secluded spot, eh? Wait till you see the garden."

The older man moved onto a small front porch with two modest wooden pillars. Roy followed. Monty rang the front doorbell.

Which was what finally did it.

Such was Roy's shock that, for the barest instant, he thought he was going to faint. His hand swung out, clutching one of the little pillars, and he managed to steady himself. He stood quivering for several seconds, and then the bell rang again.

The bell! How could he ever forget that goddamn shitty bell?

Instantly, Roy realized that the familiarity had begun the moment they'd arrived. As soon as he saw his surroundings, somehow, just below the level of consciousness, he'd known where he was. This was not because of the outward details of the place, much of which had changed. It was the overall feeling; the ambience—of quiet, seclusion and, above all, secrecy.

Trevor's place.

But how could that be? Roy wondered wildly. *What were they doing here? Why had Monty lied about a woman and an art collection in order to get him to Trevor's place? How could he know Trevor? How could he have kept it secret so long? What did he want? Oh, God, Christ, sweet fuck and mercy—what was going on?*

"Good morning, Monty. You're bright and early."

"Hello, Emily. It was a lovely morning for a drive, though my associate here snoozed half the way. Emily, I'd like you to meet ... Roy—are you okay?"

Roy managed to focus on the figure in the doorway, a real person (a woman, not Trevor), and the palpable concern on her face began to bring him to his senses.

Now he recognized the woman. He'd seen her in the gallery from time to time. But what was she doing here? Instinctively, Roy raised his hand to his eyes, as if to erase her from sight, a gesture that obviously deepened her concern. At the same time, he managed to get hold of himself a little: whatever was going on here, he wasn't helping himself by acting like a vaporous idiot.

"I'm sorry," he managed to say, and then had a small, life-saving inspiration. "As Monty said, I was asleep. I must have gotten up too quick, that's all. Fine now." He held out his hand. "Hello, I'm Roy. We *have* met, I think, a while ago. So nice to see you again."

The concern on Emily's face faded. Monty gave a hearty, if slightly embarrassed, chuckle. The door was held open and they all entered.

Roy was enormously relieved to see that the interior of Trevor's place had changed completely. Not so much that he had any doubt about its identity. The physical layout was just as he remembered: hallway; door into the dining room at the right, door to the guest bedroom (his old room) at the left; ahead, archway leading to the large living area and, just visible on the far side of that, the fatal entrance to the master bedroom—the chamber of horrors, as he still thought of it. Oh, yes, it was Trevor's place all right.

And yet, at the same time, it wasn't. To start, every single colour had changed. The walls, which had been a stylish but austere white throughout, were now of varying hues: cool green in the hall; warm bronze in the dining room; soft tan in the guest room; pale, vibrant yellow in the living area. The polished hardwood floors, which had once been severely unadorned, were now so liberally covered with colourful rugs and throws as to be scarcely visible. Every stick of furniture was, of course, different. Finally, starting in the hall and continuing upon every wall in sight, was a veritable cascade of magical art.

Only one item was unchanged from former times: on the far side of the hall, in exactly the same place on a very similar table, was the telephone. Which, if not left stupidly ignored on one fatal night, might have changed his life.

Monty and their hostess (the real, live, art-collector lady) were now headed along the hall toward the back of the house. Still working hard at the task of recovering his wits, Roy followed. Passing the telephone (it was a different instrument, of course, but it leered from the same location) he instinctively veered off, but the others were ahead of him, so at least that went unnoticed.

They entered the living area, a bright place into which the outside garden seemed almost physically to flow. This room, with its hanging plants, ornaments and a forest of paintings, the morning sun streaming golden through spotless glass, was so stunningly aglow with beauty and peace that here, at last, the spectre of the past was almost laid to rest.

The lady made offers of coffee. Monty was already starting the rounds of the paintings, stopping inevitably in front of the Jack Shadbolt. Roy, beginning to feel a little more relaxed, moved to where he could see out into the garden.

This was even more transformed from the old days than the house's interior. Before, as Roy remembered all too well, since he'd spent much of his time as Trevor's "nephew" closeted behind its hiding hedges, there had been mostly ground cover and shrubs, easy maintenance, requiring minimal attention from intrusive outsiders. Now the place was a veritable wonderland of beds, lawns, walks and rockeries. Careful arrangements of colourful plants and blooming bushes, rows, clumps, gatherings and massings of flowers, some quite common, others truly exotic, all created a vision quite comparable to high art.

"Do you like my little garden?" said a voice at his elbow.

Roy swivelled to see Emily, holding a loaded tray, regarding him curiously. Words leaped into his head, an automatic phrase about

how much the place had changed, and he almost choked in his horrified hurry to stop those words coming out.

*Christ! Fucking idiot! What was he doing? Trying to hang himself with
his own stupid mouth?*

"I think your garden's beautiful," he managed to say and then,
regretting it instantly, "I'd really like to see it."

Emily smiled. If she'd noticed his fleeting twinge of dismay she
made no indication. "I'd love to show it to you. Later—after we've
had our little meeting?"

"That'd be wonderful."

*Oh, yes, sure it would! And, since Emily was obviously a very special
gardener, perhaps he should take her down back and show her where he'd
planted Trevor ...*

THE COFFEE WAS good enough to settle Roy down a bit. They
drank it, sitting in the living area, while Emily outlined what she had
in mind. She started off quietly, but with an odd intensity, "Very few
people know this yet—and I'd appreciate it if for the moment you'd
keep it to yourselves—but the unfortunate fact is that quite soon I'm
going to die ... " Then, after the inevitable interjections of surprise
and condolence, she continued. "To be brief, this is the situation.
Here, around us, you see the sum total of my life. A wonderful old
house, a beautiful garden, plus a very special   and by now, I believe,
valuable—collection of art. I've been very fortunate and though,
sadly, I'm going to have less time than I'd hoped to enjoy it, I now
find other things bother me more. First, I have no one—no one—in
the world to leave it to. Next, and this is even more important, I can't
bear the thought that, after my death, all this will be broken up.
The house sold, the garden changed or neglected and my wonderful
paintings scattered, perhaps even sold out of the country.

"You see, I've only known about my illness for a short time. I was just beginning to get over the shock, and starting to realize the problems I've mentioned when, quite by chance, I met a man. It was a most unusual situation and, I'll be honest, for a time I even thought this person might be my son. But he isn't and though I'm thankful for the happiness, and the special insights I obtained because of our meeting, I have to say I'm glad. Finding an actual relative at this stage of my life would only complicate things even more ... "

Roy listened with mixed emotions. He hardly knew Emily, and was too self-involved to be easily moved by problems outside his own. But something about her, plus the fact that this strange scene was being enacted in a place so crucial to his own past, really affected him. It was all too weird.

Emily was continuing. "But somehow, meeting this man—who, incidentally, had come to the Island on an unusual quest, looking for someone called Doris Day, helped to clear my mind. He didn't tell me what to do, or give me advice about anything; but it wasn't long after we parted company that I understood what was necessary, and that, Monty, is where you come in."

Monty, who had been listening raptly, gave a little start on hearing his own name. "Me?"

"Yes. You see, I realized that the solution to all of my problems was simple: I've decided to leave my entire estate, house, garden and art collection, to the place where I spent so many happy years—the University of Victoria. The only stipulation is that everything be kept together. The college has been given several properties in this way and though mine is small by comparison, it would still be useful, I believe, as a retreat, for small conferences, and as a permanent art gallery.

"Now, the only problem universities have with gifts like this is the expense of maintenance and upkeep. I know that if I want all this to stay together, I'll also have to provide a decent sum as an endowment.

I do have a little money, but not nearly enough. What I want you to do, Monty, is look over the collection carefully and then to do a sort of little tightrope act."

Monty's eyebrows rose. "I beg pardon?"

"I need you to pick out a few paintings for sale, balancing which ones might provide the most money against how to do the least damage to the collection. As I said, a tightrope act. I would only entrust it to someone with your background and skill, Monty, who is also a friend. What do you say?"

Monty blinked several times, frowned, flushed and abruptly stood, turning to scan the paintings that could be seen from his position. "God, it's an awful responsibility ... "

"Yes, but will you do it?"

Despite the buzz of his own concerns, Roy found himself irresistibly caught up in the drama of the moment. Everything he'd learned while working at the Balshine had taught him that Monty was indeed the perfect choice for the task. His knowledge of the field was impeccable, his honesty beyond question and his dedication to the city and its art community almost a matter of legend.

"He'll do it," Roy said quietly, then added hastily, "Won't you, Monty?"

Both of the others now looked at Roy. After a surprised moment, Monty gave a little chuckle. To Emily, he said, "I think this young man must have been reading my mind."

"He knew you'd do what I asked?"

"Not exactly." Monty's eyes twinkled, or was it a glint? Roy wasn't sure. "Assistants aren't supposed to speak for their bosses, saying they'll do things without checking first. Roy knows that quite well. So the only reason he'd presume to speak for me is ..."—the glint definitely became a twinkle—"he must have known I was about to make him a partner."

WHILE MONTY WAS off by himself, studying the paintings, peering, listing and beginning to make careful notes, Emily said, "Congratulations, Roy. Monty must think a lot of you."

"I guess so. I just hope I can live up to his expectations."

"I'm sure you will. Do you want me to leave you alone to look at the paintings too?"

"No, I think I'll let Monty do that right now. I still haven't—um—gotten up to speed enough to concentrate properly. If Monty wants me, he'll yell."

Emily smiled. "Then perhaps, while you're getting up to speed, you might like to look around my garden?"

Roy realized that he might have expected this. His earlier reaction to the idea had been one of dismay. But now, looking at Emily's kind face, and knowing the fate that she herself was facing, the feeling of threat vanished completely. That this was Trevor's old house was bizarre, certainly, but just a coincidence. The dreadful things that had happened here involved a different person, a different life. And Emily's invitation to view the garden was as innocent as the place itself had become. There were no ghosts here, only greenery, and what could be more appropriate than that?

"I'd like to see it very much, thanks," Roy said.

"Good. I think the light is best at this time of the day, though the late afternoon is beautiful too. Come on. Bring your coffee, if you like."

The garden was even more spectacular than it had seemed from the window. Exiting the French windows onto the back deck, then meandering along a path that wound below the rockery, passing beds of poppies and peonies and roses and foxgloves dressed in early summer splendour, they came at last to the pond at its centre. Unusually for him, Roy said little, avoiding trite phrases of praise or wonder, and understanding instinctively that, in this place, with this person, the highest accolade was silence.

The pond had a small fountain, water lilies and the occasional glint of darting fish. By its side were an umbrella and chairs. Passing, Emily stopped a trifle suddenly and, after a pause, sank into one of the chairs.

Roy, who had noticed this, stopped himself as he was about to ask if she was all right. *Damn it, of course she isn't. Didn't she just tell us she was dying, for Christ's sake?* Without a word, he settled himself in a chair nearby.

From this angle he got his first good look at the line of rhododendrons along the far limits of the garden. Even when he had known them, the plants had been huge; now they were massive, a veritable small jungle, luxuriant foliage overlain with the lighter green of new growth after the spring flowering.

Following his gaze, Emily said, "Aren't those rhodos magnificent? I know you wouldn't think it now, but when I first moved here, they were about the only flowering plants in the garden."

"Really?"

"And their colours are wonderful. A good thing they get it over with early in the season, or they'd put the rest of the place to shame."

After all, they're well fertilized. Roy hurriedly put that idea away. The last thing he wanted to think, or talk, about was the damn rhododendrons. He said quietly, "I'm sure you're exaggerating. Nothing could spoil this. I don't want to sound corny, but I think it's one of the most beautiful gardens I've ever seen."

"Thank you," Emily said simply. Then, after a pause, "You can see why I want to try to keep it just as it is?"

"Absolutely."

They sat for a while in contented silence, agreeably serenaded by a small orchestra of birds and the tinkle of the fountain. Emily closed her eyes, apparently at ease enough with her new companion to relax. Or perhaps, Roy thought, considering the brief time she had left, she was at the point where she just didn't care. For her sake, he certainly hoped so.

But, come to think of it—sitting here on this glowing day, the sun nuzzling his cheek and each inhalation sweetened by a profusion of buds and blooms—Roy realized that he didn't much care either. In fact, despite everything that had so recently occurred, he came to the remarkable conclusion that he'd seldom felt so relaxed, despite being at the very epicentre of where he'd lived the most horrid and harrowing drama of his life.

How could that be? Despite the ancient pain and fear and anxiety, one thing Roy had never felt was guilt: at the time, he'd done what he had to, and that was that. Looking back, the whole thing seemed more like a bad dream, or a particularly scary movie: hardly something that had involved him at all. And sitting in this garden, from which everything but the—literal—bones of the twisted creature who had once ruled this place had been expelled, Roy now knew that Trevor was truly gone.

And he was free.

Emily rose from her seat. She stood looking about quietly, but with such intensity that Roy was pulled from his thoughts by a feeling of alarm. Then, with quick intuition, he understood what was happening: Emily was not just looking at her creation; she was drinking it in, memorizing it. As one with a lifespan known and limited, she was using every last moment, even these polite ones with him, to immerse herself in the essence of her garden, an artist reliving years of creativity in the contemplation of one last great work.

But, as suddenly as it had begun, the moment was over. Emily turned to Roy and said, "Come on, let's finish the tour. Then we'd better get back to poor Monty."

They started down another path, circling toward, beside and finally away from the rear of the property. Heading back in the direction of the house, they passed a little shed. It was a neat building, just large enough to hold a mower and a few garden implements. It had a single door and a small window with a vine-covered trellis on each side to disguise and beautify. A pleasant and practical place, well weathered now, but definitely an addition since the old days. Passing the shed, Roy glanced casually in at the open door.

Sitting on the floor in the back, its obscenely oversized phallus outlined by a shaft of light from the window, was the statue.

ROY STOPPED DEAD in his tracks. He couldn't help himself. In that first moment, it was all he could do to remain upright; he felt as if he'd been hit on the head with a hammer.

For he recognized the object immediately. In fact, such was the wave of grisly familiarity emanating from it that it was as if, in shocking refutation of all he'd just been thinking, no time had elapsed between the present and when he'd last held the monstrosity in his hands.

Held it? Wielded it! Used the thing as weapon extremis, its ugly great cock, in a plunging instant, annihilating the dark universe that had been the brain of Trevor ...

Transfixed, like an insect impaled, Roy stared at the image of Pan. Then he began to move. Even as he did so, he was aware of not wanting to, of desperately, sickeningly wishing to stop, but he could not. It was as if the repulsive bronze was not merely alive, but sentient, possessed of demonic power, drawing him to itself, like moth to spiteful flame. Unable to resist, Roy walked across the yard, in the doorway of the shed, and across the brief—hideously brief—distance to the statue. Then, at last, mind a-tremble, agape, aghast but powerless to dampen his momentum, he bent and picked it up.

He grasped it in precisely the same manner as on that night so long ago: around the goat legs, just above the hooves. It was heavier than he remembered, but the force of reflex was strong, swinging his arm around so that the statue rose behind him like a club ...

Then, just as swiftly as it had come, the compulsion passed. Magically, strength drained away and with it, all trace of enthrallment and déjà vu. His hand dropped and he only just managed to hold onto the statue, staring at it in surprise, as something tawdry and not quite real.

A voice said, "Now that definitely is not part of my collection."

Roy lifted his gaze to the owner of the voice, who of course was Emily, now standing in the doorway of the shed and regarding him unreadably. Roy heard himself saying the one thing he didn't want to say, asking the only question to which he definitely didn't want an answer. "Where did you get this?"

Instead of replying, Emily moved in and took the statue from his hand, depositing it back on the floor and covering it with an old green trash bag. "I'm sorry," she spoke hurriedly. "No one was meant to see that nasty thing."

With concealment, what remained of the psychological impact of the statue departed. On that level, Roy was relieved, but still the question he had asked hung in the air, begging at once to be ignored and satisfied. Because, of course, he knew where the statue had come from. His real question was not where it had been found, but what had been found with it.

Something he definitely didn't want to know.

"Oh, dear!" Emily said. Her tone was intense, so quiet that Roy almost didn't hear.

"What is it?"

She stood staring up into his face. *What the hell is going on?* he thought. *Is this woman nuts?* And then, *Is this some kind of game? Did she let me see that thing on purpose? Fuck! —does she KNOW!?*

As if answering his thoughts, Emily reached out and took his hand. But her expression had no indication of accusation or hidden knowledge. Instead, she caused fresh bewilderment by leading him, like a child, out of the shed and across the garden. Roy, now somewhere between fright and hysteria, let himself be guided. They came to the pond, where Emily gently but firmly pushed him into a chair. She then dragged up a seat of her own and sat close.

Glancing in the direction of the house, as if checking that they were quite alone, Emily asked, "Roy, can you keep a secret?"

Bemused, as in a dream, Roy listened to Emily's tale: about the simple garden task that had led by chance to the discovery of a body beneath the rhododendrons; about how her first notion to call the authorities had been aborted by the realization of what would happen to her privacy—and her garden.

"I just couldn't bear the thought," she said softly. "My beautiful little haven, dug up and mutilated, police stomping about, endless, pointless questions, impossible to answer. And, God, even worse, the publicity. Reporters poking and prying, ghoulish sightseers trampling on what little is left of my life. I just couldn't do it. So I wrote a note, telling about the bones and giving directions to their location, and put it with my will, to be opened only after ... you understand. So for a while that seemed all right.

"But then, perhaps because the person in the garden died violently—that awful statue you saw was used to kill him, I have to believe—and because he—I somehow assume it's a man—was buried secretly, and also, I think, because of knowing I would be joining him, I got to thinking of him as a real character. It sounds bizarre, I know, but I began calling him my garden guest ... "

Roy, thinking of Trevor, dead or alive, as anyone's rural muse, didn't know whether to grin or gag, but he managed to remain expressionless as she continued. "What really affected me was not so much what had happened to him, but that he'd been hidden away so secretly. Just made to vanish, with no one to know or care ..."

Emily, who had been staring off toward the rhododendrons, looked sharply back at Roy. "I was perfectly aware that my reaction had nothing to do with the individual under the ground. This was just my own sad little fantasy, because I would so soon be in the same position. You've maybe heard of that old tombstone inscription, 'As you are, so once was I—as I am, so you will be.' Well, that's the connection I felt with my guest. And I began to think that if I could just find out one thing, his identity, so that, for me, he could emerge from this state of anonymity, of being so entirely nothing, then somehow that would make things—well, not right exactly, but perhaps nearer to some sort of harmony ...

"Once I'd made up my mind, it didn't take long to find out who he probably was: from the neighbours. Before I bought this house it was occupied by a Trevor Devereaux, a senior civil servant who lived a very private life here all by himself, and one day he just up and vanished. Apparently his car was found abandoned at some airport and it was thought he'd flown off and possibly been killed abroad.

"I thought I knew the truth, but somehow I wasn't satisfied. Once I'd started, it was like a drug. I had to discover more about him. It didn't matter that I was beginning to feel unwell, and that I was wasting what precious time I still have. I went off anyway to search, starting at the provincial archives. I thought I might find some old newspaper articles about the man or his disappearance ...

"That didn't work, because almost as soon as I arrived I fainted, but because of that I met this man I mentioned earlier. He'd come to the archives searching too—for an old lady. I think I already told you about his hunt for Doris Day. Anyway, neither of us had any luck, because he was in the wrong place and I got ill. But you see, by that time it didn't matter. Because the extraordinary thing was that this man, Jack, happened to look so much like my family that at first I thought he was the son I'd had and lost when I was very young. In fact, he wasn't, but our meeting turned out to be much more significant than that. Because of it, we both realized that our searches were being conducted for the wrong reasons, his to avoid facing important decisions in his life, and mine to avoid facing the fact of my death.

"Jack didn't know I was dying. Not at first. I didn't mean to tell him. What I wanted to reveal was my discovery in the garden but I couldn't do it. Jack's a policeman, and it wouldn't be fair to expect him to keep quiet. But that reasoning came later. What happened at the time was that when I tried to confide about Mr. Devereaux, instead I blurted out that I was going to die.

"After that our entire relationship changed. He told me what had brought him to Vancouver Island, about his frustrating search and the personal breakthrough our meeting had enabled him to make. For that he was grateful, but no more than I was. Through hearing his story, I realized what was happening to me. My fascination with my garden guest was really quite simple: because of the life I've led, with no family, few friends, hidden away in my little haven, when I die I will be as lost and forgotten as those old bones.

"Then it came to me. What I did have was a very special legacy, my garden and my paintings. Even more important, the fact that I had no family to leave them to was not a misfortune but a bonus, because now I could leave them to everyone.

"That would be my legacy, my reason for having been here at all, my one small chance of knowing that at least I wouldn't be forgotten instantly. To a few people, for a short time at least, this place might quietly say, 'Remember me.'"

A WHILE LATER, Emily said, "I didn't expect to tell you all this,

Roy. It's just ... when you found that statue I got this overwhelming urge. I can only suppose I've needed to tell someone for a long time and it can be easier with strangers. Also, the statue seemed to affect you too. Almost as if you'd had an intuition ... I hope it hasn't bothered you too much?"

Roy, who felt himself to have aged several years but was now filled with a wondrous composure, shook his head slowly. "No bother. It's been a privilege."

"Thank you. I'm glad."

"Also a relief."

"Oh?"

"To—to know that this place, your painting collection, this garden, all of it, will remain as it is. That nothing will ever be disturbed."

"Including the garden guest?"

"Especially him!"

"Then you'll say nothing of any of this to anyone?"

Roy looked at her, unblinking. "You have to know I wouldn't. You have to know I'm the last person in the world who would ever tell."

"Yes. Actually, I think I do know that." Emily smiled quietly. The look they shared held a long time. Then Emily stood. "Goodness, look at us, chatting the day away. Come on! Poor Monty will think he's been abandoned entirely."

They headed for the house. On the way, to break the mood, Roy said, "Oh, by the way, I meant to tell you earlier. You said your policeman friend was looking for a Doris Day? I think I may know where he can find her."

TEN

When they arrived in the parking lot of Arbutus Lodge, Jack stopped the engine and sat staring into space. Margie, who had chatted happily during the drive up from Victoria, was quiet now, not watching Jack but feeling, almost as a physical presence, the weight of this moment of conclusion. After a while one small question, which had been niggling at her since she'd arrived and heard the news, edged to the threshold of intention. For Jack's sake, if not for her own peace of mind, just once it had to be asked.

"Jack?"

"Yes, I think I do."

She pretend-pouted. "You knew what I was going to say!"

"You were going to ask if I really wanted to do this."

"Right. How did you know?"

"It's been on my mind. And the reason I thought it was on yours too is, well, lately you seem to have been making a habit of getting inside my head."

"Ah! And how does that feel?"

"Believe me, Margs, it feels fine. This old head's been rattling about by itself far too long. Also this old carcass. So, if you can stand it, they both say welcome aboard." He leaned across and kissed her, then put his hand on the door handle. "But, as I said, I think I do want to do this. Her son, Joe, said it was up to me, but I think he wants it too."

"Lovely. But you seemed to be hesitating."

"Just savouring the moment, I guess." He opened the door. "Want to come along?"

Margie shook her head. "No, copper. This is something I feel you should do alone. I'll wait here with Doug."

He nodded, touched her hand lightly, got out of the car and walked toward the lodge.

A pleasant woman, who seemed to be in charge, greeted Jack as he entered. When he introduced himself and stated that he wished to visit Anita Gillespie, she issued directions crisply. She also gave him a glance that made him think she had some inkling as to his purpose, but if she did, she didn't say.

Jack set off along the corridors of what looked more like a posh hotel than a nursing home. In moments he came to the door of the one who had been Doris Day. Without pause he walked in the open doorway, then stopped.

The room had a single bed. Lying there, propped on many pillows, was an old woman. At first he thought she was asleep, but he saw that under deep brows, her eyes were open, alive with intelligence and regarding him curiously.

Jack approached the bed. He put his hand in a pocket and drew out its small cargo: the plain gold band that, for 50 years, had waited at the bottom of Christina Lake.

He said, "I think maybe this belongs to you."

ABOUT THE AUTHOR

Ron Chudley was born in New Zealand and immigrated to Canada in 1964. He has written extensively for television, including *The Beachcombers*, and several scripts for The National Film Board of Canada. He has written many dramas for CBC Radio's *Mystery*, *The Bush and the Salon* and CBC *Stage*. His stage plays have been mounted at a number of Canadian regional theatres. He has published one play and one other mystery novel and now resides, with his wife, Karen, on Vancouver Island, British Columbia.